MUCH *Ado* ABOUT *Mother*

CELIA BONADUCE

Kensington
KENSINGTON PUBLISHING CORP.
www.kensingtonbooks.com

First Electronic Edition: May 2014
eISBN-13: 978-1-60183-126-2
eISBN-10: 1-60183-126-9

First Print Edition: May 2014
ISBN-13: 978-1-60183-127-9
ISBN-10: 1-60183-127-7

Printed in the United States of America

To my nieces and nephews, in order of appearance:

Matthew, Brigid and Chris, John, Dominic, Cecilia, Declan, Isabella, Emily S., Maeve, Andrew, Emily B., Kelan, Dante, Augie, and Lincoln

The world is yours. Take a bite.

PROLOGUE

SUZANNA

It was the first chance Suzanna had gotten to look at herself since she'd been turned into a zombie. The pale skin, the sunken eyes, the stringy and matted hair. Her clothes were torn and stained—disintegrated in the sun. She looked a mess, all right.

And somehow I still look fat.

Her sister, Erinn, came up behind her. Erinn looked equally undead and studied her own reflection alongside Suzanna's.

"I thought we weren't supposed to look in the mirror," Erinn said.

"That's vampires," Suzanna replied. "They have no reflection."

"I know that," Erinn said, in her tired "I know everything" voice. "I mean, I thought we weren't supposed to look at ourselves in case we hated the way we look."

"Dear God, how Hollywood is that? I don't think you're supposed to like the way you look once you're a zombie," Suzanna said.

A siren sounded and the sisters exchanged a glance. A male zombie in rags lurched past them, out the door of Suzanna's tea shop and onto the Venice Beach Walk, where he fell into lurch with a group of other zombies: men, women, and children. Suzanna and Erinn got in step behind him, trying not to bump into the doorframe while attempting to match his pace, their arms outstretched and groaning in a low, feral tone. Suzanna felt clumsy as she tried to navigate her walkway. The zombie lurch was not as easy as it looked.

I'm the worst zombie ever.

CHAPTER 1

SUZANNA

It was always stress that sent her soaring.

It had been at least three years since Suzanna had floated to the ceiling, but there she was, bobbing among the porch eaves. She knew if she could just relax she might even enjoy watching over her tea shop below: customers sampling her famous epic scones and drinking a variety of classic and eclectic teas. But she couldn't relax. She never floated during good times. Nothing in the past three years—the general stress of marriage, new motherhood, and running a thriving business—had so much as lifted a heel off the ground. Not even Zelda, the ancient ex–movie star who held court in the tearoom every Tuesday, ordering one scone and greeting other customers for hours, could get a (literal) rise out of her. But today, clearing the tables on the porch and looking out on the view that never got old, that of the Pacific Ocean, just past the Beach Walk where her tea shop and bookstore stood, she was sure she saw him.

Rio!

Rio, the man who had once elevated Suzanna's self-loathing to a fine art.

He'd disappeared from her world without a word. He'd been not only her fantasy, but her dance instructor—the dance being salsa— one incarnation seamlessly merging into the next. Rumor had it that he had taken off for New Zealand with a dance student named Lauren. Suzanna hadn't seen him since she'd gotten engaged, let alone married and had a baby. She never thought of him. Well, she tried never to think of him, which wasn't the same thing, but she always pushed him out of her mind as soon as he started dancing around in her head. The dreams, well . . . she didn't really have any control over them, did she?

Nothing had been good, let alone real, about Suzanna and Rio's relationship—if you could call it that. It wasn't a relationship at all. The whole thing sort of boiled down to some ill-thought-out grappling at Rio's convenience. But she never hated him. If anything, she was grateful to him. The months of her obsession with him turned out to be the impetus she and Eric needed to finally admit they had been crazy about each other since high school. Love, marriage, and a baby carriage all fell right into place after that.

Suzanna carefully avoided the cobwebs clustered in the porch eaves as she tried to talk herself down. Maybe it wasn't Rio she saw Powerblading down the Beach Walk. This was Venice, after all. There were lots of fit men in their late thirties who were either so rich or so self-employed or so unemployed as to be skating in the middle of a workday. And besides, this guy didn't have Rio's signature ponytail. He wouldn't have cut that, would he? No, she decided, it must not have been him.

Then what am I doing up here?

She heard her husband's voice coming from inside the Rollicking Bun . . . Home of the Epic Scone, where he ran the bookstore part of things. That brought her back to earth. He was deep in conversation with someone, but she couldn't tell whom. Shaking from her float, she tried to calm her nerves and peeked into the tiny book area they had nicknamed the Nook. There he was, her darling husband, Eric.

She loved to tell people their story, about how they had finally admitted their love and now were living happily ever after.

Well . . .

Suzanna thought perhaps the phrase "The rest is history" might fit their story better. She was still madly in love with Eric and he, apparently, was still in love with her. They definitely had their passionate moments. But Eric had always been a man with a lot of interests, and he was very easily distracted by a good cause. Suzanna knew better than to think that would change, that he would be consumed with her . . . well, she knew it intellectually. But she had to admit his zeal for life sometimes exhausted her.

She peeked into the Nook. Eric was sitting at a table with Bernard and Mr. Clancy, two guys she and Eric called the Grumpy Old Men. Mr. Clancy was the owner of a brick courtyard a few establishments down the Beach Walk. It was full of shops that probably wouldn't find a clientele anywhere else in the world. If you were looking for incense, kites, fabric from Bali, or a nice henna tattoo, you'd probably wind up at the humbly named Mr. Clancy's Courtyard. Bernard, a photographer and general artiste, was one of his tenants. The two of them had battled over the years, mostly over little things such as how much merchandise could be displayed in the windows facing the Beach Walk without looking tacky, but now it appeared that they were in some sort of war.

Eric loved nothing more than mediating. When it came to keeping harmony on their block, Eric jumped right in. Suzanna and their little girl, Lizzy, hadn't seen much of Eric these past couple of weeks. She didn't know what the whole thing was about; she was sure he'd told her, but she got his causes mixed up and had stopped paying close attention.

Suzanna went into the tea shop to get ready for the day ahead. She knew that she was the luckiest woman in the world to have married her soul mate. She knew that Rio was a missed bullet.

But her heart was pounding to a salsa beat.

CHAPTER 2

VIRGINIA

Staring into the kitchen cupboard, Virginia realized she was out of dog food. After several moments of trying to will a bag of Royal Canin Mini Chihuahua Dog Food into existence, she gave up and rubbed a fist-sized area of steam off the window. Squinting into the murk, she watched the snow clustering in the gutters and turning gray. Picturesque snow seemed to be in short supply this winter. Everyone in the city was wearing black, as if in mourning for the glory days of summer—the pollen, the sweltering streets, and the humidity.

The kettle whistled, which startled Piquant, the teacup Chihuahua, as much as it did Virginia. As she made tea, Virginia stared down at the little dog, who looked like a miniature deer. He looked back at her with his wet black eyes.

Blink, damn it.

Virginia had gotten used to Piquant's disconcerting stare, although he had developed a wheezing cough over the last couple of weeks, which was starting to concern her.

When Virginia's kids were growing up, they always had dogs, often several at a time. In sprawling, casual Napa Valley, dogs just showed up and stayed. But they were, as her late husband, Martin, always said, "real dogs," meaning that they were all mixed, usually unfortunate-looking, big animals that could basically fend for themselves. A little food and they were good to go. Martin would surely roll over in his grave if he got a look at Piquant, who not only needed special food, but also a coat for venturing outdoors on all but the most temperate of New York City days. Piquant had booties as well, per the vet's recommendation. Virginia followed the doctor's orders: that Piquant was not to venture out in the wintertime without shoes. But she only put them on the dog when she and Piquant were safely outside and no one in the building could see them. Virginia wasn't sure who felt more foolish, she or the dog.

Momentarily ignoring the dog food situation, she tried to get close but not too close to the radiator, which tended to whistle and spit if it sensed you were getting near enough to access some heat. The radiator was even more skittish than her dog.

Three years ago, Virginia had been a professor of history in Napa Valley in sunny . . . sunny . . . sunny California. Her late husband had taught English at the same university. They both loved teaching, but Martin lived and breathed it. She hadn't admitted it, maybe she hadn't known it consciously, but sometimes all those bright young minds wore her down, while Martin's enthusiasm for his students never seemed to ebb.

Virginia peered out the window again, remembering how her husband would gleefully challenge his students to defend the Oxford comma. He would write: "I walked down the street with a doctor, a lawyer and a stamp collector" on the chalkboard. He would then ask his students how many people were walking down the street with him—two or three? Was the lawyer a stamp collector in his off-hours or were the lawyer and the stamp collector different people?

No one in the history of the world got more joy from the Oxford comma than Martin Wolf.

It's funny that I seem to remember his work more than I do my own.

Virginia was initially horrified when thoughts like that invaded her head. She was of the hard-core feminist generation, clearing the road for younger women who could now take their professions for granted. Professor? Sure. Doctor? Of course. Astronaut? Why the hell not?

But when Virginia thought about Martin happily arguing with students, he didn't seem quite so far away, so she cut herself some slack. She had been as good as any man at her job and had nothing for which she needed to apologize. And so she thought whatever politically incorrect thoughts popped into her head about her husband and savored them. Once he was gone, the thought of teaching exhausted her, as much of a sad surprise to her as it was to her dean.

Virginia had been at loose ends since her husband died in a car accident and Suzanna and Erinn, her two girls, had grown and moved to big cities. The sting of irony was certainly not lost on her that she and Martin, who were both born and raised in cosmopolitan eastern cities, had decided to raise their daughters in bucolic Napa Valley, only to have both girls at one time or another pronounce the area boring. Virginia declared she would move to New York, where her husband and she and Erinn, when she was small, had spent a few very happy years. Her girls, both living in Los Angeles by this time, were shocked by the news. Virginia's goal was to shake things up, and her daughters' reactions just added a little extra zing to the entire idea.

When she first moved east, Virginia filled her days with museums and theater and other Manhattan-centric activities. She tried all the Chinese restaurants, bagel shops, delis, cafés, and cupcakeries in her neighborhood. Just being new to the city kept the pain of widowhood at arm's length for several months. But pain did show up. Sitting on a park bench, right in the middle of a fresh H&H bagel, the understanding that Martin was dead finally hit. Really hit. It felt as if she had just been acting the part of the devoted widow and now, in a flash, she was living it. She started to choke on the bagel and was grateful that she managed to swallow the dough before attracting attention to herself. How would she explain that she'd just realized her husband was dead, when his death certificate was already eight months old? Virginia closed her eyes, hoping her reality might somehow change. She was retired. She was three thousand miles from her daughters, and she was, at least for the time being, a New Yorker. It took a while before she could bring herself to open her eyes.

After the bagel incident, Virginia's love affair with the city started to wilt. She tried to keep herself distracted. On her daughter Erinn's advice she joined a book club and on her daughter Suzanna's advice she joined a knitting group. On her own she took up mosaics; she found an old table on the corner and lugged it into her apartment. She had to admit, she had done a pretty good job creating a blazing red, orange, and yellow sunburst, which she realized, after she had finished it, had nothing in common with any other furniture in her apartment. She looked for other things to divert her and now had Mongolian clay pot cooking lessons, jewelry-making, and stained-glass classes under her belt. But nothing brought her any joy. She couldn't admit it to anyone but she felt trapped and bored by everything.

She was a little sheepish feeling trapped and bored in what was touted as the most exciting city in America, if not the world. She had started putting out feelers to her girls. Her "girls" were now women in no uncertain terms. Erinn was in her forties and Suzanna in her thirties, but to Virginia they were still "the girls." She would let a gentle hint slip out now and then in phone or e-mail conversations . . . wondering what they thought about her MAYBE moving back out west. She always tried to stress the word MAYBE . . . MAYBE back to Napa. MAYBE somewhere around Los Angeles; it was a big place; she wouldn't have to crowd them. Mothers know their daughters (like it or not) and Virginia knew that Suzanna would love it if they were closer, geographically. The MAYBE wasn't for her—it was for Erinn. Virginia's eldest had always kept her own counsel. Virginia didn't doubt Erinn's love for her, but she could always detect a note of exasperation in Erinn's voice when she felt Virginia was getting too close . . . either geographically or emotionally.

Piquant stood forlornly over his bowl, craning his head to peek passive-aggressively up at Virginia. Virginia sighed. She looked on-line and read that grains were good for Chihuahuas. She poured gluten-free Rice Krispies into the bowl. The dog's little charcoal briquette of a nose sniffed at it. He looked up again. Virginia poured some rice milk over the cereal, hoping that might help tempt the little beast into eating. The cereal lived up to its advertising and let out a loud SNAP, CRACKLE, and POP! Piquant leaped into the air and scuttled under the kitchen chair, shivering in that little-dog way that drove Virginia crazy.

"How do you even call yourself a dog?" she asked.

It was Virginia's doctor who first suggested she get a furry friend, on the theory that "older people need companionship and something to take care of." Virginia was a tiny bit affronted at both implications, that she was an "older person" and that she was in need of "something to take care of." Weren't raising a family and four thousand college students enough for a cosmic pass into sloth-hood?

She had not consulted her girls when she got the Chihuahua. Why should she? She was her own woman now, not a conscientious professor, a devoted wife, an eagle-eyed mother. With the exception of whisking herself off to New York City, adopting Piquant was her first solo decision. A nurse in Virginia's doctor's office announced that he'd found the perfect dog for her (she hadn't said she was ready to take on a dog, but in all honesty, she didn't say she wasn't ready to take on a dog, either). The dog had belonged to a socialite, who carried it around town for photo ops. Then named "Hotstuff," he apparently was subject to red eye in photographs, and the starlet decided she couldn't be seen with an un-photogenic dog. Erinn, with her recent television and photography background, explained later that red eye in dogs could not be fixed with the simple application used to fix the problem in humans. The starlet put the word out that she was looking to retire her pooch and hoped for "a quiet home with an elderly woman."

"Elderly woman" is even worse than "older person." These people need a lesson in P.R.

Virginia arrived at the doctor's office looking as youthful as possible, thanks to a drawer full of ancient cosmetics. She had a half-formed hope that the doctor and nurse would take one look at her and announce that they had made a mistake—anyone with Virginia's energy and vitality was certainly not the right owner for Hotstuff. The socialite was looking for retirement—and all the calm that the word conveyed—for her pup. A life with someone as vivacious as Virginia would surely be too much for Hotstuff's diminutive heart.

This proved to be another one of Virginia's miscalculations, and she left the office as the new owner of a Chihuahua. As hard as she tried, Virginia could not bring herself to introduce her new pet as Hotstuff, so she tried other variations: Spicy (too suggestive), Pepper (too common), and Umami (too obscure). She finally settled on Piquant, which at least nodded to the flavor of the dog's original name.

The first weeks of dog ownership had been rough. Piquant was the Smart Car of the canine world, so tiny he could hide anywhere. Virginia would come home to the apartment and the dog seemed to have evaporated into thin air. She'd put down her purse and listen for any sound. Nothing. Then she would start crawling around the apartment on all fours, looking under the bed and sofa, rummaging through closets. She never caught him in the act of hiding. As she crawled around the floor she would finally hear him crunching his dog food in the kitchen. She would leap up and run to see him, casually chomping away. He would look up at her, but not miss a bite of food. Apparently, Chihuahuas didn't go in for that adoration thing you heard about in dogs.

He never came when called and at first Virginia thought he just needed to get used to his new name, so she stood firm and never called him anything else—with one notable exception. One day, while walking him in the park, he escaped his collar.

"Piquant!" Virginia called as the little tail disappeared into some bushes. "Piquant!"

Virginia was close to hysteria, convinced she'd never find him. She frantically started calling out, "Hotstuff! Come on! Over here, Hotstuff!"

Two teenaged boys started snickering. She looked at them.

"Ain't you a little old for this, Hotstuff?" one of them said.

Showing perhaps a smattering of solidarity, Piquant crawled out from under a holly bush. Virginia scooped him up and walked away with as much dignity as she could muster while the boys catcalled behind her.

Virginia knew that Suzanna loved getting pictures of Piquant from "Grammy" (Virginia laid down the law that she would not respond to the harsher-sounding "Grandma") and sharing them with her toddler, Lizzy. When Erinn, who was more of a cat person but was clearly trying to be supportive, found out Virginia had taken on the miniature pet, she sent a "pet's perfect potty," a strip of sod in a tray that a dog could use instead of Central Park. Virginia remembered opening the box and thinking there would never be a need for this contraption (which was basically a dog litter box). Virginia knew she was starting to be a bit reclusive and one of the upsides of dog ownership was that she would now be required to get out of the apartment on a regular basis. At the very least she would meet other pet owners. This, along with most of Virginia's "becoming a New Yorker" schemes, came to nothing. Piquant hated other dogs and Virginia was reduced to holding snippets of apologetic conversation as she crossed the street whenever another canine approached, Piquant snapping ferociously, little needle teeth bared for battle.

She was now very grateful for the "perfect potty," which saved her from hitting the mean streets on frigid February evenings or scorching summer days. Basically, Manhattan lent itself to dog walking about two months out of the year ... and that was when you had a friendly dog.

Virginia rinsed out the dog's bowl. She opened the refrigerator and saw the only other "people food" in her house was a half-eaten box of lo mein. Even though the dog only needed three hundred calories a day to keep body and soul together, Virginia knew firsthand that she'd pay a steep price if she gave him leftover Chinese. There wasn't a potty on earth perfect enough to contain the carnage once Piquant's digestive system became aware that it had been served spicy noodles.

"OK, let's go out," Virginia said to the dog.

She looked out at the late afternoon gloom and tried to fool the dog into thinking this was a good idea. "Do you want to go *OUT?*"

The tone of voice seemed to do the trick. Piquant's tiny toenails started tapping on the hardwood floors. His cough was always worse when he was excited, and he started hacking joyously. Virginia bundled herself up, grabbed the leash and Piquant's plaid coat and booties. She scooped up the dog and headed into all New York City had to offer on a frozen afternoon. After nodding to the bellman she scooted around the corner and dressed the dog. She put Piquant down on the pavement and started walking. The dog stayed stock-still. Virginia gave the leash a short tug. The dog shivered and sat down.

The snow started falling steadily as she stared down at the Chihuahua, who looked alternately miserable and ridiculous. She wanted to just pick the dog up and be on her way, but the vet had warned her that she had to assert herself as the alpha in her relationship with Piquant. Virginia cringed every time a pedestrian passed by. She could see in their knowing eyes that she was the beta. It was written all over her face.

She tugged halfheartedly at the leash. Piquant coughed. She had moved to Manhattan to assert herself and she couldn't even stand up to a two-pound dog.

CHAPTER 3

ERINN

"Mom's coming for an extended visit," Suzanna said.

Erinn breathed in, absorbing the news. She stared out at the waves as conflicting emotions pulled at her like the tide. She was pretty sure that Suzanna had lured her to the beach in order to share this little nugget, and she didn't appreciate being manipulated by her kid sister. She dug her toes into the sand and tried not to look as if she were digging in her heels as well.

She glanced sideways. The muscles in Suzanna's cheeks remained smooth, seemingly free of any anxiety. Suzanna's strawberry-blond hair whipped around in the wind. Normally, when Suzanna was apprehensive, she twirled her hair around her finger, a habit from childhood. But she just stood there, peacefully looking at her daughter, who sat at the water's edge building a sand castle. Two-year-old Erinn Elizabeth was now called "Lizzy" because Erinn had made it clear she would not be referred to as "Old Erinn" or "Big Erinn" as opposed to "Young Erinn" or "Little Erinn."

Of course, Erinn understood that having a child named after oneself was a huge honor. But ground rules had to be set.

Eric, Suzanna's husband and always the peacekeeper, suggested "Junior," but that went right out the window as soon as everyone realized for every "Junior" there was a "Senior."

"I'd settle for 'Master' and 'Apprentice,'" Erinn had said to them.

But when several of Suzanna's customers made references to Donald Trump's TV show, she'd nixed that as well.

Out of sheer exhaustion, the family finally decided on "Lizzy."

Erinn looked out over the water, stalling for time, the silence crashing over them like waves.

Maybe the idea of an extended visit with Mother doesn't scare her! Maybe I should just be a little more flexible.

Twirling hair or not, Suzanna couldn't be happy about broaching the subject of their mother. Erinn didn't want to be difficult. She knew Suzanna was probably overjoyed that their mother was coming to town. Erinn decided to be kind, always an act of acute determination.

"That's great news!" she finally said. "Define *extended.*"

"I have no clue." Suzanna shrugged. "She says she wants to talk to us and she's flying in from New York next week."

"We have phones."

"She wants to talk to us together."

"We have *conference calling.*"

"She wants to talk to us face-to-face."

"We have Skype."

"Erinn! She's coming. Just be happy."

And there it was. Suzanna's simple request. Plea. Demand.

Just be happy.

As if anything in life could be that simple. Especially a visit from one's mother—a situation fraught with peril, in Erinn's book. While she had been Daddy's girl and Suzanna was always more in tune with their mother, the two sisters could always count on each other for supportive eye-rolling when the need arose. But now Suzanna was a mother herself. Where once Erinn had a reasonable ally in her battles with their mother, she now sensed resentment. Suzanna was a mother, and mothers stuck together.

Erinn decided to be quiet for a moment. Not her strong suit. But she'd learned that words, especially between sisters discussing an extended visit from their mother, possibly should be weighed before spoken. Their late father used to say proudly that their family wasn't into sports, they were into words. That was true—words were their sport and they played tackle. To be fair, Suzanna, as the youngest member of the group, certainly was the "tacklee" most of the time. Erinn thought that there probably was a real word for "tacklee," and if there wasn't, there obviously was a need. Suffice it to say, Suzanna bore the brunt of Erinn's verbiage throughout the years, and now Erinn tried to soften her approach. She took stock of her sister.

She's a good sister, a good wife, a good mother, a good daughter. She runs a crazy little tea shop and bookstore at the other end of town, and she's loved by the entire community. She's got a great epitaph waiting for her.

Erinn quickly tallied her own self-worth. She was a good playwright and TV producer.

But I'm going to be cremated, so I don't have to worry about filling up a big piece of our increasingly small world.

Lizzy toddled up and threw herself into the middle space between Suzanna and Erinn, arms joyously outstretched. She loved it when her mother and aunt each took one of her arms and swung her off her feet, as if the sisters were her own personal human swing. At two years of age she had yet to grasp the concept that you needed to alert adults that the swinging game was about to commence. Several times Lizzy had leaped into the air and landed, crumpling in her biodegradable diaper onto the floor. However, Suzanna and Erinn were by this time fully trained to *most* of Lizzy's whims. They seamlessly each grabbed a soft-as-suede upper arm and swung her into the air. For a brief second she hovered there, blocking out the sun and smiling with the radiance that only children—correction: only children you *love*—can convey.

Icarus himself could not have been more beautiful, soaring directly into the sun immediately before his wax wings began to soften.

When he was still so sure that he'd gotten it right.

Suzanna and Erinn each took a little hand and headed for the pier. Suzanna had it in her head that today would be a good time for Lizzy to discover the joys of the carousel.

Well, Lizzy is her child, and if she thinks that's the thing to do. . . .

Erinn admitted she didn't know *anything* about children, but as a TV producer who did a lot of her own camera work, she did know something about perspective. A two-year-old is small. A bobbing wooden horse with bared teeth is big, not to mention unusual. There is no reference point for a two-year-old to make sense of a bobbing wooden horse going in a fast, big circle.

But I'm not the mother. Mother. Extended . . . visiting . . . mother.

Erinn pushed the thought out of her head. There would be time for the mother situation. Right now it was more important to help her sister try to strap her toddler onto the red saddle of a prancing goat.

Because a wooden horse isn't confusing enough.

Suzanna and Erinn stood on either side of the goat. Suzanna had her arm around Lizzy, and Erinn took the opportunity to get out her new video camera, her prize possession, and motion to Suzanna that she was going to get off the carousel so she could grab some video. Suzanna nodded quickly and returned her attention to Lizzy.

It never ceased to amaze Erinn how many situations she could turn to her advantage just by having a nice camera with her. Her sister was not going to nag her about not riding the carousel *and* Erinn would be the hero who brought home adorable footage to share with friends and family. These were times when if Erinn could have surgically attached the camera to her hip she would have.

For many years, Erinn had been a successful Broadway playwright, and for more years than that she was a very UN-successful Broadway playwright. That's what brought her to Santa Monica: to be where her sister was and her failed career wasn't.

Two years ago she had stumbled onto a career in cable TV, thanks to the fact that she was pretty good with a camera. She had even won an Emmy last year for a series she had created called *Let It Shine,* a History Network reality show about two people trying to run a lighthouse like in the old days.

Let It Shine was a huge hit. Huge. But the contestants were hired for their looks, not their brains, and the cast and crew almost had a shipwreck while the challengers argued about who was getting more airtime. End of series. Erinn hoped it was not the end of her second career. She hadn't been offered anything for a few months now and was getting nervous. Her sister and mother kept telling her to be patient and something would materialize. That was easy enough for them to say—Mother had her retirement fund and Father's life insurance, and Suzanna and her husband's business was thriving, even in this loathsome economy. "Patience is a minor form of despair, disguised as a virtue," wrote Ambrose Bierce.

Erinn thought about sharing this quote with her sister, but prudence won the day. Erinn and both of her parents (well, both parents when her father was still around) were all great quoters, but Erinn suspected that Suzanna sometimes got tired of this habit as, she also suspected, did her co-workers on just about every show she worked on. Voltaire once said that "A witty saying proves nothing," but Erinn vehemently disagreed. She felt a well-placed quotation proved many things . . . not least of which was that you knew a lot of interesting quotes and were willing to share.

A hideously loud bell sounded and the carousel lurched to a start. Lizzy screamed.

Of course Lizzy screamed.

Erinn held her tongue.

As Suzanna made cooing sounds at Lizzy and apologetic faces to the other carousel riders, Erinn tried to keep them in view as they swirled in and out of frame. Every time Lizzy and Suzanna swooped by, Lizzy bobbing up and down, not crying now but looking incredibly confused, and Suzanna with a smile plastered on her anxious face, Erinn waved and tried to follow the action, all the while keeping the camera steady. Looking up from the camera, Erinn noticed a man staring at her from the center of the carousel, where the carnies stood. He had a small paintbrush in his hand and leaned against a horse that was propped up between two sawhorses and held straight by two large vise grips swaddled in cloth that Erinn guessed was to protect the paint. These were no ordinary carousel horses. Erinn had shot a documentary on them for the History Network a year or so ago, so she knew that the forty-four horses (and other animals) were all hand-carved and hand-painted. They dated back to at least 1922 and had been rescued more than once from the demolition ball by concerned Santa Monicans. Erinn studied the grounded horse while trying not to study the man. The horse was white, with a curve to its neck that made the mane look like it was blowing in the wind. With all the other horses leaping to the music, it was as if it had been given a time-out. Erinn put her eye back to the viewfinder but could tell that the man was still looking at her. He was incredibly handsome, a tinge of gray just starting at his temples. And even from across a moving carousel she could see his sky-blue eyes. Or were they ocean-blue eyes?

She could feel the color mounting in her cheeks. Firmly ensconced in her forties, she wasn't used to men staring at her so blatantly. She often felt that if that science-fiction cliché of disposing of less-than-gorgeous people came to pass it would start with middle-aged women in Los Angeles. On the other hand, the man was the right age . . . maybe he did find her attractive. It could happen. Having convinced herself of that possibility, it became even harder to focus on the video. Luckily, Suzanna and Lizzy were about to come back into frame and she tried to regain her concentration.

The music started to slow and a buzzer sounded, startling Lizzy and sending her yowling once more. Suzanna scooped her off the goat and headed over to Erinn as soon as the carousel stopped. Out of the corner of her eye, Erinn noticed that the provocative carney was also headed her way. She busied herself with the lens cap and case and pretended she didn't notice him. With her nose pointed determinedly at the depths of her camera case, she waited for whatever pathetic pretense he was going to come up with in order to speak to her.

It came as a total shock that the voice she heard was Suzanna's.

"Christopher! I can't believe it! What are you doing here?"

Erinn looked up. Suzanna was hugging the carney with the arm that was not holding Lizzy on her hip.

"I saw you on the carousel and noticed you were being photographed." He nodded at Erinn and showed off his insanely white teeth. "I figured you must be doing a mother-daughter modeling session."

Erinn stared at her sister. She couldn't believe that Suzanna was buying this claptrap, but she appeared to be enjoying herself. The carney, Christopher, poked Lizzy playfully in the belly.

"How's my Queen Elizabeth?" he asked and gave her a buss on the cheek.

He knows them? Is he a regular at the tea shop? Carneys don't stop in for tea, do they?

Erinn's questions were answered before they were completely formulated as Suzanna started to introduce them.

"This is my sister, Erinn," Suzanna said. "Erinn, this is Christopher. He is an artist on our block. His shop is next to the kite store. You know the one, right?"

Erinn did know the place. She had admired his work in the gallery window many times. He mostly painted scenes of Venice and Santa Monica but with a hipper vibe to them: hot colors and distorted, playful images. Definitely meant to attract the tourist crowd but still showing a personal flair that would leave buyers happy they had more than a postcard of their Southern California adventure. His gallery also included insightful photographs (in her professional opinion) and a few random wooden objets d'art.

"I do," Erinn said. "You have quite an eclectic collection. Is the work all yours?"

"Not all of it," Christopher said. "Some of it is my uncle Bernard's. We're both artistically OCD. We sort of jump around from one medium to the next."

Suzanna inclined her head toward Erinn.

"You're preaching to the choir," she said.

Erinn was stung by the comparison but tried to hide it. She changed careers because of necessity! She certainly didn't *dabble* like this gentleman! She realized she was glaring at her sister and recovered. She twisted her camera onto her shoulder and offered her hand for a handshake.

"You do some very nice work," Erinn said.

"Sorry, I've got paint all over my hands. Business as usual," Christopher said as he wiped his hand on his jeans before extending it. He smiled and looked her right in the eye, just the way an artist would, taking in every mole and wrinkle. "I've seen you on the Beach Walk a couple of times."

OK, enough with the teeth and cheekbones, Erinn thought, although she merely nodded in acknowledgment.

"Erinn lives just up the street," Suzanna said, tilting her head north of the pier.

"Oh, with the fancy people," Christopher said, and he and Suzanna laughed.

The Venice crowd liked to think of themselves as the bohemians of the area and lumped everyone north of the WELCOME TO SANTA MONICA sign as rich, staid, and stodgy—never mind that Suzanna and Eric probably made twice what Erinn brought home.

"What are you doing up here?" Suzanna asked, as if Santa Monica were hundreds of miles away instead of three.

"A couple of the horses were looking a little faded," Christopher said, glancing back at the horse in the middle of the carousel. "Just lending a hand with the restoration."

"Christopher is very into local preservation," Suzanna said, scooting Lizzy onto the other hip. "He started a petition to get our block designated a historic landmark."

"Well," said Christopher, "part of our block. Actually, just part of Mr. Clancy's Courtyard."

"I know the building!" Erinn said. "Well, buildings. It is a court-yard after all."

"Very true," he said hesitantly.

"I met Mr. Clancy years ago. Is he still with us?" Erinn asked.

"In what sense?" he asked. "Alive or still at the courtyard?"

"Take your pick," Erinn said.

"He's still kicking." Christopher smiled, turning to Suzanna for validation. "As irascible as ever. He's fighting us on the whole historic designation thing, so it's pretty intense over there."

"Oh, yeah . . . that historic designation thing is pretty intense, all right," Suzanna said.

She said it as casually as she could, but Erinn knew that her sister found local politics and problems a bore. Eric found it all fascinating. He was in the middle of everything, although he made it a point not to take sides. Anyone could stop by the Nook and discuss the finer points of any argument. Erinn often joined in these heated discussions, but as soon as any battle started getting interesting Suzanna tuned everyone out. Conflict was not her thing. Erinn was sure Suzanna wouldn't actually be able to explain what the historic landmark hubbub was all about if you asked her. On the other hand, Eric would probably tell most people more than they'd want to know. The two of them were so different.

Erinn wondered if this was true of all married couples.

The buzzer on the carousel sounded, announcing that the ride was starting up again. Lizzy threw her arms around her mother and buried her head in Suzanna's neck.

"You should stop by and see some of our new work," Christopher yelled over the canned circus music.

Erinn was pleased to be invited, but Suzanna spoke as if he were talking to her.

"I will," she yelled back. "Soon!"

Conversation became impossible and Christopher pantomimed that he was going to get back to work. The sisters watched him jump onto the moving carousel and thread his way to the center, where he leaped off with equal grace. Erinn stood and watched him until she realized Suzanna had already left the building.

* * *

Back at the Rollicking Bun . . . Home of the Epic Scone, Suzanna handed Lizzy over to Eric so he could put her down for a nap. She came back with two generous mugs of a new tea she and Eric were thinking of featuring in the shop. It was called Night of the Iguana Chocolate Chai. Erinn sniffed at it suspiciously.

All was quiet and Erinn knew there was no escape. The tea shop and bookstore were both closed for the day. Eric was probably reading some calming children's story to Lizzy in the rambling apartment over the store—the place he, Suzanna, and Lizzy called home—while Erinn sat trapped with a cup of vile tea.

"Mom took Piquant to the vet," Suzanna plunged in. "He has asthma and needs to be in a warmer climate."

"The vet has asthma?" Erinn asked.

"No, Erinn, the *dog* has asthma." Suzanna added some milk to her tea. "Please don't start. You know I meant the dog."

"Well, one can dream," Erinn muttered, gagging on the tea.

"I don't understand what you have against Mom."

"I . . ." Erinn took a sip of tea, realizing she didn't understand what she had against their mother, either. "I just feel as if I'm a child again whenever she's around. She takes my confidence away."

"That isn't fair, Erinn. No one can take away your confidence without your permission."

"Don't give me that tripe. Plenty of people take away my confidence and I don't recall giving any of them permission."

"If you don't mind my saying so, Erinn, you could use a little less confidence."

"What does that mean?"

"Well, you border on conceited, if you ask me."

"I didn't ask you. And for the future, I am withholding permission for you to ever call me conceited again."

Suzanna's ears visibly perked up and Erinn knew the baby must be crying upstairs. Erinn couldn't actually hear her, but Suzanna had developed that mother-supersonic hearing and Erinn just accepted that some sort of baby thing was going on.

"I'll let myself out," she said as she dashed out of the tea shop, happy to skirt yet another argument with her sister.

Erinn lived clear on the other end of Santa Monica, the "good" side, known to the locals as "Canada" because it was north of Montana Avenue. She pulled into the driveway and looked lovingly at her house. It was one of the few Victorians still standing on Ocean Avenue. When Erinn moved to the West Coast from New York she used all her savings to buy the place. The house had been completely rundown but she was determined to fix it up. Times were rough for a while, but when she rebounded with her second career in cable TV, she spent whatever money she had on the house. The house was now a jewel of Victorian architecture. She often hid behind her living room curtains and watched as tourists and locals alike stopped and studied the house. She let herself inside. What if *this* career came to a screeching halt, too? She had come to terms with being a failed wunderkind playwright—that was the luck of the gods anyway—but failing at *cable?* Where else could she go? How many times could she reinvent herself?

Caro, her cat, padded down the stairs to meet her. Erinn scooped him up. She hated to admit how much she valued her pet. He'd stood by her through all the career highs and lows and halting romantic endeavors. As iffy as her careers had been, her romantic history was worse. The last man in her life, Jude, was much younger than she was and she had known it was destined to fail from the start. Suzanna had no sympathy when the torrid affair bottomed out a year ago.

"You always said it wouldn't work, so it didn't," Suzanna had said. "You'd sabotage a relationship just so you could prove yourself right."

Erinn pretended she was so affronted that she refused to talk to her sister, but the fact of the matter was she was afraid Suzanna might be right. That whole trend about "visualizing your success" was definitely suspect, in Erinn's book. If it happened to be true she was really in trouble. But romance was not on Erinn's immediate to-do list. She had to get a job. She sat down at the computer and logged on to Facebook to see what her work associates were doing.

Erinn had resisted Facebook for as long as she possibly could, but in an industry that relied not only on "who you know" but on "who you know this minute," there was no avoiding it. Her relationship with the Internet site was, in the parlance of the medium, "complicated." There were days when she wrote something particularly clever and got instant feedback and she wondered why she had been opposed to it for so long. Other times, when it seemed that all her professional colleagues were announcing new jobs they'd been offered, or worse, when she was bombarded with pictures from around the world from friends who had gotten international gigs that had them shooting in one glorious location after another, Erinn had to wonder why she bothered.

Facebook was also a great outlet for her photography, although it annoyed her when she got more comments on pictures of her cat than she did on her real art. Scrolling through some of her pictures, she had to admit that Caro looked pretty damn charming in some of them. He was a long-haired cat, and since he was outdoors as much as he was indoors, his fur sometimes became so matted, there was nothing to do but take him to the groomer where he got shaved into a "lion's cut." Caro would leave the house a scowling, knotted mess and return a proud, regal beast with an impressive mane. Erinn was not one to romanticize animals, but still, Caro always seemed pretty pleased with himself when he came home with his new King of the Jungle hairdo. Whenever Erinn posted "before" and "after" pictures on Facebook, there was always an explosion of activity.

Work with what you've got.

She stared at her Facebook profile and saw that she had gotten a friend request from Jude Raphael, her professional colleague and recent ex-boyfriend. Her finger hovered over the Accept icon. She and Jude had parted friends, but Erinn had never really been in the habit of remaining on friendly terms with old lovers. Not that Jude was an "old" lover. He was a very young lover, more than a decade younger than she. He had always accused her of making too much of their age difference and he was probably right. But she found herself worried about her looks, her energy, her female competition on the TV shoots they shared, and she had realized she was turning into the sort of woman she just couldn't stand. For better or worse, instead of making adjustments she had broken up with him.

Caro jumped into her lap and Erinn absently petted the cat as she pondered the request. She closed her eyes as memories washed over her. Some cascaded like a warm shower, others like a bucket of ice water. Breakups, even those in which the participants agree to get along afterward, are never easy. The best you could hope for was that you could *pretend* it was easy. A quote by lateral thinker Edward de Bono came to mind:

"A memory is what is left when something happens and does not completely unhappen."

She clicked on the Accept Friend Request icon before she could overthink it. Jude and Erinn had worked together on many TV shows, he the director to her producer. She missed working with him—she missed *working*—but Jude apparently was scaling greater cable-TV heights. She clicked on Jude's profile page (she refused to call it his "wall" in Facebook-speak). There were pictures of him on his latest shoot, grinning broadly and standing in front of a sphinx. His comment read:

I've signed a confidentiality agreement, so I can't say where I am.

Erinn scowled. She knew Jude was just being his version of funny, but she personally did not think it was amusing. Contracts were signed for a reason!

She clicked through his other photos. There seemed to be pictures from all over the world, obviously work-related. She petted Caro, wondering what had happened to *her* career.

When she had to she rented out her guesthouse, which helped her stay afloat in lean times. Suzanna had been the first to recommend renting it out, and Erinn had at first resisted the idea. She didn't really like to have a stranger on the property, but by now it had become second nature to turn to the guesthouse as a means of pulling in some money. But only when she had to!

Maybe I can wait just a little longer.

The realization that the guesthouse was currently vacant made her stomach lurch. Her mother wasn't planning on staying with her, was she . . . on this *extended* visit?

Erinn quickly exited Facebook and typed in *craigslist, los angeles, rentals.*

FOR RENT: Beautiful Victorian guesthouse in prime Santa Monica locale.

CHAPTER 4

SUZANNA

Her mother had always set a good example of taking care of oneself while raising a family. Suzanna wanted to look toned and fit when her mother got here.

Liar, liar.

OK, maybe her mother wouldn't even notice that Suzanna was still carrying an extra fifteen pounds. But she should really be focusing on looking good for her husband.

Pants on fire.

I really need to speak with more adults.

Suzanna breathed deeply, admitted to herself that just maybe this sudden need to look good was inspired by the fact that Rio might be back in town. She started rummaging through her closet like an ingénue before an awards show. If that had been Rio, if he were, indeed, back in town, then another Rio sighting would certainly be a possibility. She would have to make an effort to look a little better. She pulled out a striped top and held it up to the light. It had stains on it from her year and a half of breast-feeding.

Now there's a hot conversation starter.

She threw it on the bed, starting a "give to charity" pile, then reconsidered. It would be charity to keep the top, just not wear it! Maybe she'd turn it into rags, but the thought of cleaning mirrors with a milk-stained rag grossed her out a little bit. Well, she'd start a pile and figure out what to do with it later.

Her next top was just as bad, if not worse. This one was stretched out at the neck and hem. Suzanna went through all her tops and realized how few were actually in acceptable shape.

No wonder the UPS man stopped flirting with me.

Giving up on the tops, she steeled herself to look at her jeans. She held up a pair against her hips and winced as she saw gray sweatpants sticking out on both sides of the denim.

How did she ever fit into jeans this small?

Suzanna stripped off her sweatpants. She looked at herself in the mirror and saw she was wearing baggy maternity panties. Dear God, she had let herself go. Doubling her resolve, she tugged on the jeans. They did go over her hips but were inches away from buttoning. She gritted her teeth—she would button those jeans if it were the last thing she ever did.

Inching the button and buttonhole closer together, she thought about her very first stress float in junior high school. That had involved a boy, too. She had fallen at his feet during a play and when he and the rest of the kids started laughing at her, she just . . . floated away. No one ever seemed to notice she was drifting above them, and she always did manage to return to earth. Luckily, it didn't happen often and she'd gotten used to it. But it was always awkward. From her wedding day forward, she'd been firmly planted on the ground, and it unnerved her that Rio might stir things up this way.

She sucked in her stomach until her back hurt. Her baby was now two years old and there was no longer any excuse; this was not "baby fat." Suzanna had always wanted to be one of those women who bounced back immediately after giving birth, and she had envisioned women coming into her tea shop making comments about how well she was looking.

Yeah. No.

The tips from high school about how to squeeze into jeans that no longer fit came back to her.

ONE: Button up before even attempting the zipper.

With a Herculean effort, she managed that, but her abdomen poked through the zipper opening with such force that she realized she'd have to be holding her stomach back with her left hand while trying to zip up with the right. She tried this until the skin on her right index finger was starting to bleed.

She put a Band-Aid on her right index finger.

TWO: Thread a wire coat hanger through the tiny opening in the head of the zipper and pull upward.

Suzanna tried to hold her stomach in while pulling gently on the zipper. It inched skyward, but stopped in the vicinity of her hip bones.

If I can just get them on, they'll stretch.

It was time for the final method from years ago. If this didn't work, nothing would, and she would have to give up.

THREE: Lie down on the bed, hold stomach in with one hand, and glide zipper toward button.

It wasn't working. Nothing was working. She was going to have to admit defeat, admit that her pre-baby body was as much a thing of the past as those carefree years before she was a wife and mother.

Rio.

Suzanna took a deep breath, grabbed the hanger with both hands, and yanked. The zipper closed. She tried not to breathe.

Rio sprang into her thoughts. She tried to push him out. She tried to conjure up sexy images of her husband instead, but these days Eric seemed to be miles away, worrying about some local political intrigue or another. She couldn't say what, exactly. His involvement in one political cause after another had left her exhausted.

"Hey, hon . . . I've got to run down the street for a minute," Eric called from somewhere down the hall.

Suzanna panicked and tried to sit up, but she was beached like a whale in a corset. She could hear Eric's footsteps getting closer and she rocked back and forth trying to get enough momentum to hurl herself off the bed.

"Go ahead, sweetie," she gasped.

Eric was almost at the door. She rolled onto the floor and grabbed at the quilt to pull herself up. The quilt slid silently to the floor. She heard the doorknob turn.

Thank God I locked it.

"Everything OK in there?" Eric asked, rattling the knob.

Suzanna kicked the quilt under the bed as she heard her husband picking the lock.

Damn him and his competence!

Suzanna was still on the floor, with her feet tucked under the bed where she had kicked the quilt, when he walked in. He was holding Lizzy, who was sucking on a rag doll. The doll was covered in baby slobber, which usually amused Suzanna to no end. But there was a first time for everything.

"Oh, sorry," Eric said, plopping the toddler on the bed. Lizzy pulled the doll out of her mouth and started sucking on the top sheet. Eric sat on the edge of the bed and looked down at his wife. "I didn't know you were exercising."

Suzanna lifted her head and realized that it did appear that she was doing sit-ups. She lay back down, exhausted. If Eric wanted to think it was from a great workout, so be it.

"That's OK . . . I'm done," she said. When she couldn't get up, she added, "Well, maybe just a few more crunches."

Eric put Lizzy on the floor so she wouldn't fall off the bed. Suzanna and Eric had hoped they would be breezy parents, but the apartment now resembled nothing less than Baby Prison: locks on all the cabinets and doors, baby gates at every entrance to every staircase that were so complex Suzanna usually found herself leaping over them, and cleaning supplies stored on shelves so high Lizzy might not be able to reach them until college.

Eric blew Suzanna a kiss and headed out the door. He turned back, leaning against the doorframe.

"My parents called. They want to take Lizzy to Disneyland pretty soon. That good by you?"

"I don't know, honey," Suzanna said. "I mean, she's only two years old. And she doesn't really know your parents very well."

"I think that's the point," Eric said. "The idea that your mom will be here and sucking up all the grandchild love has my mom feeling a little insecure, I think."

"Let me think about it," Suzanna said.

"I already told them yes," Eric said.

"Then why did you ask me if I was good with it?" Suzanna asked in a surly voice. It drove her crazy when her husband asked her opinion on something, just to smack her down with an "I already decided." She fell for it every time, just like Charlie Brown and his football. She realized it was a difference in upbringing. Eric always said his family was just nonconfrontational, but Suzanna felt that these "what do you think, even though I've already made up my mind" moments were passive-aggressive. When she finally brought this to Eric's attention, he said, "That's possible, but your family is aggressive-aggressive, so we're probably even."

He had her there.

"I'm going over to the community garden. There seems to be some debate about pesticides; thought I'd see what the trouble was all about," he said, looking down at her sweating form. "Don't kill yourself. . . . I think you're perfect."

Did he think she was perfect? Was he blinded by love or had he just stopped noticing? She felt guilty about her less-than-kind observations of a moment ago. He really was an amazing guy.

Suzanna felt a tingling in her nose, which was a sign that she was going to cry. Disgusted with herself, she unzipped the jeans and sat up, still breathing hard from her "workout." Eric was such a wonderful man. There was nothing to be gained by arbitrating the squabble at the community garden, but he saw it as his job to keep Venice on a happy, even keel. It was amazing how many people came in and out of the Nook seeking his advice. She was really proud of him . . . although he was often distracted. She kept telling herself that he was distracted for the greater good, but sometimes, as he headed out the door for more good deeds, she had to admit it irritated her. She knew he really did love her—even when he was preoccupied. When she was pregnant and crashing into chairs with her huge belly, he'd held her and made her feel like the most beautiful woman in the world. Well, truth be told, he only managed to get as far as making her feel like the most beautiful *whale* in the world, but that wasn't his fault.

Suzanna pulled herself onto the bed, hauling Lizzy with her. She lay back, trying to catch her breath as she watched Lizzy attempting to stand on the mattress. The toddler gave up and crawled over to her mother. She patted Suzanna on the head, which made them both laugh. Suzanna swooped the baby up and covered her with noisy kisses. Why was she even *thinking* about Rio? She had everything in the universe right here.

I'm just going to forget I ever thought I saw him.

* * *

Suzanna's resolve was short-lived.

She kept an eye on the Beach Walk for the next couple of days but there was no sign of Rio. She was relieved that she had probably just imagined the whole thing and let Rio fade into memory again. Besides, she had enough on which to focus. Their mother was due to arrive in two days and Erinn had one excuse after another why Suzanna should be orchestrating the bulk of the arrangements, including living arrangements. Erinn thought their mother should stay at Suzanna's and she was certainly persuasive in her arguments: Suzanna had Lizzy and their mother would love every minute spent in the baby's company. Erinn had a large cat that might not take kindly to Piquant. And of course Erinn was desperately trying to rent out her guesthouse to make ends meet.

Her mother called often, a little unsettled that nothing was finalized, but Suzanna told her not to worry about a single thing. The truth of the matter was that Suzanna and Eric would truly be thrilled to have Virginia stay with them. There was just something about Erinn's "It's not my problem" attitude that made Suzanna nuts. Suzanna told her mother that she and Erinn were fighting over her.

Well, that was the truth . . . in a way.

From the tearoom window, Suzanna could see clouds rolling in and a striking woman with perfect posture striding into the foyer that separated the Bun from the Nook. The woman looked around, clearly not a regular who was familiar with the place.

The Bun was closed for the day. Suzanna hoped the woman wasn't interested in tea. Suzanna hated turning people down. She couldn't stand to see the crushed spirit of a person being denied a cup of tea and a small pastry. She'd put a kettle on rather than be greeted by such disappointment.

Suzanna studied the woman. She wore tailored pants with a man's shirt tucked into them. Her hair was slicked back away from her face, sweeping across her jawbone. She wore large, round, black glasses. Suzanna thought she was attractive, in a postapocalyptic way: strong, confident, with a take-no-prisoners air about her. Something about her made Suzanna think this woman could stand the rejection of a closed tea shop.

"May I help you?" she asked, coming into the foyer from the tea shop.

"I hope so," the woman replied, smiling a crisp, toothy smile. She waved a stack of papers. "I'm showing some artwork at Willow Station later this month and I was wondering if I might leave some flyers with you."

Willow Station was a well-respected art gallery in Santa Monica.

Suzanna had forgotten about it but made a mental note that it might be a good place to take her mother. She reached for the green flyers.

"I don't hang flyers in the tea shop," Suzanna said. "But I'm sure my husband will be happy to put one up on the community board he has in the bookstore."

"That would be wonderful," the woman said. "Can I leave extra, in case anyone would want to take one with them?"

Suzanna took them and nodded. Flyers had been a bone of contention in their workplace even before Eric and Suzanna were married. Eric loved flyers. He thought the old-school approach of tacking flyers and business cards on bulletin boards and flagpoles kept a community "real." Suzanna saw them as artificial at best and litter at worst. Eric and Suzanna had reached a nice compromise. Flyers in the Nook, no flyers in the tearoom. It crossed Suzanna's mind that she and Eric had been experts at the art of compromise before they even got married. How many couples could say that?

Suzanna looked at the flyer.

"Alice?" Suzanna asked and looked at the woman.

"Yes, Alice," she said. "Thank you."

The woman took two purposeful steps and was out the door. Suzanna realized that Alice had not asked Suzanna's name in return.

"You're welcome," she said to the closed door.

Suzanna looked at the flyers in her hand. She was annoyed at herself for agreeing to hand them over to Eric. He could foster the community all he wanted, but it was Suzanna who had to go through the outdated pamphlets and multicolored sheets every week to make room for the latest batch of community outreach.

She peeked out the window of the tea shop and watched Erinn pull into an open parking space. It likely wouldn't matter to Erinn that the shop was closed; she rarely came by for tea. She was more inclined to spend hours in the Book Nook, coming in with insane requests for Eric to track down. When Erinn wasn't working, she kept her mind and Eric's time occupied with books. Erinn was much more like their intellectual parents than Suzanna was, although Suzanna (she had to admit) got along better with them. Well, that wasn't really difficult; Erinn couldn't get along with anybody.

Maybe Mom should stay with me.

Suzanna frowned. She was perfectly happy to have their mother stay with her family in their apartment over the store. Suzanna had always called the living space "the Huge Apartment." It *was* enormous, with three bedrooms, a spacious bathroom, living room, dining room, and fantastic eat-in kitchen, and there was more than enough room for their mother. As a matter of fact, their mother would be a welcome addition!

Then why am I so annoyed with Erinn?

She couldn't actually put her finger on the reason, but there was no getting around it. She was extremely annoyed. Erinn always shirked her familial responsibilities. Suzanna always had to be the one to remember birthdays, make holiday arrangements, call their mother. Erinn had been running away from responsibility for years. Now their mother was coming, and Erinn not only had enough room in her rambling house to take in a platoon of mothers, she had an empty guesthouse, too. But instead of stepping up to the plate, she was letting it all rest on Suzanna's shoulders.

As usual.

No, Mom should stay with Erinn; she'd have her own space in the guesthouse and besides, it was a matter of principle!

Suzanna heard the door creak open in the foyer that joined the Rollicking Bun to the Book Nook. Erinn stepped inside and veered immediately into the Book Nook. Suzanna inched toward the Nook so she could eavesdrop on Erinn's conversation with Eric. Erinn was like a canker sore; if it stopped bothering her, Suzanna would poke it with her tongue until she was aware of it again.

"Hey, Erinn," Eric said. "What can I do for you?"

"I was wondering if you were able to make any headway tracking down my book."

"Book? Was I supposed to find a book?"

Suzanna smiled to herself. Eric loved to tease Erinn.

"Yes, Eric," Erinn said. "The Mary Wollstonecraft."

"Hmmm . . . let me think. Mary Wollstonecraft. New mystery author, right?"

"Good God, no!"

"Mash-up writer?"

"Never! She didn't write *novels*."

"Oh! WOLLstonecraft . . . the one who wrote *Thoughts on the Education of Daughters: With Reflections on Female Conduct, in the*

More Important Duties of Life . . . that Wollstonecraft? Why didn't you say so?"

"I did. I did say so."

Suzanna couldn't resist. She peeped around the corner to watch Eric deposit a large, battered book in Erinn's hand. He was trying not to laugh, but Suzanna could only see a confused scowl on Erinn's face. She didn't know why Eric bothered. Erinn really had no sense of humor when it came to herself. Or to anything.

Suzanna caught Eric's eye as she entered the room. They both knew what was coming. Years ago, Eric had pointed out that Erinn always said your name by way of greeting. It never failed to be a shared joke between husband and wife.

"Suzanna," Erinn said.

"Erinn."

Suzanna caught a wink from Eric. God, she loved that man.

"I've come to talk about Mother," Erinn said.

"Come on in," Suzanna said, putting the pamphlets down and ushering her sister toward the tea shop. "I'm just cleaning up a bit. I'll get us some tea."

Suzanna steeled herself for a conversation with her sister. Erinn was a writer; she was *good* at conversation. But Suzanna was on her toes . . . she was not going to give in.

"I got a job," Erinn said.

"That's great news," Suzanna said. She started stacking delicate dinner plates on a sideboard. "You'll have enough money to keep the guesthouse free for Mom."

"That's true."

"It is?" Suzanna looked up, startled. She felt guilty that she had been thinking such unkind, un-sisterly thoughts. She felt the anxiety she'd been carrying in her shoulders suddenly ease.

Maybe that's why I had a stress float! This has been weighing on me more than I thought.

Erinn walked to the sideboard and took the glass dome off a cake platter containing gingerbread, a specialty of the house. She took a plate from the top of Suzanna's stack and tipped a slice delicately onto it. She sat at one of the small tables and started to eat.

"It's true that I'll have enough money . . . but it's too late. I've already rented the place," Erinn said. "This is delicious, by the way."

"To who?" Suzanna could feel her teeth clench.

"*Whom* . . . to whom."

"I said 'whom'!"

Erinn gave her younger sister her long-suffering smile.

"Well, I guess it's settled then," Suzanna said. "Mom will stay with me."

CHAPTER 5

ERINN

The drive from Suzanna's tea shop in Venice to Erinn's home in Santa Monica was only a few miles, but Erinn castigated herself the entire trip home.

Why did I lie about having a tenant? And even worse, lie about getting a job? These are very visible lies!

Erinn got out of her car and walked to the front door, digging in her purse for her house keys. She was proud of the work she had done restoring her home, but she could see that it was, once again, getting that down-at-the-heels look. Shabby but not quite shabby chic. Erinn knew the meandering front walkway by heart and was so used to the routine of lost keys that she never had to look up. Feeling the key chain in her hands, she pulled them out of her bag and held them in the air, triumphantly.

"And I have found Demetrius like a jewel . . . mine . . ."

Erinn stopped midquote as she stared at the tiny woman sitting on her step.

"Mine own . . . and not mine own," said the woman in a hushed whisper. "*A Midsummer Night's Dream,* act three."

"Act four," Erinn said.

"Is it?" asked the woman. She put tiny fists up to her mouth in dismay. "I always get everything wrong."

"No, no, that was very . . . close," Erinn said, amazed that anyone could or would finish a random Shakespearean quote.

Who is this woman?

"My name is Dymphna," the woman said, anticipating the question. "Dymphna Pearl."

Erinn shook the offered hand. Erinn was the smallest woman in her family, several inches shorter than both her mother and her sister, but her hand closed completely around Dymphna's diminutive and calloused one. "I've come about the guesthouse."

"The guesthouse?"

The fists returned to Dymphna's mouth.

"Is it already rented?" Dymphna asked. "I knew I waited too long."

"Oh! No, it isn't rented."

"Thank goodness!"

Did she really say "goodness"?

"I was selling the last of my sheep and it took longer than I thought it would," Dymphna said. "My luck hasn't been very good these last couple of years—so I figured the place would be long gone."

"Your sheep?"

"Yes," Dymphna said. "I'm a shepherdess."

"In Los Angeles?"

"No, of course not," Dymphna said. "In Malibu."

"Oh, yes . . . Malibu, land of sheep," Erinn said, instantly regretting her sarcasm. Who was she to judge this woman's ridiculous career choice?

"Well, I *was* a shepherdess," Dymphna said, her eyes filling with tears. "But it got too expensive. It took everything I had and I failed."

This woman really has a knack for alienating potential landladies.

Dymphna, who had stood up to greet Erinn, collapsed back onto the front step, put her head in her lap, and sobbed. Erinn patted her tiny shoulder awkwardly. She was never good at moments like this, moments that required tact and a few soothing words.

How strange that I'm a writer and yet I'm at a loss for words. Oh, wait, this isn't about me.

Erinn searched her brain for something, anything, to say. She suddenly remembered Massimo, an Italian cook who had once rented the guesthouse and who used to rhapsodize about lamb.

"I hope you got a good price for the meat," Erinn said.

Dymphna stopped crying instantly and looked fiercely into Erinn's eyes.

"I didn't raise them for food!" Dymphna said.

Dymphna stood up again. Standing on the step she was just eye level with Erinn. She wore a flowing skirt, petticoat, a fitted waistcoat, buttoned boots, and several scarves. Erinn thought she looked like someone who had lost her way and needed directions to a Steampunk Convention. Erinn took a step back. You couldn't be too careful around these would-be renters, and this diminutive—and over-dressed—woman didn't seem to be an exception.

"I'm raising them for their wool," Dymphna said, an edge of pride in her voice.

"You *were* raising them," Erinn corrected.

Dymphna looked as if Erinn had slapped her. She seized fistfuls of skirts in her little hands and held them to her eyes as she sobbed. Erinn looked around the yard and tried to think of a way to get this woman-child off her property. When she couldn't think of anything, she just waited until Dymphna calmed down. Finally, Dymphna dried her eyes on her skirt.

"I'm sorry," she said. "The pain is just very raw."

"I can well imagine," Erinn said, although she couldn't imagine it at all.

"May I see the guesthouse?"

"Oh!" Erinn felt a surge of panic. "I'm sorry! It's rented."

"But you said it wasn't rented."

"Did I?" Erinn asked. How was it that she could tell lie after damning lie to her sister just an hour ago and yet couldn't think of anything to say to this . . . shepherdess. "Oh, well, it's potentially rented. It's not a done deal. I'm waiting for a credit report."

Dymphna brightened.

"Well then, you might as well show it to me," she said. "I know all about lousy credit ratings."

At least she has a lousy credit rating.

Erinn let out an audible sigh. She hadn't realized she was holding her breath.

"This way," she said, leading Dymphna around back.

They threaded their way over the cobblestones through the side yard, which was full of hot pink and white mandevilla plants. Erinn watched as Dymphna took in the beauty of the plants. This was one of Erinn's secret tests for potential renters: Did they appreciate the artistry of the landscaping? As they entered the backyard Erinn tried to imagine how the yard and guesthouse must appear to a first-time guest. To her own eyes, the space took her breath away every time. The cobblestones continued from the side yard and cut a serpentine path up to the front door of the guesthouse, a beautifully replicated Victorian with a small porch and a varnished red door. Erinn noticed that Dymphna seemed more interested in the yard than the house.

"This yard is exquisite," Dymphna said. "Although you seem to have some brown patches in the grass."

"Well . . . I . . . I just can't seem to get anything to grow in those spots this year. Believe me, I've tried," Erinn said.

"It's brown patch disease," said Dymphna, looking sideways at Erinn. "I know what you're thinking . . . ."

Oh, I bet you don't.

"You're thinking that you can't possibly have brown patch disease because it's Santa Monica and it's not hot enough. But it's unseasonably warm so I think that's what it is . . . the ground is kind of freaked out."

The ground isn't the only thing that's freaked out.

"I could cure that with cornmeal and molasses if I end up living here."

That is never going to happen.

Erinn's phone rang in her jacket pocket.

"Excuse me for a minute," she said, relieved to have a respite from the Paula Deen of Landscaping. "Here is the key."

She handed Dymphna the key and walked toward the back porch of her own house.

"Hello?"

"Erinn, hi! It's Cary!"

Erinn sat down at her patio table with a thud. Cary was the supervising producer on the last two shows she had worked on, but it had been months since Erinn had heard from her. Maybe there was a new job. Could it be that she might have a job and a tenant by the end of the day and not have to admit to her sister that she'd been lying just to get out of housing their mother for an unforeseen amount of time? Erinn glanced up and watched Dymphna through the window of the guesthouse.

Well, maybe at least a new job.

"Hello? Erinn? Are you there?" Cary's voice brought Erinn back around.

"Yes!" she said, a little too loudly. "Hi, Cary. It's good to hear from you."

"Well, I've been thinking about you lately. I would love to see you."

"And I, you," Erinn said, wincing as she remembered Suzanna's admonishment not to say arcane things like "And I, you" instead of "Me too."

"Well, that's good, because I'm right around the corner!"

"On Montana?"

"No . . . the corner of your house."

Erinn looked up to see Cary, all six feet of her, loping into the backyard. Erinn, shocked, stood up and came down the porch stairs to greet her old boss. Erinn was not a hugger by nature but she knew there was no escaping Cary's exuberant embrace.

"I know this is crazy, but I was in the area and I just thought I'd stop in. I hope you're not busy."

"Oh, not at all. Not. At. All." Erinn tried to convey in three words how desperate she was for a job.

"This place is such an oasis of calm," Cary said grandly as she climbed onto the porch and looked around the yard. "It really is just a perfect, perfect spot."

"I have brown patch disease," Erinn said, not wanting her life to seem too perfect. Cary blinked in surprise, and Erinn, worried she may have overplayed her hand, added, "But I can cure it with corn-meal and molasses."

"What in God's name are you talking about?" Cary asked as she sat down at the patio table, suddenly looking very serious. "Erinn, we need to talk. I have a show coming up and—"

"I'll take it," Erinn said, sitting down across from her old—and maybe new—boss.

"You don't even know what it's about."

"I don't care!" Erinn said. "I mean . . . well, I've always enjoyed working with you and I'm sure this time won't be any different."

"It's not me that's the problem," Cary said. "It's a pilot for a real-ity show called *Red, White, and Blu*—spelled B-L-U, because it will be starring Blu Knight. Does that name ring a bell?"

This situation was exactly why Erinn didn't like face-to-face conversations. If this discussion were taking place on the phone, like it should, she could be madly pecking away on the Internet until she found out who or what Blu Knight was and not look as out of touch as she knew she was.

"No," Erinn admitted. "Should it?"

"She was a minor celebrity back in the day," Cary said. "Somehow, she's gotten one of the networks interested in doing a reality series or at least a pilot with her. She's trying to make a comeback."

"She's trying to come back as a minor celebrity?"

"No, as a shoe designer. She wants to make high heels that suburban moms will wear to make them feel fabulous or some such horseshit."

"Well," Erinn said, "you know I'm always ready to help. All I need to do is charge the batteries for the camera."

Cary looked down at her perfectly manicured nails and said nothing. Erinn could sense that there was more to the equation than the batteries—there had to be! Why was Cary on her back porch instead of calling Erinn's agent, Mimi Adams, about this?

"There is one little thing," Cary said, but then said no more.

Balzac said, "A flow of words is a sure sign of duplicity." I wonder what he'd make of Cary's fits and starts?

"It can't be all that bad," Erinn said.

"That all depends." Cary looked at Erinn. "You see, Blu has fallen on hard times. . . ."

Who hasn't?

"We need to shoot the pilot in Blu's house and at the shoe factory, you know, a day-in-the-life sort of thing."

"And let me guess," Erinn said. "She doesn't have a shoe factory."

"That," Cary said, "and she doesn't have a house."

"Well, with a wide-angle lens, we can make her apartment seem like a house. Leave that to me."

"She doesn't have an apartment, either. She's homeless."

All the puzzle pieces fell into place. Cary might need a good producer and camera op, but more than that, she needed a place for this Blu person to live. And how incredibly perfect that the guesthouse was currently empty. No wonder Cary was waxing poetic about Erinn's perfect oasis! Talk about horseshit!

"I know you're probably thinking . . . ," Erinn started carefully.

"Don't say anything until you meet her," Cary said, motioning to a figure at the edge of the house.

From the shadows of the side yard appeared an awkward child in shorts and a T-shirt. As the girl got closer, Erinn could see that she wasn't a child, just the size of one, only with huge breasts, a surgically induced pout, and hair extensions. Even as small as she was, she was wearing six-inch see-through platform shoes the likes of which Erinn had only seen while channel surfing (and quickly surfing past) movies in the middle of the night.

She must have hit on hard times after the plastic surgery.

Cary beamed her best showbiz smile.

"Blu!" Cary said. "I thought I asked you to stay in the car until I called you."

"It's hot in the car. I didn't want to frizz." Blu shook her red-and-blond-striped curls.

Erinn started to panic. Yes, she needed this job badly, but she could never work with this little spoiled starlet, let alone rent her the guesthouse.

A door slammed and all three women turned toward the guesthouse. They watched as Dymphna carefully locked the front door and walked toward them.

"That house is a riot!" Blu said. "It's so small."

Erinn bristled. *What a horrid person, what a philistine not to see the beauty and detail in the miniature house.*

Dymphna floated up the stairs and looked at the two newcomers.

"Hello," she said sadly. "I guess you've come to look at the guesthouse, too."

"Not hardly," Blu said.

"We were actually thinking . . . ," Cary said, but Erinn cut her off.

Dymphna might be an unemployed shepherdess but she knew about brown patches and cornmeal and she appreciated beauty.

"This is Dymphna," Erinn said quickly. "My new tenant."

Cary shook Dymphna's hand and didn't seem at all displeased with the turn of events, which was a relief to Erinn. Maybe the job was not lost.

"Lucky you!" Cary said.

Blu seemed completely uninterested in anything that was going on around her, and appeared ready to bolt, but Erinn wanted to seal the deal with Cary so she kept the conversation going.

"Dymphna is interested in wool. She was raising sheep until recently."

"You were a shepherd?" Blu wrinkled her stub of a nose.

"Shepherdess, yes," Dymphna replied. "But now I'm going to raise Angora rabbits for their fur."

"I love Angora," Blu said. "So . . . if you're a shepherdess when you have sheep, what are you called when you have rabbits?"

"If you were a man we could call you Warren," Cary said, and then when no one laughed said, "Sorry."

Blu, surprisingly, actually did seem interested in Angora wool and started peppering Dymphna with questions. Cary steered Erinn to the side of the porch. She took a quick look back at the two waifs. If it weren't for Cary, Erinn would feel like the largest woman in Santa Monica.

"Sorry the guesthouse was rented," Erinn said. "If I had only known you were interested . . ."

Cary looked confused and then she laughed.

"The guesthouse . . . oh, no, Erinn, you misunderstood me! Blu could never live there! There isn't a lens in the world that could make that place look big enough for our purposes. Blu has to look like she's made it to the big time!"

I took on an ex-shepherdess for no reason?

"Well, then," Erinn said, "I guess as soon as you find a house grand enough for Blu, we'll be all set to go."

Cary's face fell.

Now what?

"Erinn, this pilot is important. It could mean some real money for all of us if it hits. And we're all in need of a little career boost right now, so we all have to go the extra mile."

"I understand," Erinn said. "I'll throw in my fish-eye lens, no extra charge."

"How do I put this?" Cary said to the air. "Erinn, Blu needs to live in YOUR house for the next few weeks."

"My house? Why? Why can't the network buy her a house?"

"BUY her a house? Darling, we're talking cable! Anyway, we can't let the network know she's homeless! They are really sensitive to criticism that these reality shows aren't real."

"It won't be real. This isn't her house!"

"Nobody needs to know that! Your house is gorgeous. It's perfect. It will make Blu seem like she has . . . some substance."

"I don't think so, Cary. I'm sorry."

"Look, whatever you made on your last job, which was a while ago if I'm not mistaken, I'll double it. I'll also throw in an extra gig up the coast at a winery near Cambria. A show called *Budding Tastes*. It will be just like Old Home Week."

"Why will it be like Old Home Week?" Erinn asked. "I never lived in Cambria."

"I know, darling, but you lived in Napa. You lived near wine. The shoot is this weekend, so you don't have to be here when she moves in. I'll spearhead everything on that end. You'll be doing me a huge favor."

The shoot was a "sizzle reel" as opposed to a pilot. When Erinn had first gotten started in TV production the subtleties of the jargon perplexed her. Now she knew that it all was code for how much money the production company or network was going to put into something. A "sizzle reel" was the least expensive, followed by a pilot. In this case, Blu's pilot trumped the wine show in importance, but it was all paid employment!

But the money was a sure thing and that was enticing.

Erinn was about to say that she couldn't go this weekend, because her mother was coming into town. But having grown up in Wine Country, if not in Cambria, there probably wasn't a better producer for the show.

Maybe this weekend would be a perfect time to be away.

Let the dust settle and all that.

While Erinn silently weighed her options, Cary pulled a shingle that was hanging precariously off the side of the house, handed it to Erinn, and continued, "You really need to take care of this beautiful house and that takes cash."

Erinn took the shingle.

At least I can stop lying to my sister.

CHAPTER 6

VIRGINIA

Virginia could feel her cheeks flush as she walked Piquant through the Los Angeles International Airport. He was wearing his bright blue "Emotional Support Service Dog" vest, and in Virginia's opinion, he was not carrying it off at all. His little Chihuahua shake just added to his lack of panache. She felt ridiculous and looked around, worried that her fellow travelers would be scowling or scoffing, but this was Los Angeles, a city that prided itself on not gawking at celebrities and taking all oddities in its collective stride. Piquant sailed through the airport without a sideways glance in his blazingly blue direction.

She insisted that Suzanna meet her at the curb. Virginia was determined to establish a tone of independence. She planned on making a big show of effortlessly (a) escorting Piquant, (b) balancing his carrier, and (c) getting her own luggage off the carousel, all with the casual ease for which this city was known. The fact that she was currently only accomplishing (a) and (b) was leaving her a little anxious, since she had two very large—and overweight—bags with which to contend at the baggage claim. Looking up at the monitor to see which carousel would be depositing her luggage, she failed to notice two little hands tugging at Piquant.

"Doggy!" said the little girl as she happily twisted the Chihuahua's ears.

God, these Los Angeles mothers! What is wrong with parents these days?

"Sweetie, you wouldn't like it if someone were grabbing your ears, would you? Now let go of Piquant's ears."

The insufferably reasonable tone of the new age mother annoyed Virginia.

Just tell the kid to stop! Wait! How does this woman know my dog's name?

As the mother bent down and tried to stop her daughter from molesting Piquant, she collided with Virginia's forehead as she bent to rescue her dog. After clunking heads they looked at each other, and Virginia realized she was looking into her daughter's eyes.

"Hello, Grammy!" Suzanna said, standing up and throwing her arms around Virginia. Piquant was sandwiched between them and let out a squeak. Suzanna released her mother and patted the dog vigorously.

"So this is Piquant!" Suzanna said, scooping up Lizzy with her free hand and swirling the baby onto her hip. "I guess we both have our babies!"

Dear God, what has happened to my daughter's mind?

"I thought you were going to meet me at the curb," Virginia said as Suzanna started ushering the group toward the baggage area. "I know it's hard to park here."

"I knew it wasn't going to be easy wrangling your bags and a dog. Besides, Eric let us off; he'll circle back for us."

Virginia wondered if Suzanna and Eric thought she was getting too old to get herself to the curb but decided not to explore that in any more detail. That was an avenue she found herself traveling more and more: wondering if people thought she was too old. Clearly, all that meant was *she* was worried she was too old. Virginia consoled herself with the knowledge that she had moved to New York City by herself at an age when most people were trying to figure out if their Social Security would last through their lifetime (not that she was above wondering that herself from time to time), and here she was on an extended trip to visit her daughters, something she had planned and executed by herself. *How could anyone question her vitality?* she wondered angrily before stopping to realize no one had. She looked over at Suzanna, who appeared to be getting a little winded from carrying Lizzy.

"Lizzy can walk like a big girl, can't she?" Virginia asked, looking at Lizzy instead of Suzanna.

"Yes, Mom, Lizzy can walk like a big girl, but I don't want her connecting with all these random germs," Suzanna said.

Connecting with random germs? What does that even mean?

Suzanna continued, eyeing Piquant shivering in Virginia's arms.

"Can't Piquant walk like a big dog?" she asked.

"No, Suzanna, he can't," said Virginia. "He's a Chihuahua . . . he cannot walk like a big dog. Are we in some sort of contest here?"

"Doggy!" Lizzy leaned toward Piquant, who reared back in Virginia's arms. Virginia patted him and kissed him on his little dome of a head. Suzanna faced forward and moved determinedly with the crowd. Virginia wondered if the tension she felt was real or if she was just out of practice being around children . . . and their overprotective mothers.

They found the baggage carousel and Suzanna stationed herself at the yawning cavern that spat out bags. As the bags started to tumble out, Suzanna made happy sounds as she pointed at each one and asked Lizzy, "What's that? What's that, Lizzy?"

"Suuuuuucaaaaaa," Lizzy said.

"That's right!" Suzanna said, beaming at her mother. "Did you hear that, Grammy? She knows the word *suitcase!*"

"Isn't that something?" Virginia said self-consciously. "Isn't that something, Piquant?"

Suzanna looked at her mother thoughtfully.

"*Suitcase* is a very advanced word for a two-year-old."

"No doubt!"

"What does your bag look like?" asked Suzanna, turning back toward the bags hurtling earthward.

"Bags . . . bags plural," Virginia said. "I didn't know how long I was going to stay, so I packed for every conceivable occasion."

Suzanna laughed. "We don't have many occasions that require more than sweats or jeans. There's a lot of baby slobber going on at our house."

Virginia snuck a quick peek at Suzanna's lower extremities to see if she had chosen sweats or jeans for the occasion of picking up her mother, whom she had not seen in almost eight months.

"I saw that, Mom," Suzanna said, turning away from her mother. "I saw you check out my butt. I know I've gained a little weight, but I just had a baby!"

"Dear, I was only—" Virginia saw one of her suitcases slide down the chute and changed the subject. "There's one of my suitcases now."

"Suuuucaaaaa," Lizzy said.

Virginia melted. She had forgotten the sheer joy of watching the evolution of a new human being. She made a mental note to cut Suzanna some slack. New motherhood was certainly not easy. Virginia remembered that when she was a brand-new mother she seemed to call her own mother on a daily basis for advice. Once, when Erinn was just born, Virginia called home in tears.

"I don't know what to do," she had sobbed. "I just can't seem to get the baby to stop crying."

Virginia's mother had offered her some sage advice: "Make sure she isn't hungry, tired, or wet. Then leave your dignity at the door— make faces; soft, funny sounds; blow wet kisses on her belly. Trust me, you'll distract her."

It had been many years since Virginia had done this, but she was ready to give it another go. Lizzy was such an advanced two-year-old. Virginia looked at Piquant. Maybe she should have tried this with the dog. She watched Suzanna, baby on her hip, drag one huge suitcase and then the other off the luggage carousel. She realized that her daughter very rarely called for motherly advice. Well, she was here now and that would all change soon enough!

Each of them pulling the handle of a large suitcase, they made their way to the curb.

"Eric is driving a hybrid SUV," Suzanna said.

Of course he is.

"It's bright yellow. You can't miss it."

Virginia looked down the row of cars, packed not like sardines in orderly rows, but more like panties at a Victoria's Secret sale: brightly colored shapes heaped on top of each other and sticking out at precarious angles. Virginia wondered how this could be one of the busiest airports in the world. It just seemed so disorganized. She spotted a large, yellow, truck-looking vehicle.

"I think I see him," Virginia said and started waving.

"Mom," Suzanna said. "That's a minivan. We have an SUV. A hybrid."

Virginia put her arm down. Suzanna seemed very tense and judgmental, almost a throwback to her teenage years. *Well,* thought Virginia, *hormones then, hormones now.* Then she stopped herself. She knew better than to even THINK about hormones around her girls, especially Erinn. You could not even mention hormones to Erinn; they were a political hotbed.

"Men use PMS to keep women in their place," Erinn used to pronounce, not seeming to notice the irony that she was a top-selling young Broadway playwright. No one was keeping her anyplace but on the Great White Way.

"So . . . what then?" Virginia had ventured. "We pretend it doesn't exist?"

"Yes," Erinn said. "Exactly! No preteen hormonal crying jags, no PMS, no change-of-life histrionics. We just ignore them."

And Erinn's words became law, which Virginia found secretly hilarious since it was Virginia's generation, not Erinn's, who had done the heavy lifting. But she was thankful that Erinn took feminism so seriously so she held her tongue. But when Virginia went through The Change, she kept her hot flashes and night sweats to herself.

Erinn is so intense; it's no wonder she never married, Virginia thought, then felt instantly guilty for having thought it. Surely there was a man out there who was as equally sensitive to women's issues, political issues, environmental issues . . . issues in general. There was that nice younger man . . . what was his name? . . . Jude . . . yes, that was it. But that romance went nowhere. Although Virginia was very sketchy on the details of the dying embers of that romance. Erinn was not big on sharing.

She had forgotten how she had to dodge and weave with both her girls at different stages of their lives. This was going to take some getting used to again. She spotted another large yellow thing in the traffic. This one had a rack on the roof of some kind—surely this was an SUV. Was an SUV a car or a truck? It was a sports utility vehicle.

"What about that yellow vehicle over there?" Virginia pointed.

"That's another minivan."

"Sorry, dear," Virginia said. "I don't really interact with cars much in New York."

Suzanna looked down the line of trucks and cars and suddenly started waving.

"There he is," she said. "Eric! Errrriiiiiiic! Over here!"

A bright yellow vehicle (that looked exactly like the previous two bright yellow minivans) pulled smoothly to the curb. Eric got out of the car and hugged Virginia.

"Hello, mother-in-law," he said. "We have been counting the days."

She believed him. Eric had always been a great kid and had become a wonderful man, husband, and father. When Suzanna told her that she and Eric were getting married, Virginia couldn't believe it. She had always harbored a soft spot for Eric, having known him since he and Suzanna were both kids in Napa Valley. She'd always hoped they'd get together, but as the years dragged on without either of them making a move, even though they worked elbow to elbow at the Rollicking Bun, the dream gradually faded. But now they were making up for lost time: marriage and baby happened very quickly. Considering how uptight Suzanna seemed to be, Virginia hoped not too quickly.

Eric swung the suitcases into the back and came around to help Virginia into the front seat.

"I'm fine, Eric," she said as she tried to leap into the passenger seat. It really was ridiculously high. "I can still take care of myself."

"At least let me hold the dog," he said, reaching for Piquant.

"Oh, careful; he isn't very friend—" Virginia said, then stopped herself as Piquant went pliantly to Eric. She felt the tiniest prick of jealousy but called herself on it. These were strange new waters she was wading in.

Once Suzanna had gotten Lizzy strapped into her baby seat, a complicated, new age affair that looked like it could drive the car if it were so inclined, Eric swung into traffic and they were on their way to Venice. Virginia found herself ill at ease with this new family, a family that was hers and yet wasn't. For the life of her, she couldn't think of anything to say.

"I'm sorry Erinn isn't in town, Mom," Suzanna said, laying a consoling hand on Virginia's shoulder. "She got a job up the coast for a few days, and you know how that goes."

Virginia didn't know the first thing about Erinn's recent line of work, just that there never seemed to be enough of it. All she knew right now was that her daughter was conveniently out of town and conveniently had rented out her guesthouse just before Virginia's arrival. Coincidence? Maybe. Maybe not. But pretty damn convenient.

CHAPTER 7

SUZANNA

Why am I so rude to my mother?

Suzanna knew she was out of sorts due to the potential Rio sightings but that was no excuse. It was like plucking the petals off a daisy: "It's Rio," "It's not Rio," "It's Rio," "It's not Rio." She had seen the mysterious man a couple of times now, sometimes skating, sometimes jogging, always in motion. But he never was within identification range. Each time she saw him, a jolt went through her. Not the jolt one always read about in romance novels but the jolt from an open wire. Searing and painful, it was the kind of sensation that made you understand to the soles of your feet that you should never, ever go near an open wire again.

Even if it were Rio, Suzanna had left that world far behind her; she was now a happy if slightly out-of-shape wife and mother. Part of her wanted Rio to see her . . . see what he was missing. And a part of her wanted to make sure he didn't see her. . . . The out-of-shape part was really sinking in. But that was no excuse for being so short with her mother at the airport.

Had her mother suddenly become irritating? Suzanna didn't think so. So what if Virginia couldn't tell a minivan from an SUV? Was that a sin? So what if she had a dog the size of a mouse? There were worse flaws. Suzanna was also annoyed with Erinn for being out of town. Erinn always managed to be the sister who skated away from all responsibility when Suzanna wore the tag of "good daughter," and nothing had changed! Erinn was off doing God Knows What while Suzanna was clearing out a room in their apartment for their mother. Typical!

When they got back from the airport to the Bun, Suzanna found herself having a hard time getting her mother up to the apartment; several of the tea-shop regulars had hung around and were waiting to greet her. Piquant seemed to be causing quite a stir among the customers, too, although Suzanna noticed that the dog didn't seem to particularly crave the attention—something she could not say for her mother. Virginia had been to the shop many times over the years and was always a hit with the clientele. Apparently, the years in New York had done nothing to dim her allure. Suzanna felt the sting of remorse at her own behavior as she watched her mother interact (*elegantly* was the only word for it) with the tea-shop guests. Virginia hadn't seen many of the Bun customers since Suzanna's wedding almost three years ago, but she appeared to remember each and every name.

Eric took Lizzy up to the Huge Apartment, while Suzanna hovered in the background as her mother held court on the front porch of the Bun. Looking out toward the ocean, she felt a gentle calm until a tidal wave of emotion nearly flattened her. She held her breath as if she were underwater as the man whom she had decided was not Rio came running up the Beach Walk.

The glistening man with TV-worthy hair continued in her direction. She tried not to stare; the sun was not her friend and it blinded her. She started to squint, but realized if it were indeed Rio, her scrunched-up face was not what she intended to present. She tried to calm her heart as well as her facial features as he drew closer and closer.

Feet on the ground, feet on the ground, feet on the ground!

The sun went behind a cloud as the man was almost upon her. Whoever he was, it almost hurt her to see that his hair, jet black and wild as the wind, whipped across his face, and he had to keep tossing it back like a stallion in a storm. She had wild hair herself and when it was being blown around by the wind she looked like a circus clown. When she shook it out of her face she wound up trying to spit out the curl that ended up in her mouth.

Life could be so unfair.

As she turned back to the sanctuary of the tea shop, she felt a hand on her arm. Frozen in place, staring at the sweat-soaked hand, tanned against her pink, freckled forearm, she heard him speak before she saw him.

"Hello, Suzanna," Rio said. The soft Spanish accent was as silky as ever.

Suzanna berated herself. Why hadn't she rehearsed a stinging rebuke? On the one hand "Hello, Suzanna" didn't really lend itself to a haughty retort, but she should have been prepared. She met his eyes and prayed for something to come to her.

"Hello, Rio," she said.

Not exactly what she had in mind. She willed herself to look into his eyes. When she took a breath to try again, her strawberry-blond curls leaped into her mouth and almost gagged her. She tried to flick a saliva-covered strand out of her mouth and it snapped against her cheek with such force she was sure it left a welt.

"I thought it might be you," Rio said.

Oh? Imagine the odds of that—a woman who looks just like me standing in front of my own tea shop, she thought. But she said, "You cut your hair."

Hell.

A shadow of a melancholy smile passed over his handsome face. He continued to look into her eyes.

"Yes. My mother, she always cut my hair. When she died, I could not stand the thought of someone else cutting it. It would be as if . . . as if I lost her twice. After five years my hair was so long, I was sitting on it. So I had to cut it," he said and shrugged. "Life goes on, you know?"

Suzanna was stunned. She thought back to the days of her passionate crush. There was a day when he came into the tea shop and was showing pictures of his mother to one of the waitresses. Suzanna had thought it was a come-on strategy. She realized now that his mother was already dead and he was probably reaching out to anyone who would listen. She was so blinded by jealousy that he was paying attention to the waitress that she had never asked either one of them about it.

Perhaps he had been in mourning. His mother would have been dead at least a few years by then. Latin men could be so attached to their mothers—so sweet.

Perhaps I judged him too harshly.

"You look well, Suzanna," Rio said.

She felt herself melting. OK, so it wasn't "You look beautiful" or even "Lookin' good," but it was a start!

"Hey, you too! You're looking very well, extremely well."

And she was telling the truth; he looked irresistible. Which was a problem, because she was going to have to resist him. Plus, she reminded herself that he'd been a total tool to her!

She admitted the demise of what Erinn called their "pathetic little romance" had certainly not been all his fault. She had set her sights on him and went after him with everything she could muster. She knew that he was a dance instructor with a roster of female students practically two-stepping over one another to get his attention. She had deluded herself into thinking that she meant more to him than his other students. Well, that's one of the qualities of a great instructor, isn't it? Make every paying female feel special?

With every possible justification stripped away, the bare truth was she had thrown herself at him. In hindsight, he really hadn't paid much attention to her at all, had he? A few misguided gropings that she had practically insisted upon; she was more to blame than he was for the pain he'd caused her.

Rio leaned in, still holding her arm.

"Suzanna," he said. "I must speak to you alone."

Her feet left the ground. She tried to control her breathing but there was nothing she could do: A full-blown stress float was upon her. Because Rio had her by the arm she thankfully couldn't float out to sea, but she was floating horizontal to him, her feet in the air. She kept her eyes locked on his to make sure he didn't notice and, if he did, he seemed too overcome with some sort of urgent emotion to be aware of it.

"Suzanna?" said a voice from the patio.

POW! Suzanna was back on the ground.

Rio and Suzanna turned toward the voice. It was her mother, carrying the quaking Piquant and walking toward them. Suzanna tried to remain calm. After all, Virginia knew nothing about Rio. But mothers had a sixth sense, Suzanna knew, and she hoped her mother's own intuition was just a little rusty from being in New York for so long.

"I'm sorry to interrupt," Virginia said. "But some of the ladies were wondering if we could get tea."

"Oh! Sure, Mom!" she said, relieved that she still had the power of speech.

"This is your mother?" Rio asked, pushing his hair back and looking at Virginia in that sexy, bored way of his. Had she imagined his urgency at needing to see her?

"Yes," Suzanna said. "Mom, this is Rio. Rio, Mom. I mean Virginia. Virginia Wolf."

Suzanna studied her mother as Virginia took in the glory that was Rio. Suzanna wasn't sure what she expected: her mother to burst into flames at the sight of such magnificence? She only saw her mother's defenses go up and then lower as she realized there was not going to be a Virginia Woolf joke. Virginia Woolf jokes were definitely not Rio's style. As a matter of fact, no joke was Rio's style. Virginia offered her hand and Rio finally let go of Suzanna's arm to shake it. She tapped the ground lightly to make sure she was going to stay put.

"I am pleased to meet you," Rio said, his accent sounding like a hand stroking the nap of velvet. Smooth, smooth, smooth.

If a hand stroking velvet had a sound.

"And I, you," said Virginia, the relentless university professor.

Suzanna felt the smallest flash of irritated déjà vu. She had forgotten how annoying her family could be with their off-putting perfect grammar. She might be able to nag her sister into speaking more casually, but her mother was a different story. Suzanna worried that Rio might think her mother was stuck-up. She tried to shake off the adolescent embarrassment; she was a mother herself now. Besides, what did she care what Rio, the consummate jerk, thought of her mother? When she tuned back into the conversation, she realized her mother was speaking in Spanish.

Mom speaks Spanish?

Having no idea what the two of them were saying, Suzanna plastered on her "I'll pretend that I know what's going on" face, looking first to her mother and then to Rio as they conversed, lifting her eyebrows and nodding as the conversation appeared to warrant. It was a trick she'd picked up years ago. Her family was very intellectually inclined, and she found it much easier to look learned than actually learn a bunch of stuff. It turned out that nobody was fooled, but she fell back on old habits from time to time—like now.

Mercifully, Virginia switched back to English.

"It was very nice to meet you, Rio. I'll have to stop by your dance studio," Virginia said. "You are absolutely extraordinary."

Rio bowed slightly to both of them and jogged off. Suzanna's head was spinning.

Rio has a new dance studio? In town? Where? And why would my mother stamp him "extraordinary"? She just met the man!

Suzanna realized she was staring down the Beach Walk, watching Rio disappear around a clump of palm trees. He was running again and she took in every taut flex of his calf muscles until he was out of sight.

"Tea?" her mother asked.

"Tea!" Suzanna said, turning quickly to face her.

As the two women walked up the path to where Virginia's mini fan club waited, Suzanna hoped they would be able to confine their conversation to what kind of tea the ladies might like.

"What an interesting man," Virginia said.

"Extraordinary, even!" Suzanna replied. She seemed to be reverting to her teenage self minute by minute.

Virginia stopped walking and looked at her. Piquant sniffed the air, sensing tension.

"A man opening a dance studio for underprivileged kids seems pretty extraordinary to me," Virginia said.

Rio was opening a dance studio for underprivileged kids? That was impossible—that would just be so un-Rio. *Or would it?* She didn't really know him at all.

"Maybe you misunderstood, Mom," Suzanna said. "I mean, you were speaking Spanish."

"Yes I was, and I understood every word," Virginia replied, her voice a blend of confidence and childlike pride.

Suzanna had to admire the fact that her mother had unswerving faith in her own abilities, a trait she'd passed on to Erinn but that somehow had managed to skip Suzanna.

They started up the steps to the tea shop, both aware that the ladies were watching and probably much more interested in the body language they were witnessing between mother and daughter than any tea Suzanna might be brewing.

"He has opened a school for underserved kids. He's a couple doors down from you. It's in the back of that lovely brick courtyard . . . you know the one."

"Mr. Clancy's Courtyard?" Suzanna said. "Just the other day I was talking to someone who rents space there."

This was perfect! If Rio was working (and maybe living?) on their block, she was sure to run into him. Especially since she'd told Christopher that she'd stop down and see his latest work. And of course this was the building that her husband was working to get declared a historic landmark. Or a historic district. She really hadn't paid much attention, but she would now! She would head down there as soon as possible. It really had been a while since she'd stopped in.

Suzanna imagined throwing herself into the good fight to save the buildings on her little corner of the Venice Beach Walk. Sure, they were old and there were no tiled bathrooms and stainless-steel balconies that were all the rage in Manhattan Beach, just down the coast. But they were lovely weathered buildings and should be saved! Were the buildings in jeopardy? She really should be paying more attention to these things . . . these things that were so important to her husband. Maybe Rio was interested in all this, too.

She made a mental note to find out more about this historic monument thing so she could converse knowledgeably about it with Rio. She realized her mother was still standing beside her and Suzanna shook her head, trying to get the sweet chocolate pools that were Rio's eyes out of her mind. She turned to face her mother and found herself looking into the sweet chocolate pools of Piquant's eyes instead. They both blinked.

CHAPTER 8

ERINN

It felt good to be working again, although this was an extremely lean production. She was the entire crew: producer, director, camera operator, and sound engineer. She certainly wouldn't spread this around, but she actually preferred it this way. No negotiating with temperamental directors (if she was the camera operator) or moody cameramen (if she was the director).

If they paid me for each position, I wouldn't have to worry about money ever again.

No network had officially signed on, and it would be months before the show got any feedback, in all probability; there were notes and editing, more notes and focus groups to contend with before the show ever made it to air, if it ever did make it to air. The chances were slim at best. There were sizzle reels and pilots that Erinn had worked on that she had completely forgotten about by the time she'd heard the show had been passed over.

The concept here, the sizzle called *Budding Tastes,* was as jam-packed as the shooting was streamlined. The basic idea was that the winery, called Vermont Wines, produced not only wine but that the winery owner could also steer the viewer toward fabulous food-and-wine pairings. The show would be part business advice show, part travel show, part food show. The only problem here, as Erinn discovered as she got deeper and deeper into a conversation with Tiffany Vermont, the winery owner, was that Tiffany didn't really know anything about food-and-wine pairings, beyond the basic "red with meat, white with fish, champagne with everything." Erinn had grown up in Napa Valley; she knew her wines and had lived for years surrounded by sophisticated theater people and therefore knew her food-and-wine pairings as well. She had a professional hunch that this woman was not going to bring anything new and exciting to the production. And that had her worried. She would have to think of some kind of angle to make this show stand out from the crowd.

But what? How?

Tiffany practically hummed with ambition. As far as Erinn could tell, it was sheer willpower that got her a TV deal. She was tall, blond, and had a face frozen in a Botox-glazed stare. And most troubling of all was that she saw absolutely no irony in the fact that they were bottling California wines at the Vermont Winery.

When Erinn first arrived, Tiffany had sat on the hood of Erinn's car as Erinn singlehandedly unloaded all the camera gear. "People are always telling me that I should be on TV. Isn't that nice?"

Don't make me tell my parable.

Erinn started filming the winery and the surrounding hills. When she had to work with people and found herself becoming irritated with them, she took refuge in doing the scenic shots, beautiful landscape vignettes, or "the ubiquitous travelog shots," as Cary called them, as a way to calm herself down. She took in the winery, a California Mission-style building with a gleaming adobe front and a red-tile roof.

Erinn could guess that the wooden shutters and window boxes were probably Tiffany touches, since they had nothing to do with the architectural integrity of the building.

Behind the main building, there were two large, sleeker buildings where the wines were actually made and sat fermenting, and behind those were rows and rows of grapes. No matter what became of this pilot, Erinn was excited by the footage she was capturing. The land was beautiful.

Suddenly, a wine bottle appeared in front of the lens. Erinn stood up with a jolt, totally confused.

Tiffany was standing in front of the lens holding a bottle of wine as if she were a presenter on a game show.

"I designed the label myself. I thought you might want to shoot that."

Working with "talent," especially the wannabe variety of cast members of reality shows, was always taxing. These people, people like Tiffany and Blu, just wanted to be stars, not actors. Erinn longed for the dedication of the Broadway actors she'd known. But that was a hundred years ago. This was a new breed and they didn't appear to be going anywhere.

Secretly horrified, Erinn studied the label out of politeness and a touch of fascination. While Tiffany had added Cape Cod touches to her Mission-style winery, she went with a Bavarian theme on her labels. The labels featured Tiffany in a dirndl and low-necked top bending seductively toward the camera to show off her impressive cleavage—a more mature St. Pauli Girl. Tiffany looked at Erinn expectantly and posed again, this time with the wine bottle, mimicking the pose on the label.

There didn't seem to be any chance of ditching Tiffany.

"When do you think you'll start interviewing me?" Tiffany asked. "My hairdresser is also a makeup artist and she did my makeup for free. Wasn't that nice?"

Erinn bit her tongue. She knew better than to tell Tiffany that "for free" was a preposterous statement. Not that anyone seemed to care these days, but the expression "for free" drove her to distraction; "for" was really nothing more than shorthand for "in exchange for" and "free" was a short version of "free of charge." To say "for free" basically meant "in exchange for free of charge." Why no one used the correct "She did my makeup free" was beyond her.

But she knew she was alone in her umbrage.

Erinn tried to ignore Tiffany, who still seemed to be posing in the periphery. She looked in the viewfinder and concentrated on her shots. The land really was beautiful, and Erinn thought that if she had any time after the shoot, she might take a few still shots just for herself.

I'll bet Christopher would love to shoot up here, she thought.

Where had that come from?

Tiffany once again invaded the quiet, standing and posing in front of several long rows of grapes that stretched out over the hills like corduroy.

"I think this would make a nice shot, don't you? Me and the grapes? I could walk up and down the rows and we could chat about what it's like to create beautiful wine."

Please don't make me tell my parable.

"First of all, the show isn't about making beautiful wine. My understanding, correct me if I'm wrong, is that the show is about pairing wine and food. And second, the sun is not in the right position to shoot you. You'd be backlit and you'd just be a shadow."

"We don't want that!" Tiffany practically gulped. "Well, what about me in front of the . . ."

"Let me tell you a little parable," Erinn said.

Tiffany tilted her head to the side in confusion, a long hank of starched blond hair falling away from her slim neck.

"A hermit living way up in the Swiss Alps decides he is lonely and he goes down the mountain to find a bride. He meets a lovely young woman who agrees to go with him if she can bring her loyal donkey, who has been her constant companion since childhood. The hermit agrees; they marry and head back up the mountain. The hermit ties the donkey in the barn and they go to bed."

Tiffany snickered. "They went to bed, huh?"

"Yes, they went to bed. That has nothing to do with the story, so please concentrate. The following morning the hermit finds out that the donkey has kicked down the barn wall. The young bride, who doesn't really know anything about this man, worries what he might do. But the hermit just says, 'That's one' and goes off up the mountain with his goats."

"He has goats?"

"Yes, Tiffany, he has goats, but again, not the point. When he comes down the mountain, he discovers that the donkey has trampled all the vegetables in his garden. His bride is terrified of his reaction, but again, the hermit is very calm. He merely says, 'That's two.' "

Tiffany nodded. "He's a good man."

"Please stay with me, Tiffany. The hermit ties the donkey up and in the morning finds that the donkey has kicked over the chicken coop. The hermit looks at the donkey and then looks at his wife and says, 'That's three' and pulls out a gun and shoots the donkey. The wife, horrified, throws herself on the lifeless creature, and asks the hermit how he could be such a beast. The hermit looks at her and says, 'That's one. . . .' "

Tiffany nodded. "So . . . ," she said, "he wasn't a good man?"

"That's one!"

Tiffany gasped and her hands flew to her mouth.

"Oh!" she said and then punched Erinn playfully on the arm. "Oh, you!"

Just as Erinn thought she was going to pack up the car and go home, Tiffany's cell phone went off in her back pocket. Her jeans were so tight Erinn wasn't sure she'd be able to release it in time to catch the call, but with a flick of a pointed acrylic nail, she was focused on her phone call.

"I'll see you later," Tiffany said, *sotto voce,* waving to her like a little girl.

Erinn breathed a sigh of relief. Was this what life was going to be like with Blu? She put her eye back to the viewfinder of her XF300 HD Camcorder. She'd bought the camera when she was still flush with work, but even now that times were tight she didn't regret the purchase. The video quality was excellent and the body was lightweight. She hated to admit there were shoots she couldn't—and wouldn't—get because she couldn't physically handle the bigger cameras. Maddeningly, those jobs would always still go to the men in production. A harsh reality, but one not likely to change until the industry wrapped its collective head around the smaller, lighter cameras. There was a woman who was legendary in the industry. She could shoulder a big camera and even run through sand while shooting. Erinn tried her damnedest to work with a thirty-pound camera and got as far as getting it onto her shoulder, but after shooting for an hour, she had to have a production assistant lift it off. So she'd done her homework and came up with this lightweight beauty, which she knew she could handle. She was confident her work spoke for itself. If only a few more production companies would listen.

When she had shot every square inch of the winery and vineyard she knew she had to get back to Tiffany. There was no escape. She walked into a cool wine cellar and saw Tiffany sitting by herself with a bottle of Riesling and a bag of cheddar goldfish. She looked up—a bit drunkenly, Erinn thought—and held out the bag.

"Goldfish and Riesling is my best food-and-wine pairing idea, ever," she said. "EH-VER."

That's two, thought Erinn.

* * *

There was no "three" because the rest of the day magically turned around. Erinn seized on the idea that Tiffany, in her own way, was a food-and-wine-pairing genius! They threw out, at Erinn's insistence, the filet mignon paired with a cabernet sauvignon or a crisp, dry chardonnay with salmon. Boring! Instead, Erinn hit on the idea of a show revolving around pairing decent wines with junk food. This was more in line with what the average American ate anyway, she reasoned. The change in format was probably not what Cary had in mind, but Erinn thought it was genius!

Tiffany was the idiot savant of food-and-wine pairing. She poured out her thoughts. Hot dogs, for example, actually had nuances the average consumer never dreamed about. She recommended a dry rosé if plain, a pinot noir if the dog was served with mustard, and a humble zinfandel if it was served with chili.

At the end of the shoot, Tiffany was in tears that Erinn was leaving. She'd never dreamed anyone would ever take her junk food pairings seriously. When Erinn had finished loading the car and secured all the camera equipment, Tiffany was weeping theatrically in Erinn's arms.

"It's good, isn't it?" Tiffany asked. "Somebody will buy this, right?"

OK, maybe this is three.

"You never can tell," Erinn said, trying to peel Tiffany off her. "But we did our best, right?"

"I really want to be on TV."

"Noted," Erinn said and got quickly into her car.

Tiffany stood waving until Erinn had pulled completely out of the long driveway. Erinn hated shooting sizzle reels for any kind of lifestyle or reality TV. Production companies across Los Angeles churned out these short pilots like factories during the Industrial Revolution. Professional actors understood that the chances were a thousand to one that a show would be green-lit. But not these real people; they pinned all their hopes on one afternoon of shooting . . . even unreal people like Tiffany.

Ten minutes later, Erinn was unloading all the camera gear into her hotel room. She reviewed her footage and she had to admit it looked quirky and edgy (words she loathed but knew to sling around production company or network conference rooms). She resisted calling anyone in Los Angeles. If she called Suzanna, she'd have to feel guilty that she hadn't been in town for their mother's arrival. If she called Cary to discuss the show, she'd be trapped in a conversation about Blu Knight—and frankly, she wasn't up to envisioning the aging starlet ensconced in her guest room. Erinn realized with a shock that Blu was still several years younger than she; only in Southern California would midthirties be considered "aging."

And of course there was the new tenant in the guesthouse who was going to be raising Angora rabbits in Malibu. The one named after the patron saint of the insane: Dymphna. Erinn didn't want to think about her, either. Instead she took a bath and set her alarm. She had to start heading down the coast before dawn. She wanted to get an early start, hoping to miss the spectacular parking lot of a freeway that was sure to greet her as she neared Los Angeles if she waited until a reasonable hour.

She knew she had to get some rest; it was a long drive to Los Angeles. The pressure to sleep usually made her so tense that it became impossible, but this weekend had been pretty intense. Not only working with Tiffany but the producing, directing, and shooting all by herself, no matter how much she got to control the situation, was tiring! She was what she always thought of as "gorilla-tired" from Robert Strauss's wise words about success:

"It's a little like wrestling a gorilla. You don't quit when you're tired—you quit when the gorilla is tired."

She was asleep in minutes.

*　　*　　*

In the morning, she packed the car as quickly as possible. She drove until she saw an open coffeehouse. She popped the trunk and pulled out her camera bag.

Another problem with the whole approach to being alone on a shoot—even the Lone Ranger had Tonto—was that every time she stopped to use the restroom, get a cup of coffee, or fill the tank, she had to take her camera bag with her. She never got the hang of leaving her gear in the car and hoping for the best. She could never quite muster the optimism that the gear would still be there upon her return. At the end of the day, Erinn reasoned as she lugged her unwieldy bag through Starbucks, it is better to be a pessimist and have your camera.

As she drove through Malibu, she wondered if Dymphna might

be in the vicinity, tending to her rabbits. As she neared Santa Monica, she had some hard choices to make: Go directly to see her mother at the Bun? Go home and deal with Blu Knight? Take the footage to Cary and hope she was in a receptive mood?

Each option was fraught with unpleasant possibilities.

CHAPTER 9

SUZANNA

Suzanna tiptoed down the stairs from the apartment and into the tea shop's kitchen. She could hear rumblings from the Nook. Eric was obviously at work already, even though the bookstore wouldn't open for another two hours.

As she pulled the oatmeal, sugar, butter, and raisins from their resting places, she thought how perfect it was having her mother around. Suzanna had forgotten how hard it was to get everything ready for the day's menu while simultaneously keeping an ear and eye on the baby monitor. When Lizzy was younger, Suzanna (or Eric) could bring her downstairs without waking her and just check on her in her little basket every thirty seconds. But now that her daughter could escape her own crib, mornings had become increasingly tense.

It may have been years since Virginia had been on baby duty, but you would have thought she ran a preschool the way she was so comfortable and confident around Lizzy. And Lizzy adored her Grammy. *What else is new? Everyone adores her!*

* * *

Suzanna stepped into the Book Nook, a plate of homemade cookies in one hand and a steaming cup of coffee in the other. It was still early in the morning, and while many people might not think of oatmeal cookies as the ideal breakfast food, she and Eric had always loved them, fresh out of the oven before they had cooled, sitting like

little browned soldiers ready to give their lives for the tea-shop customers. She watched Eric pulling books off the various shelves and
putting them in a box. He turned and looked at her.

"Hey, Beet!" he said, calling her by her childhood nickname, so
given because she turned red at the slightest embarrassment. "I
smelled that coffee from across the hall and was hoping it was
headed my way."

Suzanna smiled and handed over the coffee. Eric took the cup in
one hand and with the other grabbed her around the waist and pulled
her toward him. He gave her a kiss no wife of three years had the
right to expect. She balanced the plate of cookies, hoping that they
wouldn't spill and ruin the moment.

"Hmmm," Eric whispered in her ear. "Hot coffee, hot cookies, hot
wife. I'm one lucky man!"

Suzanna giggled as she struggled out of his grasp. She put the
cookies on the table and leaped up on the counter. Eric studied the
books on the shelves, absentmindedly sipping at the coffee. When
she had his attention life was good!

"You're usually taking books out of boxes and stacking them, not
the other way around," Suzanna said. "What are you doing?"

"I'm thinning out the shelves. I was talking to Bernard at the
meeting last night and he said that one of his neighbors has started
one of those Little Free Libraries on his street. I thought I would do-
nate some books."

"Little Free Library? Isn't that the organization that puts up little
boxes all over small towns in America? You can grab a book anytime
you want?"

"That's the one," Eric said, pulling a copy of *The Complete Works
of William Shakespeare* off a shelf. He turned to Suzanna and held it
up. "We have three of these."

She nodded toward the box.

"Go for it," she said.

"I think it's an awesome idea," Eric said, adding a Charles Dick-
ens and an old Abbie Hoffman to the box. "You can take a book or
leave one. It brings the community together."

"I think that's great," Suzanna said. She picked up a cookie, but
Rio suddenly flitted through her mind and she put it back on the
plate.

"Speaking of Bernard, we ran into his nephew Christopher at the pier. He said you guys were working on . . . well . . . that thing. How is it going?"

Eric stopped loading the box and stood up, thinking.

"Oh, you mean the historic landmark designation? It's causing some hard feelings around here. It's a tough one. I'm not sure how this one is going to shake out. . . . I can see both sides."

What else is new?

"So . . . all of Venice is getting involved?"

"No . . . I wouldn't say that," Eric chortled. "But everyone on the block seems pretty into it. It would just be easier if everyone were on the same side."

Suzanna tried to digest that last sentence, but it really offered nothing. She tried again.

"Everyone on *this* block?"

"Of course, on *this* block. Do you think anyone else would spend one night a week fighting to get a tree declared a historic landmark?"

Wow, Suzanna wished she had paid more attention. A tree? Not a building? Who would care enough about a tree to get it declared historic? Was that even possible? And, for that matter, what tree?

"These things can . . . get out of hand," Suzanna said, hoping that was the right response.

One of the lovely things about Eric was that he really didn't seem to notice that she wasn't in the loop about this tree thing or half of his other town projects. There were days when this would have bothered her. On those days she took it to mean *he* wasn't paying attention enough to know she wasn't paying attention. But today it was working in her favor so she felt more forgiving.

"Yeah," he said. "Of course it's an uphill battle for both sides."

"I guess so," Suzanna said with such false enthusiasm that Eric stared at her. She toned it down. "I really need to know more about this—I think there are some holes in my understanding. Why not start at the beginning and catch me up?"

Eric looked like a kid who was just offered a new beach cruiser bike.

"Well," he said, sitting on the counter next to her, "you know that the deodar cedar tree in Mr. Clancy's Courtyard is in jeopardy, right?"

No.

"Of course I knew that!"

"Mr. Clancy wants to pull it up. He says it's taken over the place and has made the stores in the back so dark he can't rent them. He's practically renting the back space for next to nothing to some dancer who is working with underprivileged kids."

Suzanna's radar was on full force.

"Mr. Clancy was trying to draw attention to the fact that he can't even get a decent rent for the place with the tree blocking the light. He thought it would make him look like a hard-edged businessman, but everybody thinks he's a hero coming to the aid of the kids."

Suzanna tried to keep her face neutral.

"He's trying to get the city to pull the tree up. Says the roots are rippling the Beach Walk and making it hard on the bicyclists. The city says it's his problem. To compound that, most of the vendors over there love the tree and are trying to save it."

Suzanna might not know anything about the tree or its roots, but she was well aware that the Beach Walk in front of her store was cracking and uneven. She'd found herself nearly thrown from her own bike a couple of times. How could Eric be siding with the tree? Was Eric siding with the tree?

"Bicyclists have rights, too, don't they?" she asked carefully.

"Of course they do!" Eric said. "But they aren't supposed to be on this part of the Beach Walk anyway. They have their own path."

Unfortunately, there was no arguing with that.

"So, on one side you've got Mr. Clancy, who sees the tree as a liability. On the other side you have locals who want to save the tree. They want to get it declared a historic landmark."

"What makes it historic?" Suzanna asked.

"The cedar actually has a number of things going for it," Eric said. "To be designated a historic landmark, a tree has to represent a specimen that is particularly rare in the Los Angeles area and has to possess special horticultural significance."

"And does it?" Suzanna asked.

"Sure!" Eric said. "How many cedar trees do *you* see on the Beach Walk?"

"You got me there," Suzanna said.

"They got the idea from a Santa Monica designation of a cedar," Eric said. "So, there is some precedent."

"Sounds like a lot of work," Suzanna said. Reading Eric's frown she added, "For a very good cause."

"It is a good cause. If you don't fight for the trees, who will fight for you when the time comes?"

Probably not the trees.

"So . . . you're with the pro-tree people?"

"I'm with everybody," Eric said in his "All You Need Is Love" voice. "I'm just trying to keep peace in the neighborhood."

It was sometimes hard to believe that Eric had been a finance major.

Suzanna couldn't figure out a way to work Rio into the conversation; the tasty bit about the dancer and his cheap rent had come and gone, so she said, "What's the next step? For the tree?"

"Bernard and his nephew are the two most dedicated to the cause right now. They are trying to get a bunch of signatures together to raise awareness. They want to make sure Mr. Clancy can't chop down the tree before they can get the paperwork in. It's a pretty long process."

Virginia glided into the room. She had Lizzy on her hip and Piquant at her heels. It was so normal having her there; it was as if she'd lived with them forever.

"Eric is trying to save a tree," Suzanna said.

"I'm a neutral party," he said, throwing up his hands.

"Already know all about it," Virginia said. "Eric filled me in last night."

She handed Lizzy to Suzanna and spoke to Eric.

"I've been researching this whole thing. The fact that Santa Monica has set a precedent will be helpful for the locals who want to save the tree. They've saved the Fifth Street tree, the Miramar Fig on Wilshire Boulevard, and a eucalyptus with a double trunk on Twenty-second."

"That'll be great news for Bernard and Christopher, right?" Suzanna asked.

"Don't be so sure of that," Virginia said. "Trees get old and tired. People could turn against that tree before you know it. Some little sapling shows up and it's all over."

Suzanna looked at her mother.

What was that about?

"I'll make sure Bernard gets the information," Eric said. "His hook is that Venice is full of palm trees but this is the only cedar on the entire Beach Walk. Sounds like it will fit right in with the other landmarked trees."

"It should, but make sure they understand they've got an uphill battle ahead of them," Virginia said. "This is one ugly tree we're talking about."

How have I never noticed this tree?

"I know," said Eric. "But they're determined to try."

"I was over there yesterday and suggested that Bernard and Christopher take some glamour shots of the tree. No Photoshop, but make it look as pretty as possible. I volunteered to go with them, if they liked the idea."

"I thought we haven't taken sides," Suzanna said. She could feel the dollar bills racing away from her front door if she alienated half her neighbors.

"I don't have a side," Eric insisted. "Your mother is free to make up her own mind."

Suzanna saw Eric's right eyebrow twitch, a sure sign that he was annoyed. He wanted their establishment to stay neutral—could he possibly think it was OK for Virginia to take a stand? Suzanna thought not, but since she and her husband had different approaches to this sort of thing, she wasn't quite sure. She used to believe that everyone said what they thought, but now, being married to Eric, she was more aware that different people had different styles. In her own family, if you wanted someone (such as your mother-in-law) to remain outside the fray, you'd say, "Knock it off and keep your head low." But Eric's family might very well say, "You're free to make up your own mind," and, somehow, you would figure out that displeasure was being expressed. She would try to grasp this elusive approach—as if it were a goose feather floating on the breeze. As soon as she thought she could pluck it out of the air, wave it triumphantly, and shout, "I've got it!" Eric would blow it out of her hand and she'd be left with nothing.

"I just want to be helpful," Virginia said, but Suzanna knew her mother couldn't resist an underdog. "I thought maybe down the line Christopher or Bernard could do an oil painting of it; we could auction it off."

"There is no 'we' here, Mom," Suzanna said. "Eric and I are staying out of this."

Besides, who would want an oil painting of an ugly tree?

"I'm sure the boys will appreciate your support," Eric said. "But my goal is to make sure there isn't a rift in the community at large. We need to keep things as friendly as possible."

Eric was talking to Virginia more than Suzanna. Suzanna was a little hurt, but she knew that she had brought this on herself, by her rather consistent lack of interest in this sort of thing.

A knock on the front window startled them all. The morning was typical foggy coastal; no one could see who the phantom was on the other side of the glass. Lizzy started crying and Piquant ran around the bookstore, barking at shelves. Eric put his coffee mug down, jumped off the counter, and went to the front door. Even above the din of baby and dog, Suzanna and Virginia could hear that Erinn was at the door.

"I didn't think Erinn would be here until tomorrow," Suzanna said. "She just finished that shoot in Cambria last night."

Suzanna noticed Virginia visibly light up.

"She must have come straight here instead of going home," Virginia said, grabbing a sniffling Lizzy from Suzanna.

"Lizzy! Your auntie Erinn is here!" she said. "Let's go! Piquant, come meet your auntie Erinn."

"She isn't Piquant's aunt, Mom," Suzanna said to no one in particular. "Erinn would be his sister."

Suzanna stayed on the countertop, feeling like an idiot. Who cared what Piquant's relationship to the family was, anyway? Watching Virginia and her entourage leave the room, she took a sip of Eric's coffee, which was now cold. But the cookies were still warm! Maybe she could eat just half of one. . . .

Eric came back into the room, a scowl on his face.

"What's the matter?" Suzanna asked.

"We really need to keep the Rollicking Bun and Book Nook free of any controversy," he said.

"Am I being controversial?" Suzanna asked.

"Not you, Beet, your mother," he said, looking out toward the foyer, where they could hear Erinn and Virginia cooing over Lizzy.

So her mother taking sides did bother him! "She says she's just gathering facts!"

"I know that's what she says. But if she's thinking about getting pictures taken of the tree . . . well, that doesn't sound impartial to me."

"I know. But that's her generation. She always said revolt and bolstering the underdog is in their DNA."

"That's fine," Eric said, as he headed into the back office. "But she needs to keep that out of here. We have a business to run and we are *not* taking sides."

Is that an order?

As Suzanna listened to Piquant's yapping in the hallway, she thought there were two ways of looking at everything. She could be grateful that the dog wasn't a shedder or she could be irritated that her mother, without asking, had brought along a dog the size of a hamster with a bark as loud as a bear's. She could be thankful that Eric cared so much about his adopted city or she could be upset that it seemed more important than making her mom happy. She could be proud to have a sister who rushed to the tea shop as soon as she could. Or she could be annoyed that Erinn had just dropped in when it was finally convenient for her. She could be happy that her family was so close that everyone was delighted to see everyone else, that they were not one of those sad, estranged families. Or she could be hurt that her mother had raced off at Erinn's beck and call, apparently forgetting that it was Suzanna who had done all the heavy lifting.

It's all in how you look at things.

CHAPTER 10

ERINN

*W*hy, Erinn wondered, *do I slip right into the old patterns of child-hood when I'm around my mother?* She had gone to say hello at the tea shop before she had even stopped at her own house!

Shouldn't that count for something?

Erinn reviewed the visit as she drove up Ocean Avenue, to her own home, the home she got absolutely no points for having by-passed this morning.

It had started well; her mother ran into the foyer of the Bun with Lizzy on her hip and a startlingly small dog at her heels.

My cat has more presence than that dog.

Erinn of course knew about Piquant's existence; she had just for-gotten about him. He was eminently forgettable, in her opinion. But not when he was barking, which appeared to be always. Then you couldn't forget about him if you tried.

Her brother-in-law left the happy gathering early to deliver books to a box or some such thing, leaving the Wolf women to their own de-vices. They sat in the tearoom, still an hour or so before the shop opened, drinking tea and eating cookies.

"I joined a photography group," Virginia said, breaking off a piece of cookie and feeding it to Lizzy.

"Mom," Suzanna said in a strained voice, "we don't give Lizzy cookies."

"Don't be silly, Suzanna," Virginia said. "It's oatmeal."

"It's refined sugar," she replied, pulling a plastic container of hideous-looking green things out of a nearby sideboard and plopping it down in front of her mother.

"Here," Suzanna said, prying off the lid. "Give her these. She loves these."

Virginia poked and sniffed at the crackling green stuff.

"What is it?" Virginia asked.

"It's dried kale."

Virginia burst into laughter.

"Honey," she said to Suzanna. "Trust me, she does not love kale."

"How do you know?" Suzanna bristled.

"Well, dear," Virginia said, giving Lizzy another snippet of cookie, "because nobody really likes kale. They'll eat it, but they don't really like it."

In order to prove her point, Erinn guessed, their mother dropped a piece of kale on the floor for Piquant. The dog circled it, sniffed at it, and looked at Virginia. All three women stared at him—there was a lot riding on this moment. Which Wolf woman would emerge triumphant?

"Go ahead, Piquant," Suzanna urged. "Try it."

Piquant looked over at her and then sniffed at the kale again. He took a bite and started to chew as he continued to lock eyes with Suzanna. Suzanna's mouth twitched into a small smile. Then the dog gagged and threw up. They all looked at the dog in horror. Lizzy clapped. Piquant started his little dog palsy shake and went to lie down at the victor Virginia's feet.

"I'll clean that up," Suzanna said, heading off to the kitchen.

Erinn tried to get the conversation back on track.

"So, Mother," Erinn said. "Tell me about your photography class."

"Oh, you don't want to hear about that," Virginia said. "I mean, you just got back from being a *real* photographer."

"Then why did you bring it up?"

"I thought Suzanna might find it interesting."

* * *

Except for the oatmeal cookies, the visit really had been a bust, Erinn thought, as she pulled into her driveway. Her mother just didn't seem comfortable with her. She could imagine Suzanna berating her for not having enough patience with their mother. Well, maybe not today, not after the kale incident.

She unlocked the trunk of her car and was startled by her cat, who leaped into the trunk and was glaring up at her. Was he angry at her for being gone several days? Erinn used to travel for business on a regular basis and the cat had always been fine. Had it been so long that he'd forgotten?

She reached down to pat him, but Caro yowled and shot out of the open trunk. As he skidded under a rosebush, Erinn looked at him in annoyance. What kind of homecoming was this?

"At least I don't feed you kale," she said to him as she lugged her gear to the front step.

Caro meowed accusingly as Erinn struggled to let herself into the house. The front door lurched open and Cary stepped onto the landing, closing the door behind her. She wore an expression that Erinn couldn't read but whatever it was it didn't look like good news.

Maybe the deal with Red, White, and Blu has fallen through. Bad news for Cary, but I could live with it!

"Oh!" Erinn said. "I wasn't expecting you. Am I to assume Blu is ensconced within?"

"Blu's moved in, if that's what you mean," Cary said.

Erinn tried to move past her, but Cary had her handle on the doorknob. Short of tossing her off the porch, which even Erinn knew to be bad form, she wasn't sure how to get inside. She was gorilla-tired and just wanted to relax in her own bedroom and take a steaming bath in her own tub. She heard the cat let out another growl and thought, *And make nice with my cat. What is wrong with him?*

Erinn stared at Cary, who finally swung open the door. She struggled in with her gear and dropped it in the front hallway. She stood staring into her once beautiful living room. All her antiques, her overstuffed Morris chair, the rich tapestry drapes were gone. Her books were gone! The only thing that remained was her 27-inch LED monitor and keyboard, but instead of sitting on her mahogany claw-foot desk it was perched on a stainless-steel monstrosity that glinted in the harsh sunlight that was streaming through windows without any drapes. Instead they had some sort of scarflike pieces of gossamer fabric draped ridiculously over the frames.

Erinn stumbled into the room. Her Oriental carpet was gone, replaced by faux hardwood flooring. She walked around, touching the new furniture. Every single piece was a sacrilege. A sofa, pink and shaped like lips, faced the fireplace, one side flanked by a standing lamp shaped like a woman's legs.

"I'm assuming you don't love this," Cary said.

Erinn studied the coffee table in front of the sofa, which was some sort of statue of a man on all fours, with his pants pulled partway down over his rump. He grinned up coyly through the glass top of the table.

"Where did you get this?" Erinn asked. "A proctologist's office?"

"We needed to make this place look like Blu lived here," Cary said. "And she hated everything."

"But Blu doesn't live here. And I hate all of this! Where is my stuff?"

"In storage, of course. You know when a production company leases a place they can stage the house any way they like."

"I thought Blu was just going to move into the guest room."

"Well, you were misinformed," Cary said, not budging.

Erinn didn't want to fight. Cary was her most constant employer, and even though Erinn obviously hadn't read the fine print, she was getting a fair amount of money for the *Red, White, and Blu* project. She felt a little thrill when she thought about the junk-food-wine-pairing footage she'd have for Cary in the morning.

Two can play at the misinformed game.

Blu appeared out of nowhere. She was wearing impossibly short shorts and a thin cotton T-shirt that slid off her bony shoulders. She didn't appear to be wearing a bra, but her breasts still didn't move an inch.

Ah. They're that *kind of breasts.*

She was standing in the doorway with what appeared to be part of a mop in her hand.

"Cary!" Blu said, her breathy voice coming in gasps. "My hair extensions came out."

"Darling, you look divine," Cary said. "Don't worry about them. Just put them in a drawer or something."

"I do not look divine," Blu said. "I look gross. You need to call Elliot and get my extensions put back in."

Blu noticed at last that Erinn was in the room and looked at her.

"Don't I?" Blu asked Erinn. "Don't I look gross without my hair extensions?"

Erinn caught Cary's warning look and ducked the question.

"It's been a really long day and I'm ready for a bath. So, if you'll excuse me, I'm just going to feed Caro and go up to my room."

Erinn saw Blu's eyebrows flutter. What could that mean? Then she looked at Cary, who had the same expression on her face that she had had at the front door.

"I appear to be missing something. . . ." Erinn started.

"Ya think?" Blu snorted.

"Blu, darling, go to your room," Cary said. "I need to talk to Erinn."

"But what about these?" Blu shook her fists full of hair violently. Her breasts didn't move an inch.

"I'll call Elliot in a minute; now please go upstairs."

Blu shot Erinn a withering glare and tromped up the stairs. From the entrance to the living room, Erinn saw her walk into the master bedroom and close the door. It struck her that if Blu was taking over the master bedroom, she was taking over the en suite bathroom as well. Along with making any sense of what was going on, the dream of a steaming bath started evaporating as well.

"Wait, Blu, that's my . . ." Erinn stopped and looked, open-mouthed, at Cary. "You gave that cretin my room?"

"Now, Erinn," Cary said. "Look at this realistically. If this is Blu's house she can't be in the smaller bedroom, now, can she?"

"I feel the fool, you know," Erinn said. "The complete and utter fool. You sent me to Cambria so you could do your bidding with my house."

"Oh, Erinn, lighten up. We did what had to be done to make it seem real. Relax! I mean, your furniture is safe. Nobody died."

" 'To me, the thing that is worse than death is betrayal. You see, I could conceive death, but I could not conceive betrayal.' "

"Wow. That is heavy. I can't believe you just said that."

"Well, I didn't. Malcolm X said it. But if he hadn't, I would have."

Caro suddenly streaked through the foyer into the kitchen and back again, yowling the entire time. Erinn tried to catch him, but the cat flew up the stairs. At the top of the landing, he stared down at Erinn.

"My poor cat," Erinn said. "He's so confused by all of this."

"Oh," Cary said. "That's not what's wrong with your cat. Have you been out back yet?"

Erinn had completely forgotten about Dymphna, but she couldn't imagine anything being worse than having her house taken over by Blu Knight.

"What's going on out back?" she asked Cary, who threw up her hands.

"I have to call the hairdresser for Blu. The backyard is all yours, although I have to say, Erinn, I don't know what you were thinking."

Erinn threaded her way through the kitchen—thank God they had left that room alone—and let herself out the back door and onto the porch.

The ancient Roman poet Virgil wrote, "Each of us bears his own hell." And Erinn never really knew what he meant until this very moment. Against the garden wall now stood ten rabbit cages, each containing a large creature that looked like an unwieldy cotton ball with ears and teeth. Erinn tried to make herself take a step toward them but found herself rooted to the porch. She snapped back to life as Caro streaked through the backyard in a frenzy and ran back into the house. The sound of feline distress brought Dymphna from the guesthouse. Dymphna was wearing a large sack slung over her shoulder that looked as if it weighed more than she did, and she was walking a furry creature on a leash. Dymphna and Erinn locked eyes.

"It's good that you're home," said Dymphna. "You can help your cat adjust to the rabbits."

"Those are rabbits?" Erinn pointed at them from the safety of the porch. "They're the size of Volkswagens!"

"Better for harvesting wool," Dymphna said serenely.

She started to shovel a small trowel full of grayish-green pellets from her sack into each cage, talking softly to each rabbit as she went.

"Why aren't they in Malibu?"

"The sheep were in Malibu. I traded them in for rabbits, which I can raise at home."

Erinn wanted to say that Dymphna was raising the rabbits in *her* home, but she realized that logic wasn't really flying today.

"I'm not sure . . ." Erinn started. "Are you even allowed to keep thousands of rabbits in a backyard?"

"There are ten of them," Dymphna said. "And you need a permit."

"Well, I don't have a permit!"

"No. But I do."

"This is not going to . . ."

Dymphna put her index finger to her lips.

"Shhhhh. You need to speak softly. You'll agitate them and that's bad for their fur."

"Dymph—"

Again, Dymphna raised her finger to her lips, but this time she didn't look at Erinn. She just proceeded serenely with her work.

"You're projecting very negative energy," she whispered to Erinn.

Ya think?

"Dymphna . . . ," Erinn whispered. She realized the diminutive woman couldn't hear her harsh whisper from the porch. She walked down into the yard.

"We need to talk." After filling a bowl, Dymphna patted each rabbit as she went down the row. It looked as if she was making eye contact with each one, but Erinn could see no rabbit eyes. Just fur.

"I understand why you're so upset," Dymphna said quietly, the ball of wool hopping beside her.

"Well, that's a start."

"I can't even imagine what you must have thought when you saw your beautiful house destroyed like that." Dymphna shuddered. "When they moved your leather sofa out and brought in those *lips* . . ."

Erinn had forgotten the fresh hell that was her living room. Perhaps Dymphna *was* the least of her worries. Caro did another demented spin through the yard, streaking to all four corners and then blazing back into the house. Dymphna watched Caro's manic dance.

"We're going to have to work on that," she said.

"Let's have a little chat." Erinn tried again to get her attention.

I sound like my mother.

After feeding the last rabbit, Dymphna turned to Erinn with a smile.

"Sure. Come inside."

Erinn felt herself getting misty-eyed as she entered the guesthouse. Dymphna had added her own small effects to the place, but it was essentially the same. Erinn sat wearily at the little café table and rubbed her eyes. She thought about how she drove from Cambria to Venice, just to be underappreciated by her mother and sister, then home, where she had been displaced by a faded reality-TV has-been and her cat had been displaced by ten enormous rabbits.

Dymphna patted Erinn's shoulder as she placed a cup of fruit salad in front of her.

"You should eat this," she said. "I can tell by your skin that you're drinking too much coffee."

Erinn was too stunned by the day's events to do anything but take a bite of blueberries. Dymphna sat down across from her and put her little hand over Erinn's.

"How can I help you?" she asked.

CHAPTER 11

SUZANNA

Traveling with a baby made it impossible to sneak up on people. By the time Suzanna had parked the car in front of Erinn's, gotten a squealing Lizzy out of the car seat, wrapped various diaper and toy bags around her own neck, not to mention waited for Virginia to steer Piquant over to a neighboring lawn for a quick pee, a tense Erinn was walking toward them. Suzanna saw her first and called out, "Mom made Mac!"

Erinn's tight posture visibly loosened as Suzanna pointed to the casserole in the back of the car. Erinn picked it up and sniffed at it. The sisters looked at each other. Even with a baby on Suzanna's hip and a house full of outrageousness behind Erinn, the siblings traveled in a sensory time machine back to the days of eating macaroni and cheese with both their parents around a table made from an old oak barrel.

"We thought we'd pop in for a visit," Virginia said, bringing her daughters back to the present.

The previous evening, Virginia had listened, wide-eyed, over a mug of Monk's Tea, a blend of black tea and sunflower petals, as Suzanna filled her in on the details of Erinn's new living arrangements. Not only was Erinn renting her guesthouse to a woman who brought ten rabbits with her, but the pop-culture princess who prided herself on knowing *nothing* that happened in the world before 1970 was living in Erinn's completely—hideously—redecorated house.

"And Blu took over the master suite," Suzanna said, adding in an almost whisper, "even the bathtub is Blu's now!"

"Poor Erinn," Virginia said. "This must be her worst nightmare!"

"I know," Suzanna said.

Suzanna was the first to admit it, but growing up, she, not Erinn, was the daughter who usually had their parents shaking their heads in dismay. Sitting here, over a cup of tea, shaking her head alongside her mother, she tried not to let her sibling rivalry get the best of her. It did seem impossible, though, that Erinn, the woman who could make Aristotle look like a slacker, had gotten herself into such a fix.

Suzanna knew it wouldn't take long for Virginia to figure out a way to get herself over to Erinn's and inspect the situation. Suzanna knew her mother's plan as soon as she woke up. She could smell macaroni and cheese baking in the oven. Clearly, a casserole sizzling away in the oven at eight in the morning meant it was going to be a bribe, not dinner. Erinn could not resist Mom's macaroni and cheese, made with equal parts cheese and elbow macaroni. Erinn might be annoyed that her mother and sister had arrived without an invitation, but Mom's Mac would get them in the door.

It worked. Erinn grabbed the casserole and ushered them around the side of the house.

"Why aren't we using the front door?" Suzanna asked. A trip around back over the uneven cobblestones with all their gear, not to mention a toddler and a dog, was going to be awkward at best and death defying at worst.

"We're going around to the kitchen," Erinn said, leading the way. "I'm ignoring the house."

Suzanna exchanged a quick look with her mother. That didn't sound good.

Piquant was straining at his leash and whining. Virginia kept pulling him back and sternly telling him to "Heel," a command to which he turned a deaf doggy ear.

As they bumped through the side yard, Suzanna thought of pointing out that the kitchen was part of the house, but realized there was no way to make a rational argument to someone who has just said, "I'm ignoring the house."

As they rounded the backyard, it was clear what was agitating the dog. Lizzy was the first of the humans to spot the wall of rabbits. She let out an ear-piercing squeak of delight. Lizzy struggled out of

Suzanna's arms and ran at the hutches. The added excitement in the air caused Piquant to up the indignant-barking ante.

"I knew they were here first," Piquant seemed to say.

"Doggy!" Lizzy said, patting a wire cage that housed a rabbit larger and furrier than Piquant.

Suzanna wondered if Piquant thought they were dogs as well. The rabbits seemed fairly circumspect when Lizzy approached them, but started hopping around their cages as Piquant's barking got more and more insistent. Piquant's barking seemed to signal to Lizzy that all was not fun and games and the toddler started to cry. She raced back to her mother.

Virginia scooped Piquant into her arms with the same movement Suzanna used to lift Lizzy. Both women tried to quiet their armloads of unhappy little beings. The noise escalated—shrieking toddler, disgruntled dog, soothing mother sounds from both Virginia and Suzanna were now joined by weird barking sounds from all the rabbits.

Rabbits bark?

An elf in gypsy clothes suddenly came flying out of the guesthouse. Suzanna realized at once this must be Dymphna. With long hair spreading out behind her like wings, the tiny woman ignored the newcomers and crossed the yard to her rabbits in a few strides. Suzanna watched, fascinated, as the woman put her hand in front of each cage, and spread her fingers across the wire front. Suzanna wasn't close enough to hear if she was saying anything, but it appeared that it was the peaceful presence of Dymphna, rather than any words, that settled each rabbit in turn.

Once her rabbits were calm, Dymphna turned her attention to the transfixed little group standing in the yard. She smiled serenely at them and then waved to Lizzy. Lizzy stopped howling, and with a gentle sniffle, waved back. Piquant was still yapping up a storm. Dymphna, still smiling, walked toward the struggling, outraged dog. Without saying a word, Dymphna stood in front of Virginia and slowly put her hands out. She clearly wanted to hold Piquant.

Suzanna looked at Erinn, who was standing by the steps to the back porch, guarding her casserole, but clearly as transfixed as the rest of her family.

"He's not really a very friendly dog," Virginia tried to whisper to Dymphna over the barking.

Why is she whispering?

Since Dymphna just stood there with her hands out, Virginia caved in to good manners and handed the dog to her. Suzanna and Piquant were equally surprised by this turn of events. Piquant had made it very clear to everyone at the Bun, the Nook, and the apartment that while he would sporadically accept a pat from people, he was only to be held by Virginia and only to have his ears pulled by Lizzy. Suzanna watched, fascinated, as Piquant reared back in Dymphna's arms and bared his teeth. In Eric's arms, the sight of Piquant trying to look ferocious with his little mean face and snickery growl would have bordered on hilarious. The tiny dog would not have seemed menacing in the least. But this woman was so small, Piquant actually seemed like a reasonably sized threat. Dymphna walked up and down the yard with the dog, stroking his head. By now, Lizzy was quiet in her mother's arms and the yard was completely still. Suzanna could not make out any murmurings coming from Dymphna, but Piquant had stopped growling at her. Instead, he lay against her shoulder. Suzanna got a glimpse of him through Dymphna's hair. He was awake, but calmer than she had ever seen him. Dymphna walked the dog up to the rabbit hutches, turning her body sideways, so Piquant could see each rabbit in turn without having to adjust his position on her shoulder.

Dymphna walked back to Virginia, and without speaking, returned Piquant to her. He had the same look Suzanna knew she wore after a trip to a spa—totally relaxed. Dymphna stood back and folded her hands in front of her.

Suzanna realized no one in the yard had spoken in at least ten minutes. She wondered if she should be the one to break this mystical silence, when the back door to the house banged open.

An equally tiny woman, this one with reddish-and-blond-striped curls, strode purposefully to the end of the back porch. Suzanna could feel the energy in the yard change instantly—and she wasn't much a believer in that sort of thing—as the woman on the porch, who must, by the process of elimination and temperament, be Blu, scanned the group in the yard. Blu must have decided that the little band of women was of no interest, because she turned to Erinn at the bottom of the steps.

"I broke a nail," Blu said.

"You have nine others," Erinn said.

"What am I going to do?" Blu demanded, holding the offending digit out for inspection.

"I'd offer you one of mine," Erinn said, lifting the casserole for Blu to see, "but I'm using them."

Even from halfway across the yard, Suzanna could see Blu roll her eyes and head back into the house, slamming the door behind her. Suzanna absently kissed Lizzy's head and thought, *That awful woman is somebody's daughter. Dear God, please let me keep my eye on this parenting thing.*

Erinn, still clutching the casserole, started up the stairs. She turned back to her family and Dymphna.

"Welcome to the House of Blu," Erinn said. "I see you guys have met Dymphna."

Suzanna, balancing Lizzy, and Erinn, balancing the casserole, climbed the steps, but stood on the porch. No one seemed particularly eager to go into the house.

"I guess that was Blu," Suzanna said.

Erinn nodded.

"I'm really glad Mother brought Mac," Erinn said. "It's hellish here."

"I bet you just want to punch whoever said, 'There's no place like home' right about now," Suzanna said, always happy to share a sisterly moment with her older sibling.

"Do you mean John Howard Payne?" Erinn asked.

"Pardon?"

"John Howard Payne. In 1823, he wrote, 'Be it ever so humble, there's no place like home.' Is that who you mean? Or are you thinking about *The Wizard of Oz*? In that case, it would be L. Frank Baum."

Suzanna was used to sisterly moments being short-lived. The sisters waited for their mother—and the blissed-out Piquant—to join them on the porch before braving the House of Blu. Dymphna was nowhere in sight.

"Where's Dymphna?" Suzanna asked.

"She went back to the guesthouse," Virginia said. "I asked her if she'd like to come in for some macaroni and cheese, but she said she was drying rose petals."

Of course she is!

The Wolf women turned and stood staring at the door into the kitchen. Suzanna felt sorry for her sister. Erinn's home had always been a source of comfort to her, no matter how the world batted her around. Now, Erinn looked as if she were bracing herself to go in.

"Mac, anyone?" Erinn said with a forced smile and went inside.

Suzanna stood for a moment with her mother. Suzanna looked at the dog, snoozing serenely on her mother's shoulder.

"Is he OK?" Suzanna asked. "What did Dymphna say to him?"

Virginia peeked into the kitchen. Whatever she was going to say to Suzanna, she obviously didn't want Erinn to hear. Suzanna followed her gaze and saw Erinn putting the casserole into the oven. Suzanna leaned in so she could hear her mother.

"I asked her, and she said she didn't *say* anything," Virginia said. "She said . . ."

"What?" Suzanna asked. "She said what?"

"She said," Virginia whispered, "she said words have no power."

Mother and daughter stared at each other. Their eyes drifted through the door to Erinn, who was setting the table.

"Don't tell Erinn," Suzanna and Virginia said at the same time.

CHAPTER 12

VIRGINIA

Virginia was surprised by how quickly she got into the swing of life in Venice. She was able to buckle Lizzy into her Baby Jogger stroller (although, as Erinn pointed out, this was clearly misnamed since clearly the baby wasn't jogging) and Piquant into his harness and could head out the door in a matter of minutes. She loved walking out and seeing the beach and the glistening ocean as soon as she was on the porch. And Venice was such a little neighborhood! As she started down the Beach Walk, Donell, the sage salesman who put out his pot-pourri rain or shine, an enormous man in a beret and flowing caftan, waved to her with one hand. With the other he cradled a phone to his ear. He hung up quickly as she went by and shouted out to her.

"Hey, Mama Bear! Oh, I mean Mama Wolf!"

He let out a smoker's laugh, part hack and part guffaw. Virginia smiled at him.

"The booth smells lovely, as always," she said.

He reached out with a bunch of sage tied with raffia.

"For you, sweet lady. A gift."

Virginia took the sage and smelled it.

"Thank you, Donell."

"Where are you goin' this mornin'?" he asked. "Just grabbin' some sunshine?"

"No," Virginia said, tucking the sage into one of the many pockets in the Baby Jogger, possibly never to be seen again. "I'm going to Mr. Clancy's Courtyard."

"Oh, not that damn tree again! Your son-in-law is just a pain in my ass about that tree."

"Eric? He's just trying to help."

"I just don't want any trouble. I have enough trouble selling sage without some sort of coup goin' down."

"I would imagine a coup would only help business, Donell," Virginia said. "If people feel strongly that the tree has intrinsic value, they'll come see it. And even if they don't care at all, they'll still come see it just because of all the hubbub. It's win-win for you."

God, I sound every inch the retired professor.

"Yeah," said Donell, "well, maybe they'll declare me a national treasure—I'm the only three-hundred-and-fifty-pound Hawaiian in the area. Now that would really help my business."

"Maybe you'll be next," Virginia said. Then she added, "If it makes you feel any better, it's a local designation . . . not national."

She headed down the Beach Walk until she was standing in front of Mr. Clancy's Courtyard, half a block and a world away from the Bun. While her daughter's tearoom had a look that would have been more compatible with the buildings on the Eastern Seaboard, with its wide porch and whitewashed façade, Mr. Clancy's was a cluster of individual brick cottages lining an L-shaped cement courtyard. An archway curved over the courtyard, joining the two buildings in the front. She didn't like walking under the archway, which was also made of brick. Curved brick in earthquake-prone California? Not the best idea on the books, in Virginia's mind.

She bumped the Jogger up the three cement stairs and entered the courtyard. There stood The Tree. She was hoping that in time The Tree would grow on her. But no. The twisted trunk and shabby branches looked just as ugly as on the day she first saw it. It was so large, customers heading into the various shops had to climb around it. And it completely obscured the shops in the back, including that sweet Rio's dance studio. She felt a better solution might be to uproot the tree and send it to Montana or some such state where it would have room to spread out. It was obviously trying to take up more than its allotted space. But if some of the merchants felt compelled to save it, she'd do what she could to help out. Unofficially, of course.

Christopher and Bernard's art gallery was one of the first shops in the courtyard. Christopher came out, carrying a large easel.

He set up the easel among his other offerings: woodwork, beadwork, stained glass; you name it, if it was art, Christopher or his uncle dabbled in it.

"Hey, Virginia!" he said, putting a large painting on the easel and facing it toward the sidewalk. He leaned over and waved at Lizzy. "Hi, Lizzy."

Virginia was quietly happy that everyone already seemed to know her—and even appeared to think of Lizzy and herself as a unit.

Virginia studied the picture. It was a familiar subject for the local artists: the Santa Monica Pier as seen from Muscle Beach. But Christopher had added an interesting perspective. Most of the painting was soft and impressionistic, but the pier, which was in sharp focus, was seen through the long green fingers of a palm frond.

"You have such an eye, Christopher," she said.

"Yeah, but he needs to think commercial," said his uncle, who came out of the shop carrying one of his offerings, a photograph of sorts, since it had been Photoshopped within an inch of its life, of a clown wearing a Venice Beach T-shirt with a hot dog stand in the background.

"Well," Virginia said, scanning their hodgepodge of offerings, "it looks like, between the two of you, you have something for everybody."

Christopher bent over to pat Piquant, who growled, which delighted Lizzy. Christopher ruffled Lizzy's hair.

"OK, I'll pat your head instead," he said.

Virginia was used to Piquant's petulant personality and had ceased to be embarrassed by him. Her sheepish days in New York seemed like years ago.

Although all the merchants in the courtyard had shops, their bread-and-butter sales came from setting up outside on the Beach Walk. One by one the shopkeepers started setting up their wares. Virginia saw a man stick his head out of a corner shop.

"Good morning, Mr. Clancy," Christopher said tonelessly.

So this is the evil landlord!

Virginia watched him out of the corner of her eye as he pulled his merchandise onto the sidewalk. Mr. Clancy had long, thick, gray hair and a toned physique for a man of any age, let alone one who must be hovering around seventy. Virginia noticed his artistic, graceful hands. He sold what appeared to be hand-dyed T-shirts, gypsy skirts, and scarves. Not what one would expect from the resident Snidely Whiplash.

Virginia had no idea how any of these people ever made enough money to keep body and soul together. But they all did, especially, she thought, their souls.

She picked Lizzy up out of the Jogger and let her look at all the fabulous offerings. When Suzanna had first announced that she was pregnant, Virginia had had to stifle the urge to say that perhaps Venice Beach was not the greatest area in the country to raise a child. But she was glad she hadn't said anything. Lizzy was not having a conventional baby-hood, but it was sure damned interesting.

Virginia was startled as Suzanna stepped briskly into the court-yard, walking her bike.

"Hi, Mom," she said.

"Hi, dear. I thought I'd take Lizzy out, give you some time to yourself."

"That's great!" Suzanna said, looking around the courtyard. "I just thought I'd get a little bike ride in."

Virginia thought she seemed distracted.

"Well, you go right ahead. I'm just going to talk to the guys about something and then Lizzy and I will meet you at home after your ride."

Suddenly, from under the brick archway, Rio appeared with two young adults in tow, a sullen-looking boy and a goth girl. He nodded to his fellow shopkeepers and the Wolfs. To Suzanna's surprise, Virginia stopped the little group.

"Hello, Rio," Virginia said. "Who are your friends?"

Rio and the teenagers stopped in their tracks. Virginia could hear a rush of air escape Suzanna. Virginia knew her daughter was proba-bly embarrassed that Virginia was butting in, but all her years around young adults, especially hostile young adults, had taught her that kids like these were going to need more than dance lessons to make it in this world. They were also going to need manners—and as far as she was concerned, they could start learning them right now.

The boy stared at his feet and the girl glowered out from behind blunt black bangs. She was chewing gum with her mouth open, which Virginia might mention later, but she knew to tread lightly. After all, Rio hadn't asked her to lend a hand.

"Hello, Virginia," Rio said. "These are my students, Miles and Winnie."

Neither of the students responded. Virginia passed the handles of the Baby Jogger to Suzanna and stood in front of the students.

"Hello, I'm Virginia." She offered her hand to the boy, who wore baggy jeans, a white T-shirt, and gauge earrings. He had no choice but to take her hand and look at her. "You must be Miles?"

"I guess," the boy said in a frosty baritone. He did not crack a smile.

"I like your tattoos," Virginia said, nodding at the flight of exotic birds that flew up his left arm. "I don't know all the birds, but I think I recognize a Chinese pheasant and a lorikeet."

"Awesome," Miles said, forgetting his Mr. Cool composure for a moment and pointing to a blue bird with a long red beak. "This kingfisher is my favorite."

"He's lovely," Virginia said.

"One day, I want to get a full peacock on my back," Miles said.

"So he can be a walking ad for NBC," the goth girl, who must be Winnie, said.

Virginia found it interesting that Miles didn't take offense.

"That's my twin sister." Miles nudged his head toward Winnie. "She's just jealous that I'm going to kick her ass at Zumba."

Winnie smiled at her brother, but returned to her scowl when she looked at Virginia. Virginia decided not to press her luck. One out of two petulant teenagers giving her the time of day was a start.

Rio herded the students toward the back of the courtyard, disappearing behind the tree.

"How is his dance studio doing?" Virginia asked Christopher.

"OK, I guess," Christopher said. "He keeps to himself, mostly."

"He's not keeping to himself," Mr. Clancy said. "You can't see him, because the tree covers his studio like a black cape."

Christopher and Bernard ignored Mr. Clancy.

"He runs the place on donations so it can't be easy. Bernard and I feed him whenever we can," Christopher said.

"That's so sweet of you," Suzanna said.

"I feed him, too," said Mr. Clancy. "*And* I give him a break on his rent."

Virginia looked right at Mr. Clancy.

"I guess he has his hands full saving those kids," she said. "He's probably not keeping score."

"You know, we can always help with food," Suzanna said. "We could feed him at the tea shop. Or bring over some biscuits or whatever. . . ."

"Bless your heart, Suzanna!" Virginia said.

Was she missing something? Her daughter sounded out of breath and her cheeks were pink.

Suzanna seemed miles away, looking after Rio. Virginia remembered when Suzanna had taken dance lessons and wondered if she missed them. She noticed that Suzanna still hadn't seemed to catch her breath. She knew that exercise went out the window when you were a new mother.

"Suzanna?" Virginia asked. "You'd better get going if you want a good bike ride before work."

Suzanna blinked a few times and then pedaled away. Lizzy waved happily as her mother disappeared down the bike path, which thrilled Virginia (even though she would never admit it). Virginia waited until Mr. Clancy went back into his shop.

"I actually came down here for a reason," Virginia said.

Years of teaching at a university had honed Virginia's skills at getting people's attention without yelling. As if on cue, Bernard and Christopher stopped what they were doing and looked at her.

"We need to take a little field trip. Do some research. You guys up for a field trip to Santa Monica later today?"

"Sure," Bernard said. "I'll get Donell to keep an eye on the place."

"Just don't tell him it's about the tree," Virginia suggested.

She wheeled Lizzy back to the Bun and turned into the Book Nook, where Eric was deep in conversation with a quintessential California girl in tight jeans. The pair was standing over a stack of what appeared to be heavily bound comic books. The girl looked vaguely familiar, but then again, these types of overly processed girls all looked alike to Virginia with their Angelina Jolie lips and Julia Roberts noses. It wasn't until she heard the woman speak that Virginia realized it was Blu Knight, the starlet who was making Erinn's life miserable. Lizzy started fussing and Virginia rocked the Jogger back and forth so she could hear the conversation without being noticed.

"It's a superfun adventure story," Blu was saying to a nodding Eric.
"An artist friend of mine did the drawings and then we self-published it."

Eric picked up a copy and read the title out loud, *"Superblu and O'Hara?"*

Blu's hair bounced as she nodded.

"It's about a lady superhero and a detective who solve crimes,"
she said. "I'm Superblu."

"I would have guessed," Eric said. "I mean, you don't look Irish."

Blu smiled at Eric.

"Do you like my costume?" she purred.

Eric shot a quick involuntary glance at her cleavage, than righted
his eyes.

"Oh," he said, "in the graphic novel!"

"I had one made up, so I can do personal appearances once it
takes off."

"Yes, it's very . . . inspiring."

Blu laughed coyly. Virginia had to admit that it was a pretty little
tinkling sound. But it didn't mask the alarm bells that were going off
in Virginia's head. This woman could be trouble.

"So," Blu said, leaning in again. "Can I count on you to sell a couple copies for me?"

So that's what this is about!

"Sure," Eric said. "I'll put some out on the counter. They should
sell themselves."

Piquant started barking loudly. He rushed into the Nook, apparently dead set on ferreting out Virginia. Eric and Blu turned to her
and she smiled weakly.

"There's nothing quite like a good graphic novel," Virginia said.

It was clear to her that Blu's work here was done.

"I'd better get going," Blu said to Eric. "I'm shooting this afternoon with your sister-in-law, and you know how she can get if you're
late."

"I'm going to be in Santa Monica this afternoon myself," Virginia
said. "Maybe we'll run into each other."

Blu was already out the door. Apparently, women's voices didn't
register.

* * *

Later that afternoon, Virginia and the men stood regarding the Miramar Fig, more formally known as the Moreton Bay Fig Tree and more formally still as the Founders' Tree. It stood outside the Miramar Hotel on Ocean Avenue, in the hotel's circular parking lot. Cars and people swirled around it in constant motion, 24/7. She could see why it was granted landmark status. In a frenetic world, it stood, a thing of beauty in every sense of the word—massive yet graceful, reassuring yet majestic.

"Christopher, I don't think this tree is going to help our . . . I mean *your* cause after all," Virginia said as Christopher took out his sketchbook. "Our tree is too ugly duckling to this swan."

Christopher pocketed his sketchbook.

"Let's head up to Fifth Street," Virginia said, as if she were a local.

"OK," Bernard replied. "But if we're going up to Twenty-second Street, we're taking the car."

"We're not. I don't think you can whip up any enthusiasm for a landmarked eucalyptus."

As they headed up Ocean Avenue, a small film crew was suddenly in their sights.

"Is that Erinn?" Christopher asked, watching a woman with a camera backpedaling toward them while keeping a tiny woman with multicolored hair in her lens. They were too far away to make out very much detail, but Virginia was sure it was Blu. You could only see the back of the camerawoman, taking the deliberate steps that all camera people learn in order to avoid stumbling when they walk backward.

"You can tell my daughter by her backside?" Virginia asked, lifting an eyebrow.

Christopher looked at his feet and Virginia and Bernard burst out laughing.

"We're on her block," she said. "And she's working on a show."

A man wearing earphones and carrying some sort of large microphone on a pole steadied Erinn while keeping the microphone poised over the woman she was shooting.

People who live in and around Southern California seem to understand the mechanics of TV and film crews almost by osmosis. As Erinn walked backward towards them, being led by the man with the microphone, no pedestrian even glanced their way.

Virginia felt a swell of maternal pride as she watched Erinn at work. Her daughter seemed so confident, even from the back. The little group took in the woman Erinn was shooting. She was walking down the street, looking right and left, flipping her hair and deliberately ignoring the camera and microphone, touching flowers on fences and walls as she walked by. Erinn stopped walking and put the camera down.

"Blu," Erinn said. "Just be natural."

"I am being natural," Blu said.

"I don't think you are. I don't think you walk down the street touching flowers."

"Well, I do in my fake life!" Blu insisted.

Virginia thought she should not butt in, but she could tell by Erinn's posture that things were about to get ugly. How was it that this wraith of a woman could stir up so much trouble in her family?

"Erinn!" Virginia called out.

Erinn turned around. She lit up, which surprised Virginia. She thought another surprise visitation from her mother, no matter how coincidentally—and with no mac and cheese—might not be welcomed by her eldest daughter. Then she realized that Erinn was glowing because she was looking at Christopher.

Well, well, well.

Virginia was explaining their mission when Blu interrupted.

"We've been shooting for two hours. Can we be done?"

"Yes," Erinn said to her and then looked at the audio guy, who looked equally relieved. "Let's wrap for today. Call time ten a.m. sharp tomorrow, my house."

"Don't you mean *my* house?" Blu giggled.

Erinn appeared to turn to stone at Virginia's side. Without waiting to be introduced to Virginia's band of tree avengers, Blu slipped off her five-inch heels and headed up Ocean Avenue. Virginia felt Erinn shake off her anger. She was glad to see that she hadn't forgotten her manners.

"Mother, this is Opie," Erinn said, introducing the red-haired man with the microphone. "Opie, this is my mother, Virginia. And this is Bernard and his nephew."

"Christopher," Christopher said, shaking Opie's hand.

Virginia tried to hide her smile. Erinn obviously knew damn well that "the nephew's" name was Christopher.

"OK, boss," Opie said. "Ten sharp. See you at . . . the house."

Smart man.

"We're heading over to Fifth Street . . . ," Christopher said.

"I know all about it," Erinn said.

Virginia was surprised. *She* certainly hadn't said anything. Was Suzanna complaining about her?

"If you're not busy," Virginia said, "maybe you'd like to come with us."

"Yeah," Christopher said. "I mean, if you aren't busy, I'd love to compare notes on composition. Your mother is expecting miracles on these shots."

Virginia could tell that Erinn was flattered.

Erinn decided to accompany the troupe on their Fifth Street pilgrimage. Virginia noticed that Christopher, very casually, took the heavy camera from Erinn. Virginia wasn't sure if she was joining them because she didn't want to go home or because it would give her time with Christopher. Virginia didn't really care, as this was a wonderful way to spend time with her eldest.

"Now we're talking," Christopher said as the little band of would-be tree savers stood staring at the Fifth Street cedar. It was the same species as the tree at Mr. Clancy's but much larger and rivaled it in unattractiveness.

The tree sprawled across a long, narrow lot. There seemed to be no symmetry to the thing, branches sticking out awkwardly at all angles. They were gnarled and touched the ground only to curve up again toward the sky. If any tree could convey arthritis this would be the one.

"Thank God," Virginia said. "If Santa Monicans found it in their hearts to save this guy, I think you've got a chance."

"This has got to be the ugliest tree in the world," Erinn said.

"Our tree is way better-looking than this one," Bernard said. "No comparison!"

Virginia exchanged a look with Erinn. It hadn't occurred to her that Bernard actually saw the tree through eyes of love. Wasn't he just clashing with Mr. Clancy out of habit?

"Of course your tree is beautiful," she said.

"Well, now, I wouldn't go that far," Bernard said, a tinge of color spotting his cheeks above the stubble of his beard. "But it sure as hell is a lot better-looking than this one." He stabbed a stubby finger toward the offending cedar.

"OK, Bernard," Virginia said. "Please take some pictures. Lots of angles."

"I don't know," Bernard said. "Maybe Erinn should take the pictures. She's the professional."

Bernard started to hand over his camera to Erinn.

"Thank you, Bernard," Erinn said. "But I'm just going to observe."

Virginia wasn't sure if Erinn didn't want Bernard to feel slighted or if she didn't want to steal anyone's thunder. You could never tell with Erinn. Virginia turned her attention back to Bernard.

"I want to convey every emotion. Drama, solitude, anxiety, hopefulness . . . ," Virginia said.

"Hold on there," Bernard said. "This is a tree, not a Greek tragedy."

"That's where you're wrong!" Erinn said. "This IS a Greek tragedy. Or a Greek tragedy in the making. We've got all the elements: the potential for loss, the abuse of power, and the tenuous relationship between humans and their gods."

"Wow," said Christopher, already sketching the behemoth before them. "Who knew?"

Although Virginia laughed along with the men, she slipped a protective arm around Erinn. A reassuring squeeze just in case Erinn didn't get the fact that this was a good-natured joke. She was relieved that Erinn, who didn't exactly laugh, at least smiled. She felt her stiffen and was about to remove her arm when she caught her daughter's eye. Erinn wore the same expression that she had when she was little, brave and a little confused. Virginia left her arm where it was until Erinn finally shrugged her away.

Virginia thought back to Erinn's childhood. She remembered standing on the back step of their little home, and Erinn, who was just shy of three years old, standing by herself along the back fence. The toddler was walking quietly among a few scraggly pumpkins and their vines, studying them from all angles. She was too young to actually know how to count, but she took her tiny finger and touched one bright yellow gourd after another, deep in concentration. Virginia was new to motherhood, and, like all first-time mothers, thought her child was the most exceptional being on earth. But Virginia also knew that this truly was a very special child, one who looked at things in her own way. One who would not have an easy path.

Virginia wondered what Eric's response would be if she and Erinn officially declared an allegiance with the pro-tree people? Virginia knew that Erinn always took an interest in historic preservation; she fought the good fight in New York City when she lived there and had helped save several old buildings. So it wouldn't surprise Virginia that her daughter would get involved saving this little loser of a tree. And as for herself . . . well, this battle had started to get her blood pumping!

Virginia watched Erinn watch Christopher. Virginia knew that her daughter wasn't comfortable with people in general, but if she had an interest in a man she became even more awkward. So this was a brave step on Erinn's part, putting herself out there. Virginia watched as she took a tentative glance over Christopher's shoulder to peek at his drawing. But when he turned his attention toward Erinn, she ran off to take pictures with Bernard.

Virginia's heart once more swelled and she jammed her fists into her pockets to keep herself from hugging her eldest daughter. She tried not to get her hopes up—she would love to see Christopher and Erinn together. But Erinn was not an easy woman to get to know. Virginia looked over at Christopher, drawing away and chatting easily with any curious onlooker.

Will he take the time? she wondered.

CHAPTER 13

SUZANNA

Suzanna did not rush immediately to Rio's studio bearing scones and lemon cream. She was a happily married, *busy* woman with a business to run, a baby to raise, and a mother visiting from out of town. She had too much responsibility to toss it all up in the air for a visit with a hot man who had whispered that he needed to speak to her alone. He could wait. The question was: How long could *she* wait?

In a parallel universe kind of way, Rio being in the neighborhood had actually been a benefit to Suzanna's life. She had lost a few pounds and had started to tone up the rest. She had soaked up the ins and outs of local politics, was beginning to understand what it took to get a local landmark designation, and knew the difference between a cedar, a Douglas fir, and a Canadian hemlock. She knew that her husband, her mother, and her neighbors scoffed at the mighty and not-so-mighty eucalyptus. She still could not understand what the fuss was about; in her opinion Mr. Clancy's tree *was* a hazard.

But she would keep that to herself.

Suzanna was clearing out the assorted flotsam and jetsam that had managed to accumulate in her foyer. She picked up a stack of flyers and realized they were from the artist who was going to be showing at Willow Station. She had forgotten to put them in the Nook. As she headed into the bookstore, Christopher almost collided with her.

"Hey, Christopher," Suzanna said. "What's up?"

"Not a whole hell of a lot. I was just wondering if Eric was around? I need help moving a desk I just made. It's heavier than it looks."

Christopher seemed to do a double take when he saw the flyers in Suzanna's hand.

"What's this?" he asked, taking one.

"Some new artist in town," Suzanna said. "I told her I'd spread the word."

"Oh," Christopher said. "I'll take one of these, OK?"

He headed back out the door, much to Suzanna's confusion.

"Should I send Eric over to help with the desk?" she called after him.

Artists!

Virginia had come back from her research expedition to Santa Monica and told Eric and Suzanna that she felt it her duty to fight for the tree. She would keep it out of the Rollicking Bun and Book Nook, but her conscience told her she had to fight the good fight. Suzanna and Eric then had their own battle.

"This is just what my mom needs," Suzanna had said.

"This is not what our family needs!" Eric replied.

"You mean, this isn't what *you* need!"

The upshot was that Virginia was free to hold her meetings in the Bun but had to give the Nook a wide berth.

Virginia jumped in with vigor. She collected an odd assortment of women of all ages who felt honor-bound to look after the tree. She was preparing several of them for a new campaign. These volunteers would canvass the neighborhood, sniffing out registered voters who would sign their hotly worded petition. Suzanna was happy to have the extra business; the would-be petitioners spent hours in the tea-room. She felt the extra revenue would be something to show off to Eric, but she kept all mention of the pro-tree volunteer meetings to herself. As amped up as her mother was, Suzanna was drained.

Erinn came in. Suzanna was not at all happy to see her. She was treading lightly with Eric, and adding Know-It-All Erinn to the mix just seemed too much to bear. But Erinn seemed as tired as Suzanna felt. The two sisters sat drinking tea and watching their inexhaustible mother explain how to get the attention of jaded Venetians.

"Don't forget, your neighbors have seen it all and heard it all," Virginia said. "You have to do whatever it takes to get their attention and once you have it, don't let go until you get that signature."

"How do we do that?" a worried-looking lady named Clare asked. She seemed younger than most of the other women but equally committed to the cause.

"How many of you have dogs?" Virginia asked.

Suzanna looked up from her tea to see the show of hands. Where was her mother going with this? Of the eight women in the shop, five of them raised their hands.

"Five of you," Virginia said. "Good. Take your dogs with you. Southern Californians love dogs. Let them do the work for you."

Suzanna noticed that Clare looked downcast. Apparently, she did not have a dog.

"Clare, you may borrow Piquant," Virginia said.

Erinn and Suzanna exchanged a look. Poor Clare.

Erinn started picking at her sweater, which Suzanna saw was covered in long fur. At first Suzanna thought Caro must be shedding, but on closer inspection, the fur was longer and finer and blonder than Caro's. Suzanna started helping to groom her sister.

"Those damn Angora rabbits," Erinn whispered, so as not to disrupt her mother's zealous speech. "Their hair is everywhere."

"Speak of the devil," Suzanna said, looking toward the door as Dymphna wafted in.

Erinn saw her, too, and closed her eyes.

"It's either Blu or Dymphna driving me crazy," Erinn said. "I thought I could at least get away from them here."

Dymphna silently threaded her way toward the strategizing women.

"As Marcus Aurelius said, 'The object of life is . . . to escape finding oneself in the ranks of the insane,' " Erinn said while rubbing her eyes. "And I am in the ranks of the insane every minute of every day."

Dymphna sat down and Virginia broke into a huge grin.

"Hello, Dymphna," she said, greeting her with a hug. "Glad you could join us."

Erinn and Suzanna both were taken by surprise by the warm greeting. Virginia had been up to Erinn's house and met both Blu and Dymphna, but so had Suzanna, and she didn't feel as if they had any special connection. She knew it didn't take her mother long to bond with people, but this seemed quick even for her.

Virginia introduced Dymphna to the crowd.

"Ladies, this is Dymphna," Virginia said. "She lives in my daughter Erinn's guesthouse and is raising Angora rabbits to make yarn. She is new in town and I thought she'd like to be part of our community."

Everyone in the room seemed interested in her story. Shy Dymphna tucked her head into an intricate scarf she was wearing. It was light blue with flashes of darker cobalt and had a chunky texture accented with tiny pearlescent beads. Suzanna found herself mesmerized by the scarf and by the time she was listening to the conversation again, Virginia was catching Dymphna up on the petition and the idea that everyone should bring a dog as an icebreaker.

"But we don't have dogs for everyone," Clare said, firmly putting herself back in the dogless camp.

"What about rabbits?" Dymphna asked softly.

Everyone in the room strained to hear her. Suzanna saw Erinn lean in, caught up in the discussion.

"What was that, dear?" Virginia asked. "Could you speak up so the class . . . I mean, so everyone can hear you?"

"My rabbits are very friendly and they are all leash trained," Dymphna said again, although still very softly. "Maybe they could go out and help."

"That is a great idea." Erinn's booming voice shot out of nowhere. She joined the group, leaving Suzanna at an outer table by herself. "As a matter of fact, every one of you should lead a rabbit on a leash. We'll get some press that way. It will be our signature look."

Suzanna almost laughed out loud at her curmudgeonly sister using the expression "signature look." Must be Blu's influence.

Virginia was beaming at Erinn.

"I can't help it," Erinn said to her mother. "It's the producer in me."

"It's a wonderful idea," Babette, another of the dogless women, said. "I think the rabbits will get us a ton of attention."

"We need a catchy name, too," Erinn said. "I propose Cause Courtyard."

Suzanna was about to say that the word *tree* should perhaps be in this catchy name, but the group seemed perfectly happy with Cause

Courtyard, and Erinn was practically glowing from the murmurs of appreciation.

As Dymphna explained how best to walk an Angora rabbit in order to keep it healthy, calm, and knot free, Suzanna took the opportunity to slip out of the room. She peeked in on Eric in the Nook. His feet propped up at the counter, he was reading some sort of document. Lizzy was sound asleep on his shoulder. She leaned against the door frame, taking in the sight of her family. Eric looked up and she smiled at him but he didn't smile back.

"Are you OK?" Suzanna asked.

"I'm just worried that this whole thing is going to blow up," Eric said. "Your mom seems to have taken over as lead tree advocate, and I'm afraid we won't be able to stay out of it."

He sounded like he was running for office.

"She just wants to be part of things," Suzanna said, feeling silly that she was defending her mother when she was as annoyed as Eric. "She's all stirred up about the petition."

"The petition is just the first step," Eric said. "If they get past that, they're probably going to have to go to court to fight Mr. Clancy—which will be bad for community relations and cost money nobody has."

Suzanna wanted to stand in solidarity with her husband. They really hadn't had anything to bond over in such a long time (well, after Lizzy, of course). She was a little confused as to how you became an activist when the point was to remain neutral, but she would think of something. OK, so her mother and sister were movers and shakers—each in her own way—but Suzanna could be, too (she hoped). She could be so easily knocked out of orbit by the other women in her family. It was time to stand up and be counted. Suzanna studied Eric, who had gone back to his reading. She wondered if he'd miss her if she did get knocked out of orbit.

Time to go over to Mr. Clancy's Courtyard and scope out the situation for herself. She'd been immobilized because of the Rio situation. Frankly, she was hoping he'd show up again at the Bun, begging to see her, which had not happened. She now had a higher calling. She would prove to Eric that she would be his helpmate and find a way to keep the peace. She just wouldn't tell her mother. . . .

Donell, on his phone, silently offered her a bouquet of sage as she walked by. She declined. The Wolf women walked the fine line of accepting just enough of his offerings so that he was not insulted but leaving him with plenty of sage to sell. It was late afternoon and the merchants of the courtyard were packing up their sidewalk tables. She wanted to go look at a green-and-orange skirt that Mr. Clancy had thrown over his shoulder but thought better of it. Would doing business with Mr. Clancy be fraternizing with the enemy? Whose enemy? Certainly not Eric's! Her mother's? She tried not to catch his eye but he caught hers.

"Hi, Suzanna," he said, continuing to pack up his wares. "I wanted to talk to you, but I'm pretty sure I'm not welcome at the Bun any longer."

"That's not true, Mr. Clancy!" she said, although now that she thought about it, maybe it *was* true! "I'm sure everyone on the block is going to be able to work this thing out!"

Mr. Clancy waved her soothing words away.

"Yeah, yeah," he said. "I was just wondering how involved your mother is in this whole thing."

"What whole thing?" Suzanna asked. "The tree thing?"

"What other thing is there?" he groused. "I was thinking about asking her to go get a beer, but if I'm the bad guy . . ."

"I'm sure my mother does not see you as a bad guy," Suzanna replied, although she wasn't sure of that at all. Maybe her mother would be horrified by the idea of getting a drink with a man who would chop down a helpless tree. "But . . ."

"But what?"

Mr. Clancy stopped packing and looked straight at Suzanna. She was shocked to see the wariness and fear of rejection in his blue eyes.

"But . . . my mother doesn't drink beer. Better make it wine," she said as she turned into the courtyard.

Let Mom fight her own battles!

Christopher was leaning against the outside wall of his art gallery. Suzanna realized how tiny the courtyard actually was. She had just turned away from Mr. Clancy and here was Christopher, just ten feet and yet a thousand miles away from Mr. Clancy.

"Hi, Christopher," Suzanna said. "Good day?"

"Not bad. My uncle sold a lithograph and I sold a birdcage, so we'll have the rent. Can't ask for more than that."

Suzanna felt guilty. She could ask for more than that. She always did.

"Hey, listen," Christopher said. "I'm going to check out that new art installation at Willow Station tonight. I was wondering if your sister might want to go."

Suzanna hoped she didn't appear as surprised as she felt by this question. Before she could formulate any words, Bernard came out of the gallery and locked the door.

"I was thinking about heading over to Willow Station myself," Bernard said. The look he gave his nephew had a definite challenge to it, Suzanna noticed. "I thought I might ask your fine-looking mama if she wanted to go."

What the hell is going on?

"Well," Suzanna said, "they were both over at the Bun a few minutes ago, whipping up support for the cause. They're probably still there."

The men grinned at each other. Suzanna watched them leave the courtyard. It suddenly came to her. Willow Station! That woman . . . what was her name? . . . Alice . . . were they going to see her show?

Mr. Clancy was still on the sidewalk. He didn't exchange any sort of greeting with his tenants. Suzanna felt bad about this turn of events. Mr. Clancy and Bernard were always sparring but until recently it had been good-natured. She worried that Eric was right, that the animosity would sour the neighborhood long after someone declared victory about the tree. And now to have Christopher asking her sister on a date (was it a date? Or just one artist alerting another to the wonders of a local art installation?) and two old codgers vying for her mother's attention—it was too much to contemplate!

She thought of a country song from a few years back about "Viagra in the water." It made as much sense as any other explanation.

Suzanna turned around and regarded the tree. Frankly, she wasn't feeling any goodwill toward the thing that was disrupting the peace in her neighborhood. She walked around it several times, dipping under unwieldy branches and getting her footing on the uneven cement. She was lost in concentration when she heard salsa music. She stood riveted to the spot. It was the music Rio always played at the dance studio. She realized she was standing right outside his new venue. She tried to command her feet to walk away but her feet were not going anywhere. Her body turned toward the music as if she had no will of her own.

There was no denying it. She missed the music and the dancing. In a weird way, she missed the woman she had been before she became a wife and mother, when she had no one to worry about but herself. Her mistakes were hers alone. She knew she could no longer make that claim—her mistakes would echo through the Bun like a shotgun blast. But she walked through Rio's door anyway.

The rhythm of the music quickened Suzanna's pulse as she looked around the room. This group was a far cry from the fashionistas that made up most of Rio's past clientele. Rio was showing a boy the quick-quick-slow steps that made up the foundation of salsa. Rio was not a small man, but he was dwarfed by this scowling adolescent, with his enormous tattooed biceps. Suzanna tried not to smile as she watched the two men grasping forearms as Rio tried to force some rhythm into the kid. The music stopped and Rio saw Suzanna in the mirror.

She had never exactly envisioned this moment. She was glad she hadn't because it wouldn't have gone anything like this. Rio merely turned around and looked at her. No smile, no shining eyes, no sign that he was happy to see her in the least.

"Suzanna," Rio said. "Come in."

She could feel herself lifting off the ground. She tried to grab onto the ballet barre but it slipped through her fingers. She bobbed around the class of sneering teenagers, three boys and two girls covered in tattoos and piercings—she remembered three of them, Ray, Miles, and Winnie, but Rio seemed to have added two more students. He really seemed dedicated to his new venture. The kids were all too cool to take note that a neighboring shopkeeper was floating near the ceiling.

Rio spoke to the class.

"Suzanna was a former student of mine," he said. "She was not very good when she started, but tried very hard. You could learn from her."

POW! Suzanna was back on the floor. Rio put on a song she knew by heart. It was "La Ruñidera," one of his favorites. She used to listen to it over and over but deleted it from her playlist after the fantasy of Rio ended. It had all been the imaginings of a lost and lonely woman, but she had to admit, she had felt one hundred percent alive in those days before peaceful marriage and motherhood.

With the teenagers feigning boredom and the music pounding around them, Rio put out his hand. Suzanna didn't hesitate for an instant and he walked her onto the dance floor.

Although it had been three and a half years since she'd gone to a dance class, Suzanna had kept dancing. She danced in the Bun kitchen or in stores or on street corners when a Latin beat became too much to ignore. At those times she was glad she'd studied salsa. There really would not have been any way to waltz or tango effectively by herself. She'd also been dancing with Lizzy since before the baby was born. As Suzanna let herself be escorted to the dance floor, she said a silent prayer of thanks that she would not be totally rusty. But dancing by herself, or with Lizzy, was not the same as dancing with Rio.

Is there anything like dancing with Rio?

Suzanna put her left hand on his shoulder and forced herself to look into his eyes. She could hear all his instructions from years ago tumbling around in her head: "Don't let your foot slide," "Don't look at the floor," "Tilt your body forward, not backward." But she decided not to listen. She would listen to the music instead. The tree could wait. Her husband's obsession with the community could wait. Two old guys fighting over her mother could wait. She was dancing with Rio, who was even hotter now that his shiny black hair was tossing around his head.

She would play out this three-minute romance for all it was worth.

It was over in a heartbeat. Applause filled the little studio. Rio, who was still Rio even with a new cause, stood unsmiling as he applauded languidly along with the students. She tried to accept the applause graciously and not like a sponge begging for water. If she were Cinderella, the clock would be ticking. Midnight would strike as soon as she walked out the door. She tried not to feel disloyal to her life. She often thought that if she were her ten-year-old self looking at her adult self, she would be more than satisfied with what she had become. She had the best husband, the perfect child, a wonderful business, loyal friends. She missed her father but her vibrant mother was still stirring things up. But fantasy had always played a part in Suzanna's life, and she found she missed it more than she knew.

Things were different now, she told herself. She would walk out, accepting the closure that this dance afforded. She felt so light and happy, she gave Rio a spontaneous hug.

"I still need to see you, Suzanna," he said.

Cinderella had nothing on her. Suzanna raced out the studio door as the clock struck midnight in her heart. She had to get back to her life before anyone knew she had been to the ball. As she ran through the courtyard alone, her toe caught on something and she sprawled on the cement, skinning her hands.

As she sat collapsed on the ground, looking at her bleeding palms, she was feeling less than neutral about just about everything.

CHAPTER 14

ERINN

Willow Station was a strange place. An old railroad station that went the way of old railroad stations, it was turned into a local museum in the 1980s. Although it was a remodeled, cavernous space that never seemed to have enough artwork to fill it, new artists from all over the country vied for its attention. In the up-and-coming art community an exhibit at Willow Station carried bragging rights, not to mention much-needed exposure and offers to be hung in art galleries of varying reputations.

The art exhibit currently causing a stir at the little museum was called *POP! Culture*. It featured various artifacts made from the pop-tops of soda and beer cans and ribbons of aluminum cut from the cans themselves. The artist, Alice Albert, billed herself as an environmental-fiber-and-metal artist, which Erinn found gratingly pretentious. But Erinn was on her best behavior. It wasn't every day a handsome neighbor asked her out, and it certainly wasn't business as usual to be on a double date with her mother.

Virginia put on her glasses and peered at a shawl made from the pop-tops. The shawl draped and folded as if it were made of cashmere.

"We've got to get Dymphna up here to see this," Virginia said to Erinn. "I think she would find this fascinating."

Erinn tried to shake off the feeling that her mother found raising

Angora rabbits a much higher calling than following Blu Knight around with a camera.

Or maybe I'm just projecting.

"Virginia, come look at this," Bernard said.

Virginia went to stand next to Bernard as they studied a miniature train set, every tiny detail made from pop-tops and aluminum ribbons. Erinn considered herself an expert on body language and tried to read the signals, but when her mother leaned into Bernard to whisper something and he laughed and put his hand on her mother's waist for an instant, Erinn turned quickly away. Body signals were one thing, smoke signals another.

Erinn looked around the room for Christopher, who was standing in front of a large aluminum moose head, complete with mounting board. Erinn shot her mother a quick backward glance; maybe her easy chemistry with a member of the opposite sex would rub off on Erinn. She stepped lightly into the spot next to Christopher.

"She's really an incredible artist, isn't she?" he asked, although he sounded gloomy.

"Well . . . yes . . . she is," Erinn said. "Although I don't understand why she would choose this particular medium. With her talent, it seems as if she's limiting herself."

Look who's talking.

Christopher turned to her, his intense eyes looking into hers.

"I disagree. I think she took a medium that inherently puts confines on an artist and stretched the boundaries. I mean, she made a shawl and a moose head. How can you call that limiting?"

This is why I don't go out.

Erinn was more than comfortable in heated debate—and she did think that this Alice Albert was wasting her time in such a frivolous medium—but had learned from sad experience that trouncing an opponent on a first date wasn't usually the best-laid plan. Although she wasn't quite sure she could trounce Christopher anyway. He certainly had his own viewpoint.

Virginia and Bernard were suddenly at their side. Erinn gave a soft sigh of relief. Mother as backup was always a good idea.

"I love, love, love this exhibit," Virginia said. "What a talent."

"I agree," Christopher said, looking coolly at Erinn. He turned to his uncle. "Do you think we could ask if she wants to put some of her work up in our studio?"

"We can ask her," Bernard said. "She's heading our way."

The group turned to watch a severe-looking woman in her forties walking toward them. She wore a black turtleneck tucked into fatigues, which in turn were tucked into black combat boots. Her stern look was offset by a wide, toothy grin.

"Shit," Christopher said. "It *is* her."

"I told you," Bernard said, shaking his head.

"I know you did. But I didn't believe it."

Erinn and Virginia looked at each other, mystified. Did they know this woman?

"I saw her picture outside," Bernard said as the woman continued to advance on them. "There can't be two people in the world sporting those glasses."

"Christopher? Is that you?" the woman said, reaching out with both arms to envelop Christopher in a hug. A hug that Christopher did not appear eager to return.

"I can't believe it's you!" Alice Albert said.

"It's me," Christopher said, disengaging from the hug. "This is such a surprise."

"You know me," Alice said, smiling at the group. "I'm always full of surprises."

Virginia put out her hand. "Hello, I'm Virginia Wolf."

Alice burst out laughing. "No . . . no you're not! Your name is Virginia Woolf? Priceless!"

Virginia forged ahead, "This is my daughter, Erinn."

"Erinn Wolf? Erinn *Elizabeth* Wolf?" Alice's eyebrows shot skyward. "The writer? Impressive."

Erinn didn't answer. Erinn Elizabeth Wolf, the writer, seemed light-years ago. There was an awkward silence, so Virginia continued. "And this is Bernard."

"We know each other," Bernard growled, startling Erinn and Virginia.

Christopher seemed to wake from a trance.

"I'm sorry," Christopher said. "Everyone, this is Alice . . . my ex-wife."

Erinn tried to hide the jolt that went through her, but she felt her mother's hand on her forearm, steadying her.

"I think I'd heard that you had a little studio around here somewhere," Alice said. Then turning to Erinn as if they were co-conspirators against bad little boys, she told her, "It's been five years, but you hear things through the grapevine, you know."

Or through Internet stalking.

Erinn tried not to stare accusingly at Christopher. Why would he bring her to an art gallery to meet his ex-wife? Even if he wasn't sure it was his ex-wife and just wanted to check out the situation due to morbid fascination, why bring Erinn?

Her spirits plummeted. He had no interest in her! She was making a fool of herself getting her hopes up like that. All she wanted to be was gone.

"You changed your name," Christopher said. "Did you remarry, Alice *Albert?*"

Erinn tried to hear if he sounded hopeful or dejected by his own question.

Alice snorted.

"No, I just wanted to be free of preconceptions my past might have laid on me. Don't get me wrong, when you work in beer cans, you get your share of offers."

To Erinn's well-trained ear this was clearly a well-rehearsed line.

"So I went with Albert," Alice continued.

"As in Camus," Erinn offered.

"You got that right, sister," Alice said, giving her a high five, which surprised Erinn. "Good guess."

What other Albert would an artist name herself after? Einstein?

"Are you showing in any local galleries?" Virginia asked after another dreadful silence.

"No, not around here," Alice said. "I have a gallery in Sedona and one in Santa Fe, but haven't cracked L.A. yet. I'm hoping this exhibit will help."

"Best of luck to you," said Bernard. "We'd better go."

"I really would love to show my work in your gallery," Alice said, the brassy shield slipping.

"No, you really wouldn't," Christopher said.

"I would!" she said, her eyes overly bright. "I really need to show in Los Angeles, Chris."

Chris?

Christopher handed Alice a business card. "Come over after the exhibit and we'll talk."

Alice peered at it over the top rim of her glasses.

"B and C Studios, Mr. Clancy's Courtyard."

"That's us," Bernard said.

"Anywhere near the Rollicking Bun? I left some flyers there a while ago," she said. "I'll give you a call in the next couple days, when all this winds down," she added, gesturing at the entire studio.

Erinn thought that was a tad grandiose after Alice had practically thrown herself at Christopher, but she held her tongue. She offered to buy their foursome a nightcap, but when they arrived at the Four Seasons in Marina del Rey, she realized she'd made a tactical error. Willow Station, and an aluminum-can-art display, was pure funk, and she had lurched the group into elegance. It was as if they'd changed lands at Disneyland too quickly and hadn't quite regrouped.

They ordered a bottle of wine. Even though Erinn had issued the invitation and in her mind was the host of the event, Bernard took control of the smelling, tasting, and testing of the cork with a hearty sniff. Erinn and her mother exchanged a brief look. They were, after all, from Napa Valley and knew that a discreet thumbing of the cork to see if it was dried out was all that was really needed.

The conversation bumped and swirled with as much small talk as the four could generate but it finally turned to Alice Albert.

"You didn't know your ex-wife was showing at Willow Station?" Virginia asked in much more mellow tones than Erinn could have mustered.

Christopher shook his head.

"No," he said. "When I saw that someone named Alice Albert was hanging at Willow Station, it didn't ring any bells. Even the artwork is very different from anything she'd ever done. But then I saw the flyer at the Nook and thought it might be her."

Erinn wanted to ask why he'd decided that it would be a good idea to walk Erinn down Humiliation Highway but he seemed to read her mind.

"I know it was probably awkward for you this evening," he said. "And I'm sorry. I just wanted backup."

Backup? As in Tonto? As in Barney Fife?

This wasn't working. She caught her mother's sympathetic gaze and sat up straight. She was not the sort of wilting flower to be undone by this insensitive man. She looked him dead in the eye.

"I'm guessing it wasn't a civilized divorce," Erinn said.

She heard Bernard snort and take a sip of wine.

"We were both very young," Christopher said, clearly not disturbed by her bluntness. "We met in art school. She was a great artist and wanted a life I couldn't give her. For her, it was about the art and only about the art."

She's not that great. It's pull tabs!

"And you feel you owe her?" Virginia asked gently.

"I do," Christopher said, looking relieved to be understood. "Don't get me wrong, she wanted out of the marriage. But I didn't hang around to see that she was OK."

"Well, that wasn't your job any longer," Erinn said.

"Marriage is complicated," Christopher said. "So is divorce."

The conversation shifted uneasily to the idea of Alice showing at Bernard and Christopher's studio. Erinn had to admit that Alice's work would definitely fit in with their eclectic tastes.

But no use sugar-coating it: Erinn didn't need the competition.

"She was a brilliant student," Christopher said. "Alice had some very interesting insights."

"For example?" Virginia asked, always interested in people's college experiences.

"She said that if Cecilia Beaux were as pretty as Mary Cassatt," Christopher said, "*she* would have been the famous one. Even in the early twentieth century, art was still parceled out according to the male perspective."

"I think that's absurd," Erinn said, sipping her red wine. "The paintings that made Mary Cassatt famous were painted when she was older and looked like a basset hound. That's just rhetorical rambling."

"Rhetorical rambling is rhetorical rambling," Christopher said, laughing.

Is he defending Alice?

"Alice said that we needed to celebrate the women of the Industrial Revolution because they were clearly the artists of the textile factories. She wanted to do her thesis on it but couldn't find enough research to support her cause," he continued, clearly warming to the subject of Alice's intelligence. "It enraged her."

Virginia and Bernard were nodding sagely. Erinn found her temper rising, since this "observation" was commonly cited by rookie scholars debating art and history in coffeehouses nationwide.

"That, of course, depends on how you define the Industrial Revolution. One could argue that it started with the invention of the wheel," she said.

It was as if her companions had turned to stone. The waiter walked by.

"Check, please," Virginia said.

When the foursome finally got back to the Beach Walk, Christopher took Erinn's hand and asked if she'd like to go for a walk. She hesitated. She was pretty sure the evening had gone on long enough for all of them. She certainly didn't want Christopher to feel obliged to take her on a pity walk.

"She'd love to, Christopher," Virginia said, gently nudging her eldest daughter forward. Erinn wasn't sure whose romance her mother was trying to foster—Erinn's or her own. Erinn watched as her mother and Bernard headed across the sand to the ocean.

Christopher took Erinn's hand and they walked in silence down the quiet Beach Walk.

"It's hard to believe this place ever settles down," Christopher said. "It's so crazy during the day."

"Oh, I don't know," Erinn said. "It can be pretty crazy at night, too."

She knew she sounded as if she was pouting but she couldn't help herself. Christopher halted and stood in front of her. He put his hands on her shoulders and bent to look into her eyes. Erinn wished it were darker, but the floodlights from a nearby store filled the area with light. She had no choice but to look back at him.

"I know I screwed up taking you to the gallery tonight," he said. "I get it. And I know it was totally juvenile of me, but I just . . . I just wanted a beautiful woman with me. It was crazy; I was just showing off. I hope you don't hate me."

"I . . . ," Erinn said. "I can understand how there might be some satisfaction in pay-back."

Now she was glad there was light. She could see Christopher smile at her. She could see his hands as he smoothed her hair back from her face. Then she closed her eyes. She couldn't see anything, but she felt alive to her fingertips. He kissed her.

CHAPTER 15

VIRGINIA

Her daughter really was a genius, Virginia thought proudly. Erinn's idea of using the rabbits to grab media attention was brilliant. Coordinating the rabbits, which lived in Santa Monica, and the ladies of Cause Courtyard, who were all in Venice, was no easy task. Finally, Dymphna arrived in front of the Bun in a U-Haul full of rabbit crates. Dymphna could clearly tell one rabbit from the next, but Virginia could only distinguish one, a reddish hairball with a large brown circle on its back. Dymphna had named it Spot. Virginia felt anointed as Dymphna handed Spot to her. She tried not to look at Piquant, who was inside the Bun, yapping just inside the picture window.

"I thought you weren't supposed to name farm animals," Babette said, as Dymphna handed her a white Angora named Blanche.

"You don't name farm animals because you're going to turn them into food," Dymphna said. "I'm only turning their hair into sweaters."

Dymphna very calmly and carefully harnessed and leashed all ten rabbits and seemed to match each one to a particular human. She would pick up a rabbit and study the women, walking up and down in front of the Bun, until she was satisfied she had the right woman for the job. At that point she would hand over a rabbit, telling each woman in turn that rabbits could be easily frightened and she was entrusting them with precious, precious cargo. Finally, the women were able to take to the Venice streets, each walking a miniature Yeti.

"Remember that the rabbit is actually walking you," Dymphna said. "Please don't try to lead or tug the leash."

Virginia stood with Spot, not sure exactly how this was going to work. She and Dymphna watched as Babette and Blanche faltered down the Beach Walk. In minutes, she was surrounded by people who wanted to see the rabbit.

"I hope this doesn't stress Blanche too much," Dymphna said, her eyebrows knitted. "Do you think Babette will remember to hold her?"

She relaxed when Babette picked up Blanche and let people gently pat her.

Virginia couldn't hear what Babette was actually saying to anyone, but she noticed that in the middle of a conversation someone would look over toward Mr. Clancy's Courtyard, craning to see inside. In no time at all they would be signing the petition.

Virginia looked up and down the Beach Walk, where the rabbity drama was playing out over and over again. Each woman would walk the rabbit until someone came up to her. At that point she would scoop the creature into a protective embrace, according to Dymphna's instructions. Almost everyone seemed to be signing the petition.

One step closer to filing, Virginia thought.

Spot seemed eager to hop so Virginia took a few tentative steps. It took about a half hour to walk half a block. Spot decided she'd walked far enough and stopped in front of Mr. Clancy's Courtyard. Virginia could see him in the window of his shop and while she knew better than to tug at Spot's leash, she really did not want to be rallying the troops right in front of Mr. Clancy. Erinn, who seemed to thrive on confrontation, would have loved to find herself in this position, but it was not Virginia's style.

As she leaned over to scoop up the rabbit, a woman about Erinn's age came up to them.

"What have you got there?" she asked.

"It's an Angora rabbit," Virginia said, automatically cradling Spot. "We're out here drawing attention to a very important cause."

The woman signaled to two men who were standing nearby, watching, when out of nowhere they produced a camera and a boom microphone. On one hand this was exactly what Cause Courtyard had in mind when they fanned out over the beach community with their petitions. On the other hand, doing an interview right in front of Mr. Clancy seemed like bad form.

The reporter signaled to the cameraman to roll and suddenly the boom pole was dangling over Virginia's head. The newswoman lifted a microphone to her lips and spoke directly into the camera.

"Tempers are as short as the hair on these Angora rabbits is long," she said. "A band of locals is standing their ground, trying to save a tree that is moments away from destruction."

"Well, not *moments* away," Virginia said in alarm.

This wasn't journalism, this was sensationalism!

"Mr. Clancy of Mr. Clancy's Courtyard has turned a deaf ear to this dedicated local group, who are selflessly working to save a fellow earthbound cohabitant. Thousands are flocking to the Venice Beach Walk to get a glimpse of the Angora Angels as they race against the clock. Is that accurate?" the newswoman asked Virginia.

She stuck the microphone into Virginia's face. Virginia held Spot tighter as she tried to formulate a logical speech, although clearly coherent thought was not mandatory.

"We're Cause Courtyard," Virginia began, "not the Angora Angels."

The newswoman suddenly took a large step back as Spot let out a loud hissing noise. A shirtless man with bulging muscles was walking by, an anvil-faced pit bull on a lead in front of him. Spot hissed again, her powerful legs kicking. Virginia tried to control her, but Spot was strong and leaped to the ground. Virginia fumbled with the leash, but Spot was free. The rabbit ran toward the pit bull at full speed, covering the distance between them in seconds. The dog yelped in terror. Spot tore after the pit bull, which streaked madly down the Beach Walk, his owner barely managing to keep up with him. Human and dog kept glancing over their shoulders as the rabbit charged. Spot was in hot pursuit, but Virginia managed to catch her leash and scoop her up. Spot sat quietly in Virginia's arms, twitching her nose contentedly. Virginia turned back to the newswoman.

"I'm so sorry," Virginia said. "What were you saying?"

"Forget it," the newswoman said, indicating her crew should pack it up. "Nothing you can say will beat the footage of your rabbit taking that dog's pride card."

Dymphna came running up.

"Is Spot all right?" she asked, carefully taking the rabbit in her arms. "I've never seen her do that before."

"She seems fine," Virginia said, but she felt she'd let Dymphna down. "I had no idea how strong she was."

Dymphna buried her head in Spot's fur. She nodded and walked away. Virginia looked around her. All the women were holding onto their rabbits for dear life and staring at her. Cause Courtyard was over.

As the women and rabbits made their way back to the Bun, Virginia caught Mr. Clancy's eye. She wasn't sure if he had stepped outside to shoo everyone away or felt he could finally have some peace now that the rabbits and newspeople were gone. He looked years older than he had when she'd first met him and that was only a few weeks ago! She felt very sorry for him. Mr. Clancy pretended not to see her, but Virginia called out to him.

"Mr. Clancy!" she said.

He looked as if he were debating whether to talk to her or not but his indecisiveness gave her time to catch up to him.

"That was quite the show," Mr. Clancy said, not smiling.

"I hope that newswoman didn't bother you."

"No, she didn't bother me. But you and your friends sure did. You're making me out to be the bad guy and all I'm trying to do is keep from being sued. That tree is a danger to everyone who comes into the courtyard. I mean, your own daughter fell just the other day!"

Virginia wondered if Erinn was sneaking over to the Courtyard to see Christopher.

"Erinn fell?"

"No, not Erinn. Suzanna! She was coming out of the dance studio and almost went ass over teakettle, if you'll pardon my French."

Virginia was startled. Why hadn't Suzanna mentioned this? Why was she at the dance studio in the first place? Maybe she was going to volunteer to help that nice young dance instructor. After all, Suzanna did know how to dance after her salsa frenzy of a few years ago.

"I don't think it's fair that everyone is making me out to be the villain," Mr. Clancy was saying.

"Nobody thinks you're the—" Virginia started, but Mr. Clancy's look cut her short.

He was right, of course. He was being made out to be the villain.

"Maybe we should all listen to Eric and settle down for a bit," Virginia said. "Let cooler heads prevail."

Mr. Clancy finally smiled.

"I think that would be a good idea. Maybe you and I could discuss this over a bee—a glass of wine."

"I would like that, Mr. Clancy," Virginia said. She leaned into him and whispered, "But don't tell my children."

CHAPTER 16

ERINN

Erinn was still steaming over the ignobility of today's assignment. Cary had called and informed her that the latest focus groups revealed that women 18–45 wanted to relate to the people they saw on television.

"It follows the same philosophy as book covers that feature bodies with no heads. Women relate to the body but they want to put their own faces on those bodies. It's a way to make the fantasy feel more real."

Erinn found this very interesting. She had seen those book covers herself. She often wondered who was buying all those novels with decapitated people on them, referring to them as "The Romances of Sleepy Hollow."

"You want me to shoot Blu without her head?" Erinn asked, genuinely puzzled.

"We need to make Blu seem just like everyone else," Cary said. "Only more so."

"Good luck with that."

"Erinn, try to work with me. Anyway, I made an appointment with Dr. Roberts tomorrow."

"Are you ill?"

"No! Not for me, for Blu!" Cary said, sounding exasperated. "Do you mean to tell me you've never heard of Dr. Roberts, plastic surgeon to the stars?"

Luckily, Erinn's laptop was within reach and she got busy Googling Dr. Roberts. She had learned that while she was always alarmingly behind the times in all things Los Angeles, just a few clicks on a search engine and she could get herself up to speed enough to fake it.

"Oh, Dr. *Carson* Roberts," Erinn said into the phone. "Of course."

"I want you to shoot a consultation . . . maybe lipo, maybe new boobs, a new nose."

"She has new boobs and I'm pretty sure that is not her original nose. And she doesn't have an ounce of flesh on her. Why are we doing this? I thought she was supposed to own a shoe factory."

"We can't find a shoe factory willing to say it's Blu's."

Unlike me, who got suckered into losing my whole house. I can't believe I have less integrity than a shoe factory.

"We're trying to make Blu seem more like her audience," Cary said. "Aren't you listening? A trip to a plastic surgeon will make her seem relatable."

"To whom?" Erinn asked, trying not to sound annoyed.

"To the proverbial 'everywoman.' It will make Blu seem insecure about her looks."

"I'm not sure Blu can convey insecurity about her looks. She's not that good an actress. And for your information, I think when 'everywoman' is feeling insecure she makes an appointment to get a gym membership, not a high-priced plastic surgeon."

"I'll e-mail you the particulars. The appointment is at nine a.m."

* * *

Erinn and Blu headed out the next morning. Blu pouted the entire way to Beverly Hills. She was upset that Opie the audio guy was not joining them. Erinn tried to explain that her camera had a perfectly serviceable microphone and an extra person on a shoot in a tiny space would cause more problems than it would solve.

"Let's go over some ideas for the scene," Erinn said, hoping to distract her.

"I was thinking of asking for some lipo to get rid of this," Blu said, grabbing some flesh at the top of her jeans.

"That's skin," Erinn said. "You need that."

Blu rolled her eyes and looked out the window, watching Beverly Hills sail by.

"Maybe we could shoot a scene in the Coach store afterward," Blu said. "I'll bet they'll give me a free bag in exchange for the publicity."

"We need to sell this series first," Erinn said. "Let's save that for Season One."

Blu nodded, and Erinn was relieved that she gave in so easily. While it wasn't a lie that they needed the series to sell before any of this made an ounce of difference, Erinn knew that brands with the upper-crust visibility of Coach did not need the kind of publicity Blu could offer. She didn't want Blu's feelings to be hurt. She wasn't sure why she cared, exactly. It wasn't as if Blu had taken Erinn's feelings into consideration—ever. But there was no time for soul searching. Dr. Roberts's Canon Drive office was right in front of them. Blu's eyes gleamed in anticipation.

Dr. Roberts was alone in the office when they arrived. He was wearing very expensive suit pants and a silk tie; Erinn wondered if he traded services with a few Armani salesmen. He had a white coat over a pinstriped shirt with French cuffs. He handed some paperwork to Erinn.

"Here's my location release and my personal release form," he said.

Erinn was impressed. She put the papers on top of her camera case. This obviously was not the doctor's first cable station rodeo.

"I always try to do these shows before business hours," he said, leading them into an examination room. "That way, I don't have to play favorites with the staff, choosing which nurse gets to bring in the charts."

Erinn found herself grinning. This man knew his stuff . . . or at least, he knew *her* stuff!

As she set up for the shoot, she tried to hear everything the doctor and Blu were saying without appearing to be eavesdropping. This was a skill field producers had perfected. Direct questioning often led to answers the person thought you wanted to hear rather than the truth. And Erinn did try to stick to reality as much as possible in these shows, for what that was worth.

"You're pretty handsome for a doctor," Blu said.

The doctor looked Blu over, but in a completely professional way. Erinn was sure this was not the reaction she got from most men who were scanning her.

"I mean, medical school must be a lot of work," Blu continued. "You could have skipped all that and just become an actor."

Dr. Roberts took Blu's blood pressure.

"You seem to be in pretty good shape," the doctor said.

"Oh, no," Blu protested. "I am flab, flab, flab."

She held out an arm and flicked at the skin on the underside. The doctor took it in his hands and examined it.

"Two weeks in the gym and you would be fine," he said.

Erinn was of two minds. On the one hand, she admired this doctor who obviously wasn't about to sell a procedure he didn't think was warranted. On the other hand, she knew Blu would be impossible if she didn't get her way.

Blu rolled down her waistband and tucked her T-shirt into her bra, so her whole midriff was exposed, then jumped up on the examination table. Erinn flipped the On button on her camera.

"You really should be naked for this," the doctor said.

"I know," Blu said. "But my producer says I have to keep my clothes on."

"Cut," Erinn said, pulling her eye away from the viewfinder.

Blu and the doctor turned to look at Erinn.

"We're a women's lifestyle network," Erinn explained. "Our audience really isn't comfortable with a lot of nudity."

"What if it's tasteful?" Blu asked.

As if Blu could do anything tasteful.

"Doctor," Blu said, "I really need you to agree to doing lipo. That's why I'm here."

"Well, that's not why I'm here," he said. "I'm here to offer advice on what I think you do and don't need."

"My company is going to pay you, you know," Blu said.

Erinn wondered if that were true.

"It's not about the money," Dr. Roberts replied. "Television is a very powerful medium. This is my reputation we're talking about."

Erinn knew he wasn't talking to her, but she felt a tweak. What about *her* reputation? She wondered again if the universe were sending her signs.

Blu jumped down off the table.

"Well then, this is a waste of time," she said and stormed out of the office. Erinn noticed that she didn't unroll her shorts or untuck her top. Dr. Roberts shrugged and picked up his paperwork from atop the camera case.

"I guess you won't be needing this," he said.

"I guess not," Erinn said. This morning, she'd hated the idea of shooting this and now she was sorry it was over before it began. It would have been such a great scene: a high-profile plastic surgeon telling a starlet to go straight to . . . the gym! Unheard of in the annals of vacuous TV!

Erinn packed her bag quickly and shook the doctor's hand. She murmured an apology and went to find Blu.

She was sitting on the hood of the car. She jumped when Erinn pressed the sensor to unlock the car and the horn beeped. Blu got right into the passenger seat without speaking to her as Erinn loaded the trunk with gear. As they drove down Wilshire Boulevard, Blu finally said, "A Beverly Hills plastic surgeon who won't do anything for money? What's that about?"

Erinn thought of Mark Twain's famous line: "It's no wonder truth is stranger than fiction. Fiction has to make sense." But she decided Blu would not appreciate the irony. She glanced over at Blu, who was still looking out the window, but she saw her brush away a tear. Was it possible this woman *was* insecure about her looks?

Cary was sitting on the front step of Erinn's house as they pulled up. She was not smiling. Blu and Erinn exchanged a look. Could Cary somehow have heard that they left the doctor's office with no footage? Cary stood up and walked toward the car.

Why can't she be like other bosses and text?

Erinn and Blu stepped out of the car looking like guilty teenagers who had taken their parents' vehicle without permission.

"We need to stick together on this," Blu said.

"Whatever *this* is," Erinn said, as they watched Cary make her way purposely toward them.

Cary wasted no time.

"Blu, would you please give me a minute with Erinn?"

"Sure!" Blu said and ran toward the house, digging in her purse for her keys.

"Let me just get my camera inside," Erinn said, stalling for time.

"Oh, I'll take it," Blu said, grabbing the camera case and rushing through the front door.

So much for solidarity.

Erinn was used to being on the receiving end of bosses' displeasure. She never intentionally set out to annoy them, but it happened regularly. She had ceased trying to guess what her transgression was; she was never right. So she waited.

"The footage for *Budding Tastes* was finally digitized," Cary said. "I've been going over it all morning."

Red, White, and Blu had been consuming so much of Erinn's time that she had almost forgotten about *Budding Tastes* and her own executive decision to make it into a show about junk-food-and-wine pairings.

Perhaps I should have mentioned that in my notes.

Maybe this wasn't bad news after all. Maybe, just maybe, Cary would see her vision!

"What did you think?" Erinn asked.

"Let's walk," Cary said, guiding Erinn away from the house.

They crossed Ocean Avenue to Palisades Park. They made their way to the fenced edge that looked over the cliff toward the Pacific Ocean. They rounded a class of five or six people learning swordplay and skirted a yoga boot camp that took place every day. Erinn always considered "yoga boot camp" an oxymoron but thought better of sharing this with Cary in case she wasn't in the mood.

Erinn waited.

"May I ask what you were thinking?" Cary asked.

This wasn't good.

Erinn thought of changing the subject but realized telling Cary that she had nothing to show for herself from the visit to Dr. Roberts probably wasn't going to help the situation.

"I think if you just give the junk food slant a chance—" Erinn began, but Cary interrupted her.

"Of course I'm going to give it a chance," Cary said. "I have no choice but to give it a chance. The network paid for this, and I have to now try and sell them on their own show!"

"They might find it interesting," Erinn said. "It hasn't been done before."

"Erinn, there is not an executive in all of television who wants something that has never been done before."

The two women looked out over the water. Erinn was grateful for its calming presence. She willed it to soothe her boss. She racked her brain for something to say. She knew she was terrible at that loathsome thing called "small talk."

"This view never fails me," she said, hoping to ease the tension. "I wish I had my camera."

"Speaking of your camera," Cary said, turning to face her, her hand shielding her eyes from the sun. "How did today go with Dr. Roberts?"

Another massive small-talk failure.

Erinn was grateful that Cary was looking into the sun and couldn't read her face.

"I don't think it's going to work for our story," she said, trying to keep her voice neutral.

That wasn't exactly a lie!

"Whatever." Cary shrugged, turning back toward the street.

Erinn took this to mean the inquisition was over.

"I've got enough problems," Cary continued. "I'll work on *Budding Tastes*; you do what you can with Blu."

"Sounds like a plan!" Erinn chirped, wondering whose bumptious voice she was channeling.

"But, Erinn, please, toe the party line."

"Toe the party line," she repeated, as they crossed the street. "A mixed metaphor, but I understand your meaning."

"Don't push your luck," Cary said as she got into her car.

Erinn watched her drive down Ocean Avenue until she was out of sight. Sighing with relief, she turned toward the house. Blu was standing in the front window, peeking out from behind the curtain. Erinn looked directly at her and the curtain dropped back into place. She knew that by the time she got into the house Blu would be nowhere in sight. This knowledge gave her a sense of satisfaction, until she remembered that Blu would be hiding out in her own bedroom.

Erinn picked up Caro and carried him into the hideously redecorated living room. She sat down at the computer and clicked on Facebook. She clicked on Suzanna's page and found pictures of Lizzy and Eric. She noticed a new profile picture, which was decidedly unmotherly. To Erinn's professional eye it screamed, "I might be a wife and mother, but I'm still hot."

Poor Suzanna. She needed so much . . . feedback.

She clicked on Eric's page, which was full of links to social causes and thinly veiled advertisements for the Nook. There were no personal photos or comments. Erinn knew he used his site for more professional reasons—she did that herself—but he actually had a personal life. A picture of the family couldn't hurt, could it? Her mother's page could have passed for a travel brochure for Venice Beach. Pictures of the Beach Walk, the bike path, the tea shop, Bernard's artwork, Donell and his sage—it was all there. Erinn scanned the photos quickly, looking for a picture of Christopher, but didn't see any. Her mother had a new profile picture as well. Virginia was holding Spot up to the camera, their faces touching cheek to cheek (if rabbits had cheeks).

Erinn clicked on Jude's profile. He was still traveling the world, apparently. In his latest self-portrait (she refused to use the term "selfie") he was pretending to be passed out among giant beer steins. His caption read: *Beer, women, and song . . . OK, beer and women . . . OK, beer.* Erinn smiled in spite of herself.

Blu's page was pretty much what Erinn expected: one semiporno-graphic pose after another. Erinn saw a video post that said "Blu twerks." Having no idea what that meant, she clicked on it. Staring at the screen, she witnessed Blu squatting low to the ground, her back-side thrust toward the camera. Her tiny rear end tensed, bobbed, and weaved to a pulsing, thumping rhythm. Was this a dance? Was that music? Blu started moving around the room, continuing her strange fertility rite. Erinn realized this video was made upstairs in Erinn's own room. She closed the page.

Dymphna's offering was a "fan page," which meant you could show your support by "liking" it. There was a link to a YouTube video. Erinn watched as her own mother appeared on the scene, chasing a rabbit that in turn was chasing a square-headed dog, which was followed by a shrill, terrified man. The video had 100,000 hits. There was also a news article explaining why the rabbits were in Venice Beach in the first place: They were being used to highlight the tug-of-war about the cedar tree in Mr. Clancy's Courtyard. The article went on to say that the community was collecting signatures to show support for the tree and were now in the process of applying for his-toric landmark status.

Erinn read the comments at the bottom of the article. Viewpoints were passionate. Many agreed that the idea of landmark status for a tree that was too big for the courtyard was silly and "too Southern

California for my tastes." Others felt that the tree was deserving of protection, while others deplored the exploitation of the helpless, opinion-less rabbits.

There was a quote from Christopher, who said, "We want to be open-minded. We're going to apply for landmark status in short order and hope to raise enough funds to get a professional evaluation." Erinn wondered if Christopher hadn't put the cart before the horse. Shouldn't they have checked out the tree before making all this fuss?

Giving in to temptation, she clicked on Christopher's Facebook page. Her fingers froze. Christopher's latest post featured Alice Albert's artwork and an open invitation to all interested parties to stop by and "check out the work of this first-class artist."

Caro sensed the shift in Erinn's mood and jumped to the floor. Erinn put her head in her hands. She was a TV hack and Christopher was keeping company with a first-class artist.

Damn Facebook.

CHAPTER 17

VIRGINIA

Two months ago, if anyone had told Virginia she would be the object of desire of not one, but two men, she would have laughed . . . if she hadn't wept with relief. The malaise she felt in New York City those last few months, which she had pinpointed as missing her daughters, turned out to be a broader problem. She was missing life!

Feeling desirable at seventy was not the same as feeling desirable at twenty or thirty. She certainly felt the jolt of age when she stumbled upon the video for Robin Thicke's "Blurred Lines." She sat stunned as the topless beauties strutted across the screen with their feverishly perky breasts bouncing. She was not so old that she couldn't see the allure of these girls, but the odd props and insane platform shoes seemed more silly than sexy. She guessed she was alone in that assessment—or at least among the under-fifty crowd.

She was past the age of comparing herself to younger women. Thank God. What a relief that was! If Bernard or Mr. Clancy were interested in her, it was not because they were expecting a perfect young body. Older men seemed to be kinder than their younger brethren, but whether that was because they had to be (they were not so perfect themselves, after all), Virginia didn't know.

Virginia wasn't sure why she hadn't informed her daughters that she was having a glass of wine with Mr. Clancy. She knew from experience (at this age, didn't she know everything from experience?)

that children did not want to see their mothers as sexually attractive to the opposite sex. The fact that their mothers' sexual attractiveness to the opposite sex was wholly and directly responsible for their very existence would probably fall on deaf ears.

She felt like a teenager, sneaking out of the Huge Apartment for her rendezvous with Mr. Clancy. She had only meant to borrow Suzanna's makeup and perfume, but here she was walking out the door in one of Suzanna's lace tops. She hoped she could get it back into her daughter's closet before it was missed.

People who said "nobody walks in L.A." clearly did not live near the beach. Virginia walked more in Venice than she had in New York. She could have walked down the Beach Walk as far as Rose Avenue before heading east, but she was trying to keep a low profile. She zigged and zagged through tiny courtyards until she came to Rose Avenue, where Mr. Clancy would be waiting for her at a tiny wine bistro. Rose Avenue was a trendy street, but as a whole kept a slower pace than the hipper, more energized Abbot Kinney, Main Street, or the Beach Walk. Virginia often thought it must be exhausting being a street in Venice.

Virginia could have spotted Mr. Clancy a block away. He was the only man in the city wearing a tie. She thought back to her dating years, when all men wore ties. When Virginia was in New York, if she went to dinner alone she had studied young couples on dates. The women tended to have put some thought into getting dressed. Even if they were dressed casually, their makeup was always perfect and their shoes impressively spiky. The men, on the other hand, often looked as if they had just rolled out of bed. Unshaven, wearing un-ironed shirts, beltless pants, and no socks—Virginia thought they looked as if they were signaling, "I didn't care enough about you to make any effort," but the young women around her didn't seem to feel that way at all. Times had changed, no doubt, but she was touched by Mr. Clancy's old-fashioned gesture. He smiled nervously as she approached.

"You look so nice," Virginia said.

"Thanks." Mr. Clancy blushed. "It took me a while to find my tie."

She had spent too many years as a professional to offer the easy hug that seemed to be the common greeting in Southern California. She thought about shaking his hand, but that seemed too formal, even for her. Instead, she just said, "I've never been here. Is it nice?"

"I don't know," Mr. Clancy said, looking at the building as if he was surprised to find it standing there. "I've driven by it a couple of times and never had a reason to stop . . . until now."

Virginia felt her own color rising.

"Let's go in," Virginia said, taking his arm.

The bar was dark and it took a minute to adjust to the light. The room was small with only a few tables. A copper bar ran along one wall, red leather barstools dotting the length of it. Mr. Clancy led Virginia to one of the tables, his hand against the small of her back. They sat and he signaled the bartender. Virginia had been on her own for several years now and she found it hard to step back and let the man take the lead. Cultural submissiveness was not something she missed, but she supposed if you wanted a man to shave and wear a tie, you couldn't have everything.

"I'll have a glass of Shiraz," Virginia said, setting the ground rules that she would order for herself.

"That sounds fine," Mr. Clancy said. "I'll have one, too."

The bartender, a young woman in jeans and a buttoned-up black vest with a name tag that read *Neila* and her hair in a topknot, just nodded and returned to the bar. It was obvious Mr. Clancy was feeling as awkward as Virginia. They watched the bartender as if they'd never seen a drink poured before. When the drinks arrived, they toasted self-consciously and each took a sip.

"This is lovely," Virginia said.

"I'm glad you like it," Mr. Clancy said. "I was worried you might be a wine snob or something, coming from Napa Valley."

"Oh?"

"I mean, not a wine snob, exactly. I just meant you might know a lot about wines and not like this place."

"I do know a lot about wines, and I do like this place," Virginia said, letting him off the hook.

"Listen, Virginia, I don't want you to think I only asked you out because I wanted to talk business."

"I don't understand."

"You know. We're on opposite sides on the tree thing. I just didn't want you to think I was trying to win you over or anything."

Virginia just blinked at him. She hadn't thought that at all. They were on more solid ground when he'd called her a wine snob. He'd brought her out on a date to try to manipulate her! Who did he think he was? Who did he think *she* was? She suddenly felt very foolish in her lace top.

"I'm an old hippie chick," Virginia said. "It would take more than a glass to make me compromise my ideals."

"How about two glasses?" Mr. Clancy said, smiling.

She looked up, startled. He actually meant it—he didn't want this evening to be about the tree. She relaxed.

"OK, no shop talk. Deal?"

"Deal," Mr. Clancy said, and this time they did shake hands.

Before they had a chance to settle back, Virginia noticed that Miles and Winnie had walked in. She watched as they headed to the bar. She pointed them out to Mr. Clancy.

"Aren't those Rio's kids?" she asked.

Mr. Clancy reached in his jacket pocket and pulled out his glasses.

"Yeah. Looks like them."

"They aren't twenty-one."

"Well, I know they have to be over eighteen to be one of Rio's students. I made sure of that myself. I don't want any trouble with crazy parents. The kids are crazy enough as it is."

"Eighteen is not twenty-one. Excuse me."

She took another sip of wine, got up from the table, and approached the daring duo at the bar. They appeared to have ordered whiskey sours.

Who orders whiskey sours?

Winnie looked past her as Virginia approached, but Miles smiled at her.

"Hi, Virginia," Miles said. "Want a drink?"

"I have a drink," Virginia said, gesturing to Mr. Clancy's table. "What are you kids doing here?"

"Uh, drink-ing," Winnie said, staring through her charcoal makeup.

"May I see your ID?" Virginia asked.

Neila, the bartender, who appeared to be as surly as Winnie, stood on her side of the bar and planted her hands on the counter.

"I already checked their IDs," she said.

"I'm sure you did, dear. But it's very dark in here. I'm fairly certain you couldn't tell a fake ID in this light."

"What's it to ya, lady?" Winnie said. "We're not hurting anybody."

"Oh, I know," Virginia said. "But, you know, Rio is working really hard to give you guys something special, and the least you guys could do is meet him halfway. Now, you and I both know—even if Neila doesn't—that those IDs are fake. So, please hand them over."

"No way!" Miles said. "They cost three hundred bucks each!"

"Dude, you're such a moron," Winnie said.

Neila looked at Virginia, as the kids turned over their fake IDs.

"Somebody will have to pay for their drinks," she said.

"Oh, I don't think so. I'm sure the police frown upon establishments that serve liquor to minors, fake ID or not."

"Go ahead," Neila said. "Call the police."

"If you insist," Virginia said, pulling out her cell phone. Who knew her years of being a professor would come in so handy? She'd been outbluffing young people since before this young woman was born.

"OK, OK," Neila said. She turned to the kids. "You guys just go."

Virginia wasn't sure, but she thought she saw a faint smile on Winnie's lips.

"Later," Miles said to Virginia.

"Yeah," Winnie said, "later."

The kids slunk out of the bar. Virginia turned back to Neila, who was still glaring at her.

"May we have two more Shiraz at our table, please?" she asked.

"Sure," Neila said. "And I guess you expect those to be on the house, too."

"I hadn't," Virginia said. "But since you offered, thank you."

She headed back to the table, heady with victory. Mr. Clancy stood up as she approached.

"Wow," he said. "That was pretty impressive."

"I hope I didn't scare you," Virginia said as Mr. Clancy held out her chair.

"No," Mr. Clancy said. But instead of helping her into her seat, he turned her around and kissed her. "You didn't scare me at all."

CHAPTER 18

SUZANNA

Suzanna waited for Rio to show up at her door. How important could this conversation be if they kept not having it? Was he avoiding her? She knew how his withholding nature had been catnip to her years ago, but did *he* know it? Was this some sort of seduction tactic? The idea that he might just be busy with his fledgling studio blew into her brain from time to time, but she discarded that thought immediately.

She was grateful that her own life was busy and she couldn't be all-consumed with Rio. Lizzy was changing by the day, discovering new reasons to say, "no"; "no" to getting dressed, "no" to going to bed, "no" to eating kale (although Suzanna suspected her mother of giving Lizzy sugary treats, she couldn't prove it). No after no after no, which rattled Suzanna, but Virginia took it in stride. It was good to have a baby expert on the premises.

Lizzy loved Piquant and that horrible little dog seemed to love her back. Piquant still growled at almost everyone who came near him, but Suzanna was happy that he'd made peace with her little one. Lizzy was not the gentlest of pet lovers. She would yank on Piquant's ears and squeeze his neck, but he just endured the lovefest. Suzanna would be so overwhelmed by the dog's good grace that she would try to pet him, but Piquant reverted to Chihuahua type immediately and would nip at her. If she found she needed to pick the dog up for any reason, she would throw a towel over him and scoop him up in that. The towel would thrash wildly, like an undulating beast.

Suzanna was standing in the apartment kitchen, looking through the cabinets for nutmeg. She was always surprised how much nutmeg you could go through when you ran a tea shop. She rubbed absently at her palms, which were still scabby from her spill over at Mr. Clancy's Courtyard. Her mother came in with Lizzy on her hip and Piquant already on his leash.

"We're going for a walk," Virginia said.

Suzanna turned around. Was her mother wearing makeup?

"Where are you going?"

Her mother reddened.

"Just . . . out," Virginia said.

Suzanna had been a teenager much more recently than her mother, and those words did not ring true. Suzanna was pleased that her maternal detective skills were on high alert. But what was her mother hiding?

"OK," Suzanna said slowly. "Well, if you find yourself by the market on Main Street, will you grab some nutmeg?"

The tension visibly went out of Virginia.

"Sure," Virginia said. "We can do that."

As Virginia headed down the stairs, Suzanna listened as Piquant's tiny toenails tapped on each step. She heard her mother strapping Lizzy into the Jogger and the front door slam.

Who was "we"?

Suzanna still had an hour before she needed to head down to the tea shop. Eric was already in the Nook. Suzanna was surprised how quiet the apartment was. She didn't like it. She made Eric's favorite tea, a fruity number called Gibraltar Black Currant, and headed down to the Nook carrying two mugs. She was still in her oversized T-shirt and pajama bottoms, the ones with the rubber duckies on them. The odds were slim she'd run into a customer at this hour.

Good thing I'm not a gambler, Suzanna thought as she looked into the Book Nook and saw a customer. Suzanna looked closer—this was not just any customer, this was Blu! What was she doing here?

Taking a cue from her husband, she decided to remain neutral until she had all the facts. She studied them. Eric was on one side of the counter and Blu on the other. Their heads were together as they laughed over that oversized comic book of Blu's. Virginia had mentioned something about Blu having a book at the Nook, and Suzanna had checked it out immediately. She thought it was ridiculous, self-serving, and took up far too much counter space, but she had too much on her mind to consider it further.

Blu was wearing what looked like sprayed-on running gear and very well-worn running shoes. Could she possibly have run all the way from Santa Monica and still look this cool? She was standing on her tiptoes, flexing her well-toned calves. Suzanna was proud of herself for not overreacting, but then she saw The Sign. As Blu leaned over the counter, she squeezed her arms together under her breasts, so they heaved forward. She casually turned a page in the book.

That woman is after my husband!

Knowing she could not wage battle in her pajamas, Suzanna tried to back slowly out of the room, but her elbow thudded against the wall. Eric and Blu looked at her. She could feel her cheeks turning red as she stood there in her pajamas, with bed head, holding on to two cracked mugs of steaming tea.

"Hey, Beet," Eric said easily.

She couldn't hear any guilt in his voice but wanted to smack him for using her childish nickname in front of this slut.

Blu tossed back her hair and beamed. She was very aware that she was in control of the room.

"Oh," Blu said with her twinkly laugh. "Did you bring us coffee?"

"Tea," Suzanna said. She wanted to bite her own tongue.

Blu came over and took the cups, as if Suzanna were the intruder, not she. Blu handed one cup to Eric.

"I'm just checking on my book sales," Blu said.

At this hour?

"Oh, that's right . . . you have a comic book," Suzanna said.

"Graphic novel," said Blu.

"Superblu and O'Brian . . ." The blow glanced off Blu, who laughed and said, *"O'Hara!"* And then she shot an "It's us against her" smile at Eric.

"Blu says it's a circus over at Erinn's house and she couldn't take it anymore," he said.

"What's up?" Suzanna asked, genuinely interested.

"Oh, the paparazzi is all over the place," Blu said, shaking her curls and opening her eyes wide at Eric, even though she was talking with Suzanna. "I just get so tired of it. It's nice to just get away to someplace quiet and think."

How could her husband be such an idiot? He never was very good at picking up the signals that a woman was hitting on him, but Blu was more obvious than most.

"Oh?" Suzanna said. She was torn between retreating upstairs, giving Blu the win, or jumping across the room and throwing her out on her flat ass. "Paparazzi? That's good for publicity, isn't it?"

"Depending on whose side you're on," Eric said.

"Whose side are you on?" Suzanna wanted to scream at him.

"Dymphna is totally stressed," Blu added. "She says all the noise is freaking the rabbits out."

"I've heard that anxiety is bad for their fur," Suzanna said, horrified that she was engaging this woman in conversation.

"They might die!" Blu said. She tried to widen her eyes farther, but Suzanna noticed her face didn't move. "Dymphna says bunnies have very weak hearts."

"Poor Dymphna," Suzanna said earnestly. "She must be so upset."

Blu shrugged. She opened up the graphic novel again and turned back to Eric, pretext forgotten. Suzanna could tell she had been dismissed. Suzanna willed herself not to float—this woman did not deserve to get to her! She stayed rooted, looking at Eric. He sensed her stare and looked back at her. He gave her an easy wink, as if they were both in on the same joke. They were together in this. Suzanna headed back upstairs. She decided the morning had ended in a draw.

* * *

By the time Suzanna ended up in the Bun's kitchen, she was showered and wearing a bright new peasant blouse, which she felt hid a multitude of sins. She had put on some lipstick and mascara as well. She knew she'd never be able to compete with Blu in sheer sex appeal, but Eric loved *her*. Showing a little appreciation wouldn't kill her.

As she started to make her nutmeg-scented scones, she realized her mother hadn't returned with the spice. Suzanna instantly changed gears, rummaging through her cabinets. She had a large bag of chocolate chips somewhere and her customers loved her chocolate chip scones. She missed Fernando, who had been her friend since high school and her first pastry chef. He would know exactly where he had put the chocolate chips. She could also use someone to talk to. She had so much on her mind. Eric. Blu. Rio. Not the sort of problems you wanted to discuss with your mother or older sister. While Eric knew about the whole Rio thing, he didn't want any details, but Suzanna had spilled her guts to Fernando. However, Fernando was miles away, having opened a successful bed and breakfast on Vashon Island near Seattle. Her other dear friend from the Napa Valley days, Carla, a busy architect in Northern California, would happily lend an ear, but she'd have no time for Suzanna's fantasies about Rio, and Suzanna would be embarrassed to admit she had no idea what to do about Blu.

She was on her own.

She located the chocolate chips. The bag had been opened. Suzanna remembered that her mother used to give them chocolate chips as a treat when she and Erinn were little.

No wonder Lizzy stopped eating kale!

With not enough chips and no nutmeg, Suzanna realized she'd have to run out to the store herself. She stuck her head in at the Nook to let Eric know she was going out. She was relieved to see Eric was alone but disappointed that he didn't comment on her makeup and new blouse. She thought about taking her bike but realized that if she ran into her mother and Lizzy, she'd rather walk with them, so she set out on foot.

She passed Donell but he didn't speak to her. *That's odd,* Suzanna thought. He was busy tying raffia around strands of sage. Perhaps he hadn't seen her. She had her mind on Blu and didn't realize she was walking by Mr. Clancy's Courtyard.

"Suzanna," Rio called from the courtyard.

The voice was disembodied but she knew it was his. Why pretend that she didn't hear it? She stopped dead in her tracks. Rio came down the steps and closed the gap between them in seconds.

"Shall we walk?" he said.

At first, she thought he must have meant, "Shall we dance?" but realized that was ridiculous. They were on the Beach Walk. She nodded and started walking. He fell into step with her. Apparently, "Shall we walk?" did not include "Shall we talk?" because Rio said nothing. They continued down the Beach Walk in silence. Suzanna felt the electric charge she always experienced when he was near, but confusion was ruining the moment. Finally, Rio took her arm and led her to an empty playground. He leaned against the slide but still didn't say anything. Suzanna tried to find her voice. She really wished she had one of those clipped, disdainful English accents she'd heard on *Downton Abbey*. That would be just the ticket right now. But she only had her own voice to rely on and even that was iffy. She was afraid if she opened her mouth right now, her voice would come out wobbly or whiny. So she just stayed silent.

Rio wanted to talk? Then he could talk. Suzanna, of course, had imagined this moment since he'd come back to town. Actually, she'd imagined versions of it since he'd left Venice the first time. Variations on a theme: him telling her how much he missed her. How wrong he was to go. How he was in love with her. She also had rehearsed her part. Laughing at him while flashing her wedding ring in his face. She toyed with the idea of calling him "buster," but feared that might not translate into Spanish and would just sound as though she'd forgotten his name.

As she watched his handsome profile looking out to sea, her heart softened. If he realized his mistake, she should take pity on him. It was too late but he would mend, just as she had done. Maybe she would introduce him to Blu.

"Suzanna," he finally said, picking up her hand and gently caressing her fingers. "I made so many mistakes."

Suzanna knew she could not speak. That wobbly voice was begging to come up. She could hear it in her throat. She waited, hoping she seemed mysterious and slightly bored instead of on the verge of hysteria.

"So many mistakes." He shook his head as if he couldn't believe the pain he'd put her through. "I am happy to have my studio. I am happy to be helping those children. But I came back for you."

He kissed the back of her hand.

"Rio," she said softly, not trusting herself to say anything else.

"I'm in Alcoholics Anonymous and I am here to apologize to you. To make amends. It is step nine."

Suzanna prepared to float away, but instead lost her equilibrium. Luckily, she was standing in front of a swing set and she plunked gracelessly onto a swing. Rio put his hand on the chain and swayed her gently. Apparently, he had said what he needed to say and it was her turn.

"You're in the twelve-step program?" Suzanna asked.

"Sí," Rio said. "As I say. Amends. Step nine. You know it?"

"I know it," Suzanna said. "Everybody in Los Angeles knows step nine. Everyone is either apologizing—or being apologized to—in this town."

"Do I understand you accept my apology?"

"Yes," Suzanna said. "I mean, no. I mean . . . what exactly are you apologizing for?"

"I treated you badly," Rio said.

"That's true," Suzanna said.

"I did not take your feelings into account."

"Can't argue with that," Suzanna said.

"I was selfish," Rio said.

"Yep," she said.

Although in her imagination they were usually naked, she had pictured this scene a thousand times: the reunion, the contrite "It was me, not you." But now that it was happening, she felt surprisingly unmoved. What was wrong here?

Suzanna knew that he was saying all the right things. Then she realized: There was no passion. Was she just a name on a list of people he'd been thoughtless to? She turned to look at him. He was now sitting in the swing beside her and she could only see his profile.

"Did you apologize to Lauren?" Suzanna asked.

Lauren was the woman with whom Rio had run off to New Zealand. He shook his head.

"I brought no harm to Lauren," he said.

Suzanna wondered if that meant he hadn't used her, that somehow his connection with Lauren was more real, but decided this conversation was tough enough as it was.

Suzanna settled on: "Why apologize to me?"

Rio shrugged, but still didn't turn to look at her.

"When I was a boy in Costa Rica, I had to take care of my mother. My father left when I was six. My mother and I were all alone. I started dancing because an instructor in our city needed boys in the classroom, and he paid me to come in whenever there were too many ladies. I was tall. I picked up the dance steps quickly and made good money. After I grew up, I didn't need the dance instructor to pay me anymore. There were always women ready to pay me to be their partner."

Suzanna winced. This apology might be working for Rio, but now Suzanna just wanted it over with.

"But I always took care of my mother," Rio said. Suzanna could feel his flashing eyes fastening on her and she looked directly at him. "When she died, I just started moving around, taking jobs in studios and nightclubs, meeting women. My life was not always honorable, Suzanna, and one day, I knew that had to stop. Not just the drinking, but the running away from everything—and the womanizing."

Suzanna asked, "What made you stop?"

She steeled herself, sure the answer was going to be "Lauren." But she had to know.

"You made me stop," Rio said.

"Me?"

Suzanna tightened her grip on the swing. She faced forward again. His intensity was too much for her. She couldn't believe that her dream seemed to be coming true after all.

"You are a pure spirit, Suzanna," Rio said. "Women have thrown themselves at me my whole life, so your attention was nothing new. . . ."

Dreams take strange turns.

"But for the first time in my life, I realized I had hurt someone. Hurt someone deeply. When I would go to sleep at night, I would see your eyes looking at me, wanting me to be a better man."

She felt that powerful desire welling up inside her—that urge that only Rio brought out. Should she tell him that she never once wanted him to be a better man? It occurred to her that perhaps this was a new come-on technique. She could only hope.

"And so," Rio continued, "I am now a better man. Suzanna, I want you and my sainted mother to be proud of me."

Speaking her name in the same sentence with "my sainted mother" was like a bucket of ice water poured over her head. She stood up.

"It's OK, Rio," Suzanna said. "I forgive you."

Suzanna didn't remember what he said next or what she said next. As she walked back into the Bun, she realized she'd somehow gone to the store and bought nutmeg and chocolate chips. She had absolutely no idea what to make of Rio's confession.

She knew brooding time was over; she had a busy day ahead of her. For that, she was grateful. In the hallway that separated the Bun from the Nook, she saw the Baby Jogger and smiled. Lizzy and her mother were home. Just having them there would help her get over the sting of Rio's words.

Suzanna turned into the Bun. She had to go through the dining room to get to the kitchen, but she stopped dead in her tracks. Eric, her mother, Bernard, and Christopher were all seated in the dining room. Conversation had ceased as soon as she entered. Suzanna quickly shot a glance at the corner of the room, where Lizzy and Piquant were wrestling with a chew toy. Was she so very late? She looked at her watch; no, she had been gone fewer than forty minutes. Did they discover her rendezvous with Rio? She realized that had been nothing but an innocent encounter, one that the group would probably praise rather than condemn.

"Hi, guys," she said.

Wordlessly, Eric held up a pink sheet of paper. She wasn't close enough to read it, but it looked like some sort of flyer, with a black-and-white picture and some large text. She moved closer. Eric obviously wasn't about to explain.

He handed it over silently.

A gasp escaped Suzanna's lips as she stared down at the flyer. The word *DANGER* was written across the top and below was a picture of Suzanna in the courtyard, sprawling on the ground after being tripped by the tree roots. The bottom of the flyer was full of heated words explaining that the tree was a danger to the city and that the tree huggers who were trying to save it were putting lives at risk.

Suzanna stared at the page. What could she say?

I've always hated flyers?

While it wasn't her fault she'd tripped, she shouldn't have been visiting Rio in the first place. Would Eric be angry? It wasn't exactly infidelity, but it wasn't exactly innocent on her part, either. She met his eyes.

CHAPTER 19

VIRGINIA

Suzanna had always loved her spacious apartment but ever since the flyer of her sprawling on the cement courtyard had come to everyone's attention, the place seemed minuscule. Virginia tried to stay out of the way, making sure Piquant and Lizzy were both kept happy, distracted, and quiet.

Virginia felt sorry for Suzanna, who really was caught off guard by the unhappy quartet in her tea shop. Bernard and Christopher felt she had dealt Cause Courtyard a mighty blow, and Eric felt she had chosen a side. Virginia thought the men were being unreasonable. It wasn't as if Suzanna had taken the picture and plastered flyers all over the neighborhood. Virginia had her own concerns. Although she did have a soft spot in her heart for the tree and for the valiant warriors who fought for its survival, that glass of wine with Mr. Clancy had opened her eyes to his side of things. And now that Suzanna had taken a tumble it seemed even more possible that the tree was a hazard.

Virginia had to stay impartial. While it was flattering that both Bernard and Mr. Clancy were paying attention to her, she knew that it would not be fair to pick a side based on her attraction to either man. Virginia could call on her years of teaching at the university for strength. She'd spent years in the presence of attractive students, both men and women, who were used to getting their way. They arrived on campus sure they could charm their way into an easy A. She had always been able to stay clear-eyed about a term paper no matter how adorable the student or elaborate the excuse.

Martin was not always as tough as she was and they both knew it. If he hadn't been married to Virginia, word would have spread around campus that Professor Martin Wolf was a soft touch. His classes filled with students looking for an easy pass. Virginia prided herself on keeping him on the straight and narrow. Both Professors Wolf were highly regarded teachers with reputations for being firm but fair. Virginia had to keep those skills sharp! She wished Martin were here to talk to, but that desire only lasted for a second. Would he really want to discuss the possibility of one or two pending romances? She thought not.

Her cell phone rang. She looked down to see a photo of Erinn on her screen. When she had first arrived in Venice, Suzanna had commandeered Virginia's cell phone and added identifying pictures to the phone numbers of family members. Virginia found it disconcerting, but Suzanna was so pleased with herself, she let it go.

"Hello, dear," Virginia said.

"Mother, I need your help. The press is surrounding the house."

"Oh, I heard about that!" Virginia said, grateful for the chance to switch gears. "Eric mentioned that Blu seemed a little unnerved by all the attention."

"There isn't enough attention in the world to unnerve Blu. Besides, the newspeople—if you can call them that—aren't here for Blu anyway. That's all in her head."

"I don't understand."

Virginia could hear a long-suffering sigh on the other end of the line. Erinn had been heaving this sigh since she was a girl. That sound used to drive Virginia crazy, but now she found herself vaguely amused by it.

"They are here for the rabbits, Mother. Haven't you seen the videos on YouTube?"

"I'm not a huge fan of YouTube. And, frankly, I'm surprised you are!"

"I'm not!" Erinn said, sounding as if her mother were calling her integrity into question. "But when your yard is full of camera people and photographers, you tend to investigate."

"I know, dear, I'm sorry; I was only teasing."

"Now is not the time for levity, Mother."

Virginia wondered if there was ever a time for levity in Erinn's world.

"How can I help you?"

"Cary finally found a shoe factory where we can shoot. I need you to come up here right away."

"Please," Virginia said reflexively. She was glad she hadn't said, "What's the magic word?"

"Please," Erinn said, equally automatically.

Virginia could hear Eric and Suzanna talking. A couple didn't need a mother/mother-in-law rattling around during tense times. This would be a perfect time to get out of the apartment!

"I'll be there in ten minutes," Virginia said.

"Use the back gate."

Virginia drove north on Ocean Avenue. Once she was on the main drag of Ocean Avenue it was a straight shot for the mile or so to Erinn's house. She could see Erinn's place for several blocks. The press was indeed camped out around the front gate. The hedges were high and the gate itself was solid wood, so the press looked bored rather than hungry for a story. Even so, parking was hard to come by in Santa Monica on the best of days, so she parked a few blocks away and walked up the back alley. When Erinn's gate was in sight, Virginia slowed her pace, making sure there were no paparazzi in sight. She spied one lone cameraman skulking about half a block away. Virginia determined that she wouldn't cause any alarm; she would appear to be an older woman out for a walk. As she closed the distance between herself and the gate, she could tell by the man's body language that she had caught his interest. She sped up. He sped up. As she reached the gate, she heard him call out, "Virginia? Virginia? Wait a second."

Virginia panicked. Who was this man? How did he know her name? What was going on?

She reached for the latch on the gate. She figured that it was probably locked but she jiggled it anyway. The cameraman was so close she could see that he had a coffee stain on his shirt. Suddenly, the gate opened and a hand pulled her inside. She could hear the lock snapping back into place and the man's plaintive voice on the other side.

"Virginia, I know you're in there!" he called.

Virginia turned to face her savior. It was Dymphna.

"Erinn said you'd be coming to the back gate," Dymphna said in a strained voice. "I've been listening for you."

Dymphna guided her into the guesthouse and put a kettle on for tea.

"What the hell is happening?" Virginia asked. She was not one to swear but she was shaken to her running shoes.

"Erinn figured word would get to the other reporters in a matter of minutes that you came in through the back gate and they'll all leave the front of the house. That would give Erinn and Blu time to escape to Erinn's car and get over to the shoe factory. It probably worked or we would have heard something. That Erinn is very smart."

"Why would anyone care if I'm here?" Virginia asked. She realized her legs were shaking and she sat down.

Dymphna put the tea on the little café table in front of Virginia but did not sit herself. Instead, she walked over to the loveseat and picked up her iPad. She brought it back to the table.

"This is why," Dymphna said. She scrolled and swiped until she found what she was looking for. She handed the iPad to Virginia.

Tea was forgotten as Virginia watched herself chasing Spot down the Beach Walk as the rabbit pursued the hapless man and his dog.

"Now the rabbits are getting all this attention, and it's not good for them," Dymphna continued. "They're distraught."

Dymphna walked into the yard. Virginia took a quick sip of tea and followed her. There was plenty of privacy thanks to the hedges and gate, but she could hear the ladies and gentlemen of the press on the other side of the hedge. They weren't loud, but they were definitely *there*. Virginia also noticed the yard itself was looking a little worse for wear, with bald and yellow spots dotting the entire back lawn.

Dymphna walked over to the row of cages. Virginia saw one of the rabbits hop over to the front of its cage as Dymphna approached. Dymphna reached out and stroked the rabbit's fur.

"See what I mean?" Dymphna asked.

Virginia studied the rabbits, trying to think of something soothing to say. They all looked fine to her. Some of them were drinking water, others eating, others thinking their rabbit thoughts, as far as Virginia could tell.

"I'm sorry, Dymphna," she finally said. "I don't know the signs of a distraught rabbit."

"Look around the yard," Dymphna said, sweeping her hands in an arc to encompass everything. She lowered her voice so as not to attract any attention from the newspeople.

Virginia looked around the yard. Clumps of little furry tumbleweeds rolled across the lawn with every hint of breeze.

"They're losing their fur?" Virginia asked.

"Yes," Dymphna said.

She unlatched the cage of the rabbit she was petting and put it on the ground. Virginia remembered that this rabbit, with his little black booties, was named Paws. Paws hopped a few steps then halted, looked around, then hopped again and stopped again. Virginia wondered if perhaps his name was actually Pause. She looked up to see Dymphna putting more rabbits on the ground.

"Rabbits need to be free for several hours a day," Dymphna said.

So that's what's happened to the lawn.

"And they need to feel safe," Dymphna said. "How can they feel secure with all of *that?*"

She pointed accusingly toward the newspeople.

A slight wind wafted through the yard and a great cloud of bunny fur lifted into the air.

"They are very hairy," Virginia said, treading carefully. "Isn't it reasonable for them to lose some fur?"

"Not like this," Dymphna practically wailed as they watched the tufts of fur float away. "I brush them twice a day. Molting like this is just angst."

Angst?

Caro appeared out of nowhere, plopping down on all fours in the middle of the rabbits. Virginia's breath caught at the sight of him. He was sporting his lion cut and looked more the predator than ever as he turned his head slowly from right to left, scanning the rabbits. Virginia started toward him, but Dymphna put her hand on Virginia's arm.

"Don't worry. They're all friends."

It was true. Virginia watched in amazement as Caro jumped gleefully around the rabbits. He'd bat at one and the rabbit would hop at him. Caro would dart away and begin the game again with another bunny. Virginia was relieved but thought the majestic cat looked ridiculous in his new role of rabbit whisperer.

Virginia suddenly picked up Caro and held him up to the sunlight. She studied him from several angles. Caro stared back, clearly displeased by being interrupted in his game of cat and rabbit.

"What is it, Virginia?" Dymphna asked, looking up at the cat, her eyebrows knit.

"Let me see your iPad," Virginia said.

CHAPTER 20

ERINN

"Goldfish do not need air," Blu insisted. "I brought one home in a plastic bag from a fair once. He was fine."

"He was fine for an hour or so, Blu. Not for long," Erinn said. "Fish need air. You'll just have to trust me on this."

"But I want to make a five-inch-heeled see-through shoe with a goldfish in the platform," Blu said. "I can't do that if the fish needs air."

"That isn't the fish's fault," Erinn said, not quite believing that she was being subjected to this conversation. "Besides, there are other problems. You couldn't feed the fish, the fish would be . . . concussed, for lack of a better word, when you walked."

"Not to mention, when the fish pooped you would see it," Mac, the shoe factory owner, added.

He and Blu burst into guffaws. Erinn chided herself for not asking more questions before they got to Shoe-B-Due, the hole-in-the-wall shoe factory. Blu bought many of her custom five-inch platforms from Mac and had convinced him that he would be getting incredible media exposure if he would just let her TV crew shoot here. Erinn was impressed that Blu had been so resourceful, but now she was having second thoughts.

Mac's interest in Blu was certainly not conveyed with the same professionalism as Dr. Roberts's had been. Mac ogled Blu at every opportunity. This would make for just the sort of lowbrow TV that

Cary was looking for; a series about an aging starlet needed this sort of heat. However, Erinn just couldn't stand to shoot it.

She looked around the factory. It was a long and narrow space in an industrial park in the San Fernando Valley, a half hour and a world away from Santa Monica. "The Valley," as it was called by friends and foes alike, was a giant suburb of Los Angeles that was always a good ten degrees warmer than the Westside (of which Santa Monica was the farthest point west). Besides housing thousands of families, a few studios, and a well-known sushi restaurant or two, The Valley's main claim to fame was its dubious distinction of being the porn capital of the United States. It was probably the porn industry's need for flamboyant hooker shoes that kept Shoe-B-Due in business.

The factory had several long tables, filled with various samples of colored leather, heels of impossible heights, platform bases, and an entire table full of sparkling add-ons, like rhinestones, charms, and buckles.

"Let's see what else we can come up with," Erinn said, leading the group to the accessory table. She looked at Blu. "Tell me exactly why you own a shoe factory."

Blu blinked. "I don't."

"I know you don't," Erinn said. "But you came up with the idea, didn't you, that you'd like to own a shoe factory?"

"Oh, that." Blu giggled and looked at Mac through long lashes. "Yes, my idea is that I want to sell five- to seven-inch heels to housewives so they'll feel better about themselves."

"How do you envision that working?" Erinn asked.

"They'd feel hot. Ya know . . . sexy," piped up Mac.

"Thank you, Mac," Erinn said. "But I was addressing Blu. I need to know why Blu would think housewives, who have to shop and clean and chase kids and drive cars, would feel better about themselves if they were attempting to do all that in ridiculous shoes."

"You don't understand anything," Blu said. "You don't see any value in being sexy."

Erinn felt as if she'd been slapped. She caught Opie's surprised reaction, which obviously embarrassed him. He suddenly became engrossed in the dials on his audio rig.

"Perhaps I just have a different definition of sexy," Erinn said, although she wondered why she felt she needed to qualify this insult.

"Perhaps I think being well read and up-to-date on world events is a kind of sexy."

"Well, you'd be wrong," Mac said. "The women who are going to buy these shoes don't give a rat's ass about world events and neither do the men who fuck . . . uh . . . marry them."

Erinn knew this conversation was getting them nowhere. She focused on the task at hand: selling the idea that somewhere there were women running busy households who would be lining up to buy hooker shoes from Blu Knight's fictitious factory.

Erinn picked up a little charm from the accessories table. It was two small red rhinestone cherries connected to a green stem. Erinn paired it with a platform base with a hole cut out.

"What about this?" she asked, holding up the charm inside the cutout of the platform. She held it out to Mac to inspect. "Would you be able to create something like this?"

"Yep," Mac said. "And if the charm falls off, we can say Blu lost her cherry again."

Erinn stood stock-still as she waited for Mac and Blu to stop their convulsive laughter.

"I'm glad we have a consensus on the design," Erinn said.

She called Opie over and put the camera up to her eye. She knew it was going to be a long afternoon. One good thing about these days with Blu was that they took all of Erinn's concentration. She couldn't dwell on Christopher or the fact that he was moving Alice's art pieces to his studio.

She sometimes felt that her maturity level was dropping as she got older. In her younger days, she would have accepted the fact that the few kisses she and Christopher had exchanged meant nothing. Even as a teenager, a kiss did not make you exclusive. But, as a teenager, nobody had an ex-wife. The harsh reality of Alice brought back painful memories of coupledom. There were many possibilities for explaining Christopher's actions: Christopher still loved his ex-wife but was using Erinn to shore himself up emotionally. OR Christopher had no residual feelings for his wife and was just being honorable showing her work at his studio. OR Christopher was showing her work at his studio because he thought she was a great artist.

Of all the possibilities, the idea that Christopher thought Alice was a great artist pinched the most. Erinn was used to coming in last when the man she was interested in just wanted a showpiece. In her Broadway years, she had practically stepped aside when a beautiful woman came into the domestic picture. She once told Suzanna that if a man were interested in physical beauty alone, there really wasn't anything she could do about it. It was as if a man announced he was gay and leaving her for another man. She couldn't fight that. His desire lay in the opposite direction of her very essence. Fighting for him would just be silly. But if intellect, wit, and artistry were on the menu, watch out. She would go brain cell to brain cell with anyone.

That confidence seemed to have leaked away over the years. Could her work on reality TV stand up to a moose head made of beer cans? In Christopher's mind, probably not. In her own mind, definitely not—and she wasn't overly impressed with the moose head in the first place. Sure, it took a lot of patience, but was it art? It occurred to Erinn that perhaps that was the scariest part of this. Alice seemed to have a lot of patience. Alice could visualize what she wanted. And Alice could wait.

Erinn snapped out of her thoughts, back to the juvenile antics of Blu and Mac. There was nothing to do but muscle through. Mac put a pair of shoes together in record time; in minutes, he had a Lucite pair of five-inch heels, a three-inch platform base with the cherry charm dangling in the middle. Blu studied the shoes. Erinn had to admit that the woman seemed to know what she was looking for. Blu had a practiced eye when it came to shameless footwear.

"What size shoe do you wear?" Blu asked Erinn.

"A seven."

"Good. These are a seven. Put them on."

"No."

"Oh, come on," Mac said. "Why not?"

"As Ralph Waldo Emerson once said," Erinn replied, " 'Common sense is genius dressed in its working clothes.' "

Mac turned to Blu.

"What?"

"Ignore her," Blu said to Mac and then turned to Erinn. "You need to try these on so you can see how sexy you'll feel. You're all judge-y for no reason."

"Yeah," Mac said. "You need to walk a mile in her moccasins before you get all judge-y."

"*Judge-y* is not a word," Erinn said.

Blu held out the shoes and said, "I really think you'll be surprised how you feel about yourself."

"It doesn't matter how I feel in your five-inch-tall moccasins. This isn't about me."

"I'm not shooting anything more until you try them on. I think you'll stop being so stuck-up."

"I'm not . . . ," Erinn began and then reached for the shoes. "All right, if we can get back to work after I put these on, I'll put them on."

Erinn hoisted herself onto the table and slid off her Keens, which were the shoes she always wore while working. The large rubber outer sole that curved over the toe was not particularly attractive (even Erinn admitted it made your foot look like a hoof) but it was first-class protection from falling production equipment. When a battery pack landed on your toe and you walked away—that *was* a thing of beauty. She put her foot into the shoe and hooked the ankle strap. She flexed her ankle. She certainly didn't feel any overwhelming sense of sexiness overtaking her. She looked up to see Mac, Blu, and Opie staring at her. She put on the other shoe.

"All right?" Erinn said. "I have the shoes on. Is everyone satisfied? Can we get back to work now?"

"No," Blu giggled. "You have to walk around in them."

Opie put out his hand and helped Erinn off the table. She took a tentative step. Then another. Once she had her balance she walked around the table.

"No," Blu said. "You can't stomp around like a truck driver. You need to walk like this. . . ."

Blu straightened her shoulders and swung her hips back and forth, strutting to the end of the table and back, hair extensions swinging. Mac whistled. Erinn stood teetering at the edge of the table.

"Try it again," Blu said.

Erinn took a step. She wondered if perhaps she did feel a little sexier after all.

* * *

In the end, Blu had to drive them back to Santa Monica. Erinn had an ice pack on the knee that had crashed into the cement as she took another step. She was just grateful that Opie had managed to catch the camera before it smashed into the floor.

"Do you think it's broken?" Blu asked, not daring to look at Erinn.

"No. I don't have time for it to be broken and neither do you."

"I could teach you how to walk. It wouldn't kill you to act more like a girl once in a while."

"You know, Blu," Erinn said, massaging her aching knee, "when girls are little, they all think they're beautiful. Then, as they are growing up, they find their rightful place in the world. Some go to Pretty Girl Camp, some go to Smart Girl Camp. It defines them."

"Uh-hum," Blu said.

"Do you have any idea what I'm talking about?"

"Yes! You're saying that I went to Pretty Girl Camp!"

As they neared Erinn's house, she wondered how she was going to outrun the paparazzi in the front yard with a bum knee. As they pulled up to the Victorian, it was clear the newspeople were no longer there. Were they still camped out by the back fence? Erinn directed Blu to drive through the alley; no one was around but a few of the locals walking their dogs. Relieved, though a little perplexed, Erinn had Blu drive through the neighboring alleys and back out to the front of the house. Blu parked the car, and the two of them unloaded the gear from the trunk.

Erinn could hear her mother's voice deep inside the house. She could also smell a rich chocolaty aroma wafting from the kitchen. Erinn beamed at Blu.

"My mother is making fudge!" she said. Nothing would heal a bruised knee like her mother's fudge.

"Oh? I've never tasted fudge."

Erinn stared at Blu.

"How is it possible that you've never even tasted fudge?"

Blu shrugged, then said, "I guess they only serve it at Smart Girl Camp."

Erinn limped after Blu into the kitchen. Her mother was at the stove, peering into a large pot. Dymphna was seated at the table, stroking Caro. Caro looked at Erinn in acknowledgment but didn't get up.

Her mother lit up as the women entered, but as soon as she saw Erinn was limping, her smile fell.

"Oh, dear, what happened?" her mother asked, coming toward her.

Erinn limped to a chair and sat down.

"I'm fine, Mother," Erinn said. "Don't stop stirring!"

Virginia went back to the pot. Blu looked out the back door. She turned around with a pout.

"Where are the news crews?" she asked.

"Your mother got rid of them," Dymphna said. "She's amazing!"

"What did you do?" Erinn asked.

"What did *you* do?" Virginia replied, indicating the torn jeans and purpling kneecap.

"Occupational hazard." Erinn swept the question away. She was too embarrassed to admit she fell off a shoe. "Come on, Mother! I've been trying to get rid of those pests for days."

Virginia was obviously enjoying herself. She had a little smile on her face as she stirred the fudge. Dymphna jumped up.

"Erinn, can you walk to the backyard?" Dymphna said. "I'll show you!"

"Oh, Dymphna, don't make Erinn get up!" Virginia said from the stove.

Erinn got up. "No, no . . . whatever it is, I want to see it!"

Erinn and Dymphna headed into the backyard, passing Blu, who stood in the doorway with her arms crossed.

"You want to come with us?" Erinn asked her.

Blu didn't answer but unfolded her arms. She followed the two women into the yard.

"Look at the pens," Dymphna said.

Erinn limped over to the rabbit cages and let out a gasp. The rabbits were bald!

"They look gross," Blu said.

"That's the idea," Dymphna said. "Your mom got the idea from looking at Caro's lion's cut. She figured if we sheared the rabbits and showed them to the news guys the show would be over! It took all day but it worked. I sheared six of them and your mother sheared four. I didn't even have to help her."

Erinn was affronted that her mother didn't think Caro looked handsome. She went back into the house just as her mother was pouring the liquid fudge into pans.

"Mother, how did you learn how to shear rabbits?"

"YouTube, dear," her mother said. "How else?"

CHAPTER 21

VIRGINIA

Virginia remembered her own mother and mother-in-law weighing in on her fights with Martin. It was always grim. She knew better than to interfere. Obviously, Suzanna hadn't tripped on the tree root on purpose. Virginia's motherly instinct was to check her daughter's palms on a daily basis to see the progress of healing. The sight of that flyer had sent Eric into a snit, but she ignored the iciness between the couple when the three of them were together.

Virginia admired Eric's determination to stay above the fray. Because she was a child of the 1960s, she couldn't resist taking sides, but having been a professor at a university she understood, all too well, the undercurrents of local politics.

"Eric isn't being fair," Suzanna said to her mother as they bathed Lizzy in the claw-foot tub.

"Every community needs an arbitrator. Eric's role is really important."

"I know. But it doesn't help if the community's arbitrator has a mother-in-law running around shaving rabbits to help save a tree," Suzanna said, sitting back on her heels to look at her mother. "I mean, that's a little too perfect, isn't it? Cute animals *and* a tree?"

"It doesn't help the community's arbitrator if his wife goes tripping over tree roots, proving it's dangerous," Virginia said, feeling just a touch guilty. She didn't actually believe it was Suzanna's fault.

A wet sponge slapped Virginia in the face.

Virginia sucked in her breath. Had her own daughter slapped her with a sponge? Suzanna stared at her mother in horror. Lizzy was squealing and clapping her hands.

"Yay, me!" Lizzy said, patting her chest.

Suzanna stared at her soggy mother, then turned to Lizzy.

"Good girl," Suzanna said to Lizzy, and all three started laughing and clapping.

After Lizzy was put to bed, Suzanna and her mother sat at the kitchen table, sharing a tea Suzanna had created, a blend of chamomile, valerian root, and cornflowers. She had worked long and hard to come up with a tea that would put you naturally to sleep. This was as close as she'd come. As Suzanna said, "It's soothing, but it ain't NyQuil."

Suzanna called the tea Twilight since it made you sleep like the undead.

Eric strode by the kitchen, stopping in the doorway.

"Hey, guys, I'm going down to the Nook to get more books for Bernard's Little Library," he said.

Virginia jumped up and said, "I have a few paperbacks I just finished. Do you want them?"

Before Eric could answer, Virginia was out of the room. She stayed down the hall, trying not to listen in on the conversation in the kitchen.

"How long are you going to punish me?" Suzanna asked.

"I'm not punishing you," Eric said. "You've just made things harder around here. I'm sorry if I'm not jumping around saying it's OK, because it's not."

Virginia scooped up the books as fast as she could and headed back down the hall.

"Eric, I wasn't—" Suzanna stopped when her mother entered the room.

Virginia briskly plunked the books down in Eric's hands. "Here you are," she said.

Virginia wasn't sure if stopping this conversation was a good idea or not, but she went with her instinct.

Eric kissed one then the other on their cheeks and headed downstairs.

"I don't know what to say to him," Suzanna said, absently touching the spot on her cheek. "I . . . I feel bad about everything."

Virginia went to the kitchen counter and got out the cookie jar. Soothing tea was one thing, but this conversation required the big guns: homemade peanut butter cookies.

"I mean, Eric is wrong to accuse me of choosing sides," Suzanna said.

"I don't think that's what he meant," Virginia countered carefully. "I think he just meant it's harder to give the appearance of neutrality when one side can use damaging photos of the supposedly neutral arbitrator's wife to their advantage."

"That isn't my fault," Suzanna said.

"But . . . ," Virginia offered.

"But," Suzanna said, wiping away a tear. "Maybe I shouldn't have been there in the first place. If I hadn't been in the courtyard, I wouldn't have tripped, and Mr. Clancy couldn't have taken that picture of me."

Virginia sat up straight.

"What makes you think it was Mr. Clancy who took the photo?"

"Who else?" Suzanna sniffled.

"Well, he's not alone in this. There are other merchants who think the tree is a hazard."

"Mother! Who cares? Who cares who took the stupid picture?"

I care.

Virginia focused on the crisis at hand.

"You were saying you shouldn't have been at the courtyard," Virginia said and took a wild guess. "Why not?"

Virginia was caught off guard as Suzanna let out a sob and put her head on the table.

"Dear!" Virginia said, scooting her chair closer to her daughter. "Do you want to tell me what is going on?"

"Remember when I was taking dance lessons?" Suzanna asked. "Well, I know I made it sound like I just wanted some exercise . . . but I . . . I was in a weird place. I was chasing my dance instructor all over the city. I threw myself at him. It was pitiful."

"I don't understand," Virginia said, and then suddenly she did. "Was this dance instructor Rio?"

Suzanna gulped and nodded.

"When he showed up at the tea shop after being gone for years, I just . . . I just . . . I don't know. I know I'm the luckiest woman in the world and I must seem completely ungrateful, but part of me has felt like . . . like I'm asleep. Just seeing Rio made me feel awake again. God! I sound like something out of a bad fairy tale."

Virginia got up and poured more tea, not because she wanted any but because she knew she had to choose her words carefully and she needed time to think.

"OK, we're going to have to take off the mother-daughter suits right now, because I'm going to tell you something you probably don't want to hear from your mother."

"If you're going to tell me you had an affair, you're right," Suzanna said, blowing her nose. "I don't want to hear it."

"Oh, honey, I worked at a university surrounded by brilliant men. I would have had to have been dead not to want to take those flirtations further."

"How much of this do I have to listen to, Mom? I really don't want to know that."

Virginia put her hand on Suzanna's arm and squeezed.

"I hope mothers stop reading fairy tales to their little girls," Virginia said. "Because even the good ones are bad for you. You think once you get married to the love of your life, you'll never be attracted to another man as long as you live. That's just not true."

"I wish it *were* true," Suzanna said, biting into a cookie. She didn't even think about her skinny jeans.

"Don't we all!" Virginia said, sitting back in her chair. "I was young, but I already had Erinn, when your father and I started working at the university. I was overwhelmed with being a teacher, being a wife and mother, remodeling that old barn so we'd have a place to live. On top of that, I felt invisible to the men of the world. Then, one day I was making copies in the Xerox room and this handsome professor of visual arts came in. He bent me over the copier and kissed me!"

Suzanna's eyes widened. "You're kidding."

"I'm not," Virginia said, sounding giddy. "It was crazy. He finally let me up and we both went on making copies of our assignments as if nothing had happened."

"Do I want to know the rest?"

"That was it. That's the whole story. But I felt great afterward! I felt beautiful and mysterious! When I went home that night, I looked over at your father, who was feeding your sister some macaroni and cheese. I'll never forget it: a normal family, a father, a daughter, macaroni and cheese, and a mother who just got kissed in the Xerox room. And I knew that it was OK to keep a part of myself to myself."

"Please, Mom, I feel like I'm going to pass out. . . ."

"Yes, well, everything took a little while to figure out," Virginia said, looking up at Suzanna, who was looking very pale. "I decided that I could have *one* affair, in my whole married life. So what I had to decide every time I was attracted to a man was: Is this the one? Is *this* the one?"

Virginia looked Suzanna in the eye. Woman to woman, not mother to daughter.

"Do you need another cookie?" Virginia asked.

Suzanna shook her head.

"And nobody was just right. In all honesty, it took less time deciding to marry your father than it did deciding if I was going to sleep with this man or that man."

"I can't believe we're having this conversation," Suzanna said.

"Well, I might have saved you some pain—or at least some guilt—if we'd had it earlier. The progression was always something like this: I would meet a man I found attractive. Every so often, the feeling would be mutual and I would find myself thinking, *Maybe he's the one.* It was so exciting! I would find myself comparing your father to him and thinking, *Oh, if Martin were only a little more like this . . . or a little more like that.* As I was deciding if this was going to be my grand affair, I would get to know the man a little better and, after a while, I would think, *Oh, if only he could be a little more like Martin, he'd be perfect.* Then, of course, I knew he wasn't the one."

"Mom," Suzanna said. "That's nuts."

"Oh, it gets nuttier," Virginia said, stirring her tea. "After a while, I realized that I could never have an affair with someone I knew well, since he'd never measure up to your father, so I changed the rules and decided I'd have to have an affair with a complete stranger."

Suzanna gasped so loudly that Virginia looked up.

"Should I stop?" Virginia asked.

Suzanna seemed incapable of speech. She shook her head again.

"I won't go into the gory details," Virginia said.

"Thank God!" Suzanna said, finally pushing out the words.

"But I finally thought I'd found the guy. He was foreign. I couldn't understand a word he said, so it wasn't any of the Romance languages. But as we were leaving the bar—did I mention we were at a bar? Anyway, as I was leaving the bar, I realized that I could never sleep with a man who would knowingly have sex with a married woman. I couldn't believe this man would enable me to cheat on your father! I was outraged! So I just turned away and went back into the bar alone. He probably thought American women are very strange."

"Is that the end?" Suzanna asked.

"Yes. I kept my option open, because just knowing I had one made me feel . . . just a little bit . . . free. I always felt I had a Get Out of Jail Free card. Just in case. And you know what?"

"Apparently, I don't know anything!"

"When your father died, I was really glad I'd never used it."

"I'm not sure what to make of all this."

"Make of it what you will." Virginia took another sip of tea, kissed Suzanna on the head, and went to bed.

* * *

The following morning, Virginia was up early, buckling Lizzy into the Baby Jogger. She didn't really want to be in the kitchen when Suzanna appeared. That woman-to-woman chat seemed a little more embarrassing in the light of day. Besides, Virginia had something she needed to do. She stopped at Piquant's dog bed.

"Do you want to go out?" Virginia whispered, but was given the Chihuahua stink eye, so she left him to sleep.

What kind of dog didn't always want to go out?

She took the few steps to Mr. Clancy's Courtyard slowly. She wanted to know, needed to know, if Mr. Clancy had taken the damning photo of Suzanna. She could understand his take on the tree and felt she had been more than fair in hearing him out. But all that open-mindedness would come to a screeching halt if she found out he was behind that flyer. She found this bothered her more than she thought it would. She had grown very fond of Mr. Clancy.

She noticed Donell setting up his sage stand with one hand and talking on his cell phone with the other, business as usual. He waved absently and turned his back to her. Virginia was perplexed. Donell had become increasingly standoffish. Was he upset that the tree situation seemed to be escalating? That would be odd, since more and more people were stopping by and checking out the tree for themselves. That had to be good for business. Hadn't she mentioned that to him before? Donell had his own way about him, that was for certain.

Virginia took one more step toward the courtyard and then stopped dead in her tracks. She turned back to Donell and waited for him to get off the phone. When he noticed her, he pointed to the phone, signaling that he was on it.

"I can see that." Virginia smiled. "I'll wait."

Donell finally rang off.

"You looking for some sage?" Donell asked, pulling a bundle out of a box. "Always got sage for a pretty lady."

"Oh, thanks, Donell," Virginia said. "But I was wondering if I could use your phone for a minute. Mine is out of battery."

"Why, sure," Donell said, and handed over the phone. "It's real easy to use."

"Oh, I know," Virginia said as she stepped out of his reach. "It's the same one I use."

She turned her back to him and quickly selected the icon for Photos. She looked up and made sure Donell was busy setting up his table. She quickly flipped through the photos and there it was: a picture of Suzanna taking a tumble in the courtyard.

Virginia looked up just as Donell spun around. Guilt was written all over his face.

"Well, lovely lady, you said the tree was good for business," Donell said, almost, but not quite, apologetically.

Mr. Clancy came out of his studio in the courtyard and waved.

"Does Mr. Clancy know you put up those flyers?" Virginia asked.

"No, ma'am. I'm not sure if he would like the idea of causing trouble like that."

"But you do?"

"Just being a good capitalist!"

Virginia looked at him sternly, deleted the photo, and gave Donell back his phone.

"I'll be keeping an eye on you," Virginia said.

Donell shrugged. Virginia jogged over to Mr. Clancy.

"Good morning, Virginia."

"Good morning, Mr. Clancy." She gave him a quick kiss on the cheek and headed off for her jog with Lizzy. Lizzy put her fists in the air and let out a whoop.

"Faster, Grammy!" With a huge grin on her face, Virginia ran as fast as she could.

CHAPTER 22

SUZANNA

Suzanna was beside herself. First Lizzy had stopped eating kale and now she was off boiled beets.

"What child in her right mind would eat a boiled beet?" Virginia asked.

"It's good for her," Suzanna said.

"So are sweet potatoes. You were probably too small to remember, but I used to make you a sweet potato, carrot, and yogurt thing that you just loved."

"Did it have raisins in it?" Suzanna said, instantly remembering. "You called it Sweet Potato Surprise or something like that?"

"That's the one." Virginia beamed. "You thought I called it 'Surprise' because of the raisins, but it was actually because I got you to eat it—you were so fussy! Your father would come into the dining room and you'd be covered in sweet potato. You and I would both throw up our hands and yell—"

"Surprise," Suzanna said.

"Now, if you had to eat boiled beets or my Sweet Potato Surprise, which would you choose?"

When Virginia had asked them over dinner (while Lizzy ate her Sweet Potato Surprise) how Suzanna and Eric would feel about hosting a party, Suzanna could only gape at her. The idea behind the party was that Dymphna needed help preparing all that Angora fur so it could be turned into yarn.

"You don't usually shear all of your rabbits at the same time," Virginia said.

"And whose fault is that?" Suzanna asked.

"It's nobody's fault," Eric said. "It is what it is."

Did Eric want to have this party? She was treading lightly ever since that damn flyer of her tripping over the tree root found itself plastered all over the neighborhood.

"Where would we have this party, Mom?" Suzanna said.

"In the tearoom?" Virginia asked.

"I can't have the tearoom covered in rabbit hair, Mom. What would the health department say?"

"We don't have to tell the health department. We can always stop if we get busted."

Suzanna winced. She hated when her mother used words like *busted.* That was not a motherly word.

"Besides, it's for the greater good," Virginia said. "It doesn't have anything to do with the tree. Anyone can help with the rabbit hair."

"It can be a time of healing for the community," Virginia continued, clearly playing to Eric, which annoyed Suzanna. "We can put up flyers."

"No flyers!" Suzanna said, remembering not only her own handbill debacle, but also her sister's run-in with Christopher's ex-wife. "And not in the tearoom."

"What about the Nook?" Virginia asked Eric.

Suzanna gaped anew! Her mother was the one who'd chosen sides, and now to ask Eric to throw his principles to the wind over a bunch of fur?

"We can't use the Nook," he said.

Suzanna's mouth dropped open. Her mother had some nerve. Eric had made it clear time and time again that the Nook was a neutral zone!

"There isn't room," Eric continued.

Suzanna could see the disappointment in her mother's face and she couldn't stand it. She shot a pitying look at Eric, who had obviously noticed the same look.

"But I can fix up the backyard," Eric said. "This is a great idea, Virginia. It will bring people back together."

* * *

Eric transformed the backyard into a quaint extension of their commercial space. He sandblasted the brick patio and put out ten assorted tables and chairs, now painted bright colors. He strung twinkly lights from the rooftop to the fence, creating a little canopy of stars. Virginia got into decorating mode and found large baskets to hold the fur. She thought she might spray paint the baskets, but Dymphna nixed that idea—the rabbit hair had to be housed in an organic environment.

The night of the big event, Eric made a quick adjustment to his decorating scheme. The weather report said a rare and frisky storm was headed their way, so he added a tarp roof. Although perfect weather was business as usual, the random storm that turned up to say hello could be potentially pretty spectacular. But most storms blew over quickly, Eric had said. Suzanna looked at him significantly, but he didn't seem to understand the subtext.

Suzanna was distracted, but try as she might, she knew she was not being as helpful as she could be preparing for the big yarn-making extravaganza. Eric's parents Red and Wanda, true to their threat, swooped in to take Lizzy on an overnight to Disneyland. Suzanna had never been separated from her daughter for more than a few hours, and usually her own mother was watching the toddler if she wasn't. But Eric continued to think it was a great idea for his parents to have some bonding time, and Suzanna thought it would be an olive branch, so she said yes. As the Coopers drove away to the Happiest Place on Earth, Suzanna felt as if she were living in the Most Panicked Place on Earth. She was grateful for the massive preparations ahead of her.

Virginia had done an amazing job getting people in the neighborhood to rally 'round the rabbits, but the dream of getting them all to set aside their differences didn't exactly pan out. When word spread that there was going to be free tea and scones and a lesson on making rabbit hair into yarn, which was right up the collective Beach Walk alley, both literally and figuratively, the neighbors turned up ready to eat and learn. But they kept to their philosophical corners. Mr. Clancy was at one table against the fence, apparently trying to catch her mother's eye, while Bernard sat at the other, also vying for Virginia's attention.

Suzanna tried not to watch the door for Rio. It was a long shot that he'd show up, but you never knew about these things.

Erinn was setting up her camera and tripod at the back of the lawn when Christopher came through the side gate. Suzanna's antennae were up as she watched Erinn pretend she hadn't seen him. Suzanna smiled to herself. While her mother really wasn't conscious that two men were watching her every move, Erinn was pretending she wasn't aware that Christopher was nearby.

Two very opposite approaches!

Christopher went over to Erinn, draping a hand casually over the tripod as they chatted. Suzanna couldn't hear what they were saying. She grabbed a basket of Angora fur so she could walk past without looking like a snoop.

"Isn't Alice coming?" Erinn asked. "I would think this would be right up her alley."

"She says she already knows how to turn rabbit fur into yarn." Christopher shrugged.

"Of course she does," Erinn said.

Christopher waved to his uncle. When he saw Erinn wasn't about to engage further, he went to sit with Bernard. Suzanna thought it was amazing that Erinn could sound like a snob even in a bout of jealousy.

A storekeeper named Mavis, who was sitting on what Suzanna now thought of as "Mr. Clancy's side," signaled Suzanna, which unfortunately meant she would be forced to move away from Erinn and Christopher. She'd have to catch up with their story later by gathering her own intel; God knows Erinn would never pour her heart out to her own sister!

"What can I do for you, Mavis?" Suzanna asked.

Mavis pointed to the pile of fluffy white Angora fur nestled in its basket in the center of the table.

"I don't really like this color," she said. "Can you bring another?"

"Well, we really only have beige, brown, and white."

"I want to make a red sweater."

"That's a little bit down the line," Suzanna said, although she realized she didn't actually know exactly how far down the line it was. It was as if her mother sensed she was at a loss because Virginia was suddenly at her side.

"I'm sure there would be many, many people who would trade

their brown fur for this beautiful white," Virginia said. "As a matter of fact, I'd be happy to trade with you myself. I have a nice drab brown."

"No, that's fine," Mavis said, pulling the basket toward her. "I like white."

As Virginia and Suzanna walked away, Virginia said, "You just have to subscribe to the theory that every tactic you use as a mother, you can use on the world."

"Sort of like, 'Everything I know I learned in kindergarten,' " Suzanna said. "But from the mother's perspective."

"Exactly!"

A few of the Cause Courtyard ladies, including Zelda and Babette, as well as complete strangers dotted the backyard. The oddest of odd couples, Dymphna and Blu, stood at the entrance of the tea shop, which was serving as the stage. Eric had rigged up a spotlight of sorts, and now that dusk was finally here, he turned it on, signaling to the crowd that the lecture on all things Angora was about to begin.

Dymphna was wearing one of her voluminous dresses, which looked like something out of the Renaissance, and Blu wore a skirt that looked like it could have been made from the material left over from a pocket. Blu clapped her hands and everyone quieted.

"Thanks, everybody," Blu said. "When I found out that Dymphna and Virginia had sheared all the rabbits, I was like . . . what?! But then Dymphna said she was going to turn the fur into yarn and make sweaters and things, and I was like . . . oh!"

Suzanna and Virginia went to stand near the back fence where Erinn was shooting.

"Is this for Blu's reality show?" Suzanna whispered to her mother.

"I don't know," Virginia whispered back.

"The rabbits were up at my house and we were desperate to get the paparazzi away," Blu said.

"I guess that answers your question," Virginia whispered to Suzanna.

"Now, my good friend Dymphna is going to show us how to make yarn!" Blu said, gracefully extending her hands toward Dymphna like a poor man's Vanna White.

Suzanna saw Erinn pop her head up from behind the lens and signal to her. Blu stood beaming and Dymphna stood still, obviously wondering what to do now that Blu was not exiting the spotlight. Virginia started applauding, loudly. Everyone else followed her lead. Blu had no choice but to leave the stage to Dymphna.

"OK, everybody," Dymphna said. "Thank you all for coming."

She clearly did not crave the spotlight like Blu did. She stood looking around the patio. Virginia came back to stand next to her and spoke to the crowd.

"In front of you, you'll see two paddles with little bristles that look like dog brushes and beautiful piles of Angora fur. The first step in making yarn is to clean the fur."

Mom knows how to make yarn?

Suzanna watched Mavis check out everyone else's basket of fur and almost burst out laughing. Her smile dimmed as she watched Blu sidle up to Eric. Suzanna tried to read their body language: Eric was relaxed, one foot propped up against the side fence, and Blu's body language practically screamed, "Let's have sex right now."

Suzanna could see her mother drawing Dymphna out of her shell.

"What do we do next?" Virginia asked.

"Everybody pick up your paddles," Dymphna instructed. "We're going to do something called carding. We'll use the paddles to brush the wool between them until the fibers are more or less aligned in the same direction and are sparkling clean!"

Suzanna watched Blu pick up her paddles.

"She could turn carding Angora into a porn film," Erinn whispered to Suzanna.

"I know!" Suzanna whispered back as she started brushing a small handful of fur with the paddles, transferring the fur from paddle to paddle as instructed. "Do you think I should be worried?"

"I don't think you should be worried," Virginia said, also concentrating on the carding. "But I don't think you should be blind, either."

"Oh, what do you know?" Suzanna retorted.

"I know my microphone is picking up this conversation and it's going to be hell to edit," Erinn said.

Suzanna tried to keep her eyes off Blu and Eric while at the same time watching their every move. It was a technique Suzanna had been working on ever since Lizzy started to walk. Suzanna would let Lizzy think she was exploring the world on her own, but she knew what was going on every second. She was very grateful to have perfected the skill before tonight's event.

Suzanna noticed a few raindrops had fallen on the tarp overhead. She watched Erinn scoot the camera and herself under it. Suddenly, an enormous thundercloud rolled in. Rain poured down as if a cloud had opened up a mile-long zipper. People started grabbing the baskets of fur, the carded fiber, and anything else they could get their hands on and running into the Rollicking Bun and Book Nook. Suzanna and Virginia grabbed the tea service, and Suzanna caught a glimpse of Blu trying to snuggle inside Eric's jacket. Eric shot her a surprised "I have nothing to do with this" look and led the way into the shop.

Erinn was the last in, her coat thrown protectively over her camera.

Everyone was laughing as they shook off the rain. It continued to pelt the building, the drama accentuated by thunder of Biblical proportions. Lightning lit up the sky for a few theatrical seconds at a time. The electricity flickered but appeared to be just goofing around. The lights held.

While Blu and Erinn consoled Dymphna that everyone would reassemble outside as soon as it stopped raining, Virginia and Suzanna opened up the tearoom and ushered the crowd inside. Most of the food was rescued in time, and while the pro-tree people and the anti-tree people kept their distance from one another, the mood was upbeat. The rain stopped but nobody seemed in a hurry to leave, so they headed back outside to finish what they had started.

The lighthearted mood of the crowd changed as a loud crack rocked the building.

"What was that?" someone asked.

"Sounds like something got struck by lightning," Eric said, a protective arm around Suzanna.

Suzanna kept her eyes forward, but she could barely keep from turning to Blu and saying, "So there!"

The door to the foyer swung open. Everyone turned to see a drenched Rio breathing heavily. Something was terribly wrong, but Suzanna couldn't help noticing how great he looked in his rain-soaked shirt and trousers.

"El patio está en llamas!" Rio said.

Half the people in the foyer gasped in comprehension, the other half murmuring, "What? What did he say?"

Virginia and Mr. Clancy were the first to reach Rio. The three of them raced out the door.

"Let's go," Eric said to everyone. "The courtyard is on fire!"

CHAPTER 23

ERINN

"How can the courtyard be on fire?" Dymphna asked as she and Erinn ran toward the blaze. "It's been raining."

"And the courtyard is brick," Erinn added. "Not the most flammable substance that comes to mind."

They could see flames shooting skyward. Erinn realized that the tree, the poor tree that had withstood so many battles, had lost out to an act of God.

Virginia, Eric, and Suzanna raced past. Erinn was surprised to see the entire family sprinting toward the courtyard; usually someone was left behind watching her niece, but then she remembered that Lizzy was staying with Eric's parents at Disneyland. Erinn was grateful that Lizzy wouldn't be involved in such a traumatic experience as a neighborhood fire. She thought of the poet Edward Young's words, "How blessings brighten as they take their flight."

She hoped more blessings were on their way. If that dance instructor had been at the courtyard he must have been teaching. Were his students all right? The stores were all closed and almost everyone was at the Bun, but who else might be there? Then it hit her.

Alice. Alice was at the courtyard.

She looked around for Christopher. He caught her eye and grabbed her arms.

"Alice is in there," he said. "I've got to get her out."

"I know, I know!" Erinn yelled over the crowd that had gathered.

The fire department was already at work by the time the band of people from the Bun showed up. There were barricades already in place. Rio was standing with a group of stunned-looking students.

Everyone watched as the fireman sprayed the tree with a torrent of water.

Christopher was looking wildly around and ran at the barricade when Alice ran toward him through the smoke.

Erinn stood looking helplessly as they embraced. Erinn slowed her footsteps, realizing she had no part in this. As she turned away, she heard Alice's voice.

"Mandy is in there," Alice said to Christopher. "You have to save her!"

"OK," Christopher said, looking at the courtyard. "Wait here."

Erinn took a step toward him; he couldn't go in there. But she was too late.

She watched in horror as Christopher ducked under the barricade at the far edge of the building nearest the studio. No one else saw him. Everyone was focused on the tree, still lighting the night sky with its branches going up in angry flames.

Erinn tried not to panic. Should she go in after him? The building itself didn't seem to be on fire but the smoke would be terrible. The smoke was getting thicker and she could barely see Christopher's door.

Suddenly, she heard a fireman yell, "Hey! What are you doing? Get out here!"

She saw Christopher, covered in ash, coming out his door. He was choking on the smoke, but signaled the fireman that he was OK. He crossed the barrier, carrying the moose head.

Mandy.

Was this man so in love with his ex-wife that he would risk his life for her *artwork?*

She thought wistfully of David Grayson's "Looking back, I have this to regret, that too often when I loved, I did not say so." She stood, watching, and realized that this love affair, which she so very tentatively had dreamed about, was over before it had begun.

Erinn felt rooted to the ground. She knew she should join her family and friends as they watched the firefighters put the tree out of its misery. But she could only stare at Christopher and Alice. Alice had stepped back from him and was surveying the damage to the moose head. One antler broke off in her hand. Christopher caught Erinn's eye. He handed Alice the entire art piece, patted the top of his ex-wife's head, and walked toward Erinn. She tried to will herself to walk away, but she remained where she was.

"That was . . . brave of you," Erinn said, as the firefighters finished spraying down the tree and started the cleanup.

"Really? I would have thought you would have found it . . . unwise."

"Well, it was unwise. But brave."

"Yeah. But it had to be done. For us."

"I can see that." Erinn looked up at the sky and hoped she wouldn't cry. "I mean, what woman could resist a man who saved her moose head?"

"Wait, no," Christopher said, taking Erinn's face in his hands, tilting it so he was looking into her eyes. "Not Alice-us, us-us. You-and-me-us."

"You had to risk your life for us-us?" Erinn asked. "I don't understand."

"First of all, I wasn't really risking my life. The studio wasn't on fire. I'm not an idiot."

"So it was just a dramatic gesture?"

"Don't tell Alice, but yes. I rescued her damn moose. She and I are even now. No more guilt. I'm free."

Erinn tried to think of an appropriate quote to sum up her feelings, but the only thing she could think to say was, "Free to be us-us."

They wrapped themselves around each other and watched the cedar smolder, a few dying embers drifting into space. Erinn felt sorry for the tree and for the Cause Courtyard people, of which Christopher was one. She studied him as he watched the tree lose the battle.

"All that hard work literally up in smoke," Erinn said.

Christopher looked at her.

"I don't know," he said. "We wanted to let that tree live out its life in the courtyard. But in a way, it has done just that."

Looking at Christopher, Erinn thought that life was inexplicable. Here she was, standing near the rubble of a fire in her sister's neighborhood and yet she was totally happy. Nothing made any sense. She felt a tap on her shoulder and spun around to see Blu and Dymphna looking at her.

"The tree is toast," Blu said. "Can we go home now?"

"I really need to make sure the heat lamp is on for the rabbits," Dymphna said.

Yes, Erinn thought, *nothing made any sense.*

CHAPTER 24

SUZANNA

One thing about Venice Beach: It was a resilient little town. A month after the fire, and fences were literally and metaphorically mended. Dymphna's wool got spun into yarn, thanks to the Cause Courtyard ladies. Mr. Clancy's insurance covered some of the repairs to his establishment, but not all. Volunteers from both sides of the tree issue labored toward restoring Mr. Clancy's Courtyard to its former glory. Mr. Clancy and Bernard worked side by side cleaning up the courtyard. Virginia seemed to be playing the field, first favoring one and then the other. Eric and Suzanna brought food to the volunteers, who scrubbed the charred bricks and painted windowsills. Bernard moved his Little Free Library to the courtyard. Christopher built the book box a gorgeous stand, which would have a place of honor at the front of the courtyard, surrounded by wrought-iron chairs.

"You better be careful with that library, Christopher," Eric said. "You'll put me out of business."

When the city came to take away the remains of the cedar, it seemed the entire neighborhood came out to bid it farewell.

"It's amazing how one ugly tree could tear the community apart and also bring it back together," Virginia said to Erinn and Christopher.

They had been accepted as a couple almost immediately.

"I just don't understand why Alice is still around," Erinn said to

Suzanna as they hauled broken concrete to the sidewalk in front of the courtyard.

Suzanna looked at her sister. Suzanna, as well as everyone else, including Erinn, knew why Alice was still around. She was creating a metal tree sculpture to replace the cedar.

"It's the least I can do," Alice had said grandly. "After you've all been so kind." She flashed her white teeth at everyone.

"Why?" Erinn asked Suzanna. "Why is it the least she can do? Nobody asked her to build a tree! I mean, no one was overly kind, except Christopher."

Suzanna continued to tug at a sack of concrete chunks. She really did not want to hear, yet again, the story of how Christopher had saved the moose head in order to free himself from the guilt of his divorce. But Suzanna always wished that she and her sister would find more common ground. She was happy to give Erinn a turn as the obsessed sister in love. Suzanna had to admit that it was more fun than listening to her discuss gerunds.

"Alice says she'll leave for Santa Fe as soon as the tree is dedicated," Erinn said. "I'm sure she is expecting some sort of madness to break out over her artistic genius. The woman has delusions of grandeur!"

Suzanna tried to change the subject.

"How is the show with Blu coming along?" she asked.

"It's terrible," Erinn said. "She comes across as spoiled and demanding . . . even more spoiled and demanding than she is in real life."

"I don't know," Suzanna said. She didn't want to be overly sympathetic to a woman who flirted brazenly with Eric, even if Eric seemed—for the most part—oblivious. "She must have a fan base that likes that sort of thing."

"I can't imagine," Erinn said.

"Eric sold one of her graphic novels."

"One?" replied Erinn, who had listened to Suzanna's rages against Blu. "I bet some hormonal teenage boy just shoplifted it."

Suzanna smiled. Only Erinn would think shoplifting sounded supportive.

"The best footage we have is of the rabbits," Erinn continued. "Their fur has grown back, and I have fantastic video of Blu combing them and feeding them. She seems almost likable."

"How is Dymphna with that?"

"She only really cares that the rabbits are happy. You know Dymphna."

"Yeah, she marches to her own beat."

"As Thoreau once said, 'If a man does not keep pace with his companions, perhaps it is because he hears the beat of a different drummer. Let him step to the music which he hears, however measured or far away.' "

"Are you sure that was Thoreau?" Suzanna asked, trying not to smile.

Erinn stopped dead in her tracks.

"Of *course* I'm sure!"

"I'm just teasing." Suzanna laughed. "I swear, Erinn, you can be such an easy target."

Erinn laughed and the two sisters started lugging the concrete again. As they dumped the bag of debris in the recycling pile, Erinn caught sight of Christopher. Suzanna knew her older sister would be useless now that her man was in her eye line.

"Go see Christopher," Suzanna said. "I don't think I could haul another bag of concrete if they paid me."

Which they didn't.

Rio's studio was hit the hardest by the smoke damage, but he was still giving dance lessons to kids out in the open by the skateboarding area. Suzanna watched him at work. He was just so damn sexy she couldn't stand it. He was in control of every muscle in his body—quite impressive to a woman who had trouble not soaring into space when the going got tough. She and Eric mended some fences of their own, but Suzanna couldn't get her mother's Get Out of Jail Free card out of her mind. Maybe Rio was the one?

Suzanna noticed her mother had made her way over to the group. Virginia was laughing with a few of the teenagers who were standing around. She didn't want to interrupt whatever was going on, but she couldn't tear her eyes away. She wasn't close enough to hear, but it was obvious that Rio had turned on some music. He put out his hand and Virginia took it. She and Rio started doing some sort of disco routine that had the kids laughing and howling encouragement.

Mom knows how to dance?

There was no denying that her mother was full of surprises these days. A day after the fire, her mother had practically adopted Rio and his kids. It was her idea to continue the dance lessons outside.

"You've got beautiful weather all year long here," Virginia had said.

There was something about the way she said, "You've got beautiful weather," instead of "We've got beautiful weather," that sent up a warning flare in Suzanna's mind.

It wasn't long until she was proven right. Her mother had plans.

Virginia spent most days with Rio and his kids. She seemed renewed. Two weeks ago, after putting Lizzy to bed and taking Piquant out for a final stroll, Virginia joined Eric and Suzanna in the kitchen. She made small talk until Eric went to check on Lizzy. Suzanna saw her mother's eyes follow him as he left the room. She could tell her mother had something on her mind and the fact that she had waited for Eric to leave the room was not a good sign.

"I need to talk to you about something," Virginia had said. "I'm not sure how you are going to feel about this."

"OK," Suzanna said.

"I've decided to move back to New York after the metal tree is dedicated."

"Why?" Suzanna asked abruptly. She was hit harder than she expected. Her mother had fit so seamlessly into their lives. Yes, she drove Eric crazy with her passion for causes, but Suzanna took some satisfaction that Eric was, in the gentlest way possible, getting a dose of his own medicine. What would life be like without seeing her mother smiling every morning as Suzanna staggered into the kitchen to start the day? She had gotten used to a lovely routine: Her mother and her daughter would greet her every day, having already returned from their morning run. She could feel tears forming but blinked them away. Piquant was in a corner of the kitchen, resting in his doggy bed. He looked up at Suzanna and a tear finally escaped.

Hell, I'm even going to miss that damn dog.

Suzanna wiped at her eyes. It wasn't fair to guilt her mother with tears . . . at least not yet.

"There's more," Virginia said.

Suzanna tried to figure out what it could be. Was Virginia bored just being a grandmother? Had she started a romance with Mr. Clancy or Bernard and not told anyone? Did one of them break her heart? No, she decided, that would be impossible. Her mother was . . . well, her mother. Men weren't supposed to fall in love with a *mother*—especially hers!

"Well, Mom," Suzanna prompted. "What is it?"

"I'm moving to New York with someone," Virginia said.

Suzanna couldn't wrap her head around this announcement. So it *was* love! This was crazy. Suzanna commanded herself to keep a grip on her emotions. She knew this could not be easy for her mother. She was about to announce the man who would be replacing her own husband! Replacing Suzanna and Erinn's father. Suzanna wasn't sure she wanted to hear, but hear it she must!

"And . . . who is it?" Suzanna asked. "Mr. Clancy or Bernard? Who won?"

Suzanna tried to keep the moment light.

"Well," Virginia said, "I hate to disappoint you, but neither one."

"Oh?"

"Suzanna, when you get to be my age, your needs are different."

"Please, Mom, you know I can't handle talking about your needs."

"I just mean, Mr. Clancy and Bernard are both lovely, lovely men. But their lives are just fine without me. Neither of them *needs* me. A serious relationship with either one of them never really entered my mind. And besides, it would ruin the friendship they've had for all these years. I'm sure as hell not interested in that."

"Who then? Who is it that needs you so badly?"

Virginia drew circles on the table with her finger, stalling. Suzanna stayed focused and waited. She would give her mother all the time she needed.

"Rio," Virginia said, averting her gaze.

Suzanna grabbed the edges of the table. Usually when a stress float was upon her she was aware that liftoff was imminent. This time, her thighs banged instantly into the tabletop, which held her in place. She concentrated on the conversation as her legs banged again and again on the bottom of the table, trying to break loose, so she could float away and feel safe.

"Rio!" Suzanna almost growled, before trying a different tone. "I mean . . . Rio?"

"Yes, dear. I know this is probably coming as a shock."

OK, understatement was never her strong suit.

Eric popped his head through the doorway.

"You guys good? I thought I'd go for a bike ride."

Suzanna and Virginia waved him away. They were so in tune with each other. Neither of them spoke until they heard the soft click of the back door below them.

"So, Mom, you were saying . . ."

"I'm sure you're aware of how much time we've been spending together."

Yes! I have noticed and I've been damn grown-up about it! And now I find out my own mother is a traitor and a slut! Well, slut is probably too strong . . . a floozy, maybe—Suzanna thought. But she knew she had to hold her tongue. Instead she said,

"I have noticed, yes. But I thought it was for the good of the kids."

Virginia reached out her hand imploringly and placed it on Suzanna's arm.

"It was. It was about the kids. But he needs studio space. He can't keep teaching kids on the street. It's a fine stopgap, but the idea is to get them off the street. Rio got a call from a church in New York City that wants to offer him studio space—they have ten kids who have signed up for dance class. They're getting funding to start a citywide program. They are focusing on younger kids and they really, really need him."

Suzanna couldn't help but think that Rio had sold her mother a bill of goods, but she kept quiet.

"He couldn't take the job because he wouldn't have the money for a place to live. He's such a good man, Suzanna. He should have this chance."

"What has that got to do with you?" Suzanna asked.

"I've loved feeling needed again."

"Oh, now I get it. Rio needs a place to live in New York, and you just happen to have one, so suddenly you guys are madly in love and all his problems are solved!"

So much for holding my tongue.

Virginia stared at her as if she'd been slapped.

"Now, that's a bit harsh," Virginia said.

"I'm sorry, Mother, but—"

"But what?" Virginia interrupted. "There's no fool like an old fool?"

"Now who's being harsh? Mom, he has you bamboozled. I told you who he was!"

"You told me who he *used* to be," Virginia said. "By the way, *bamboozled*. Good word."

Suzanna stared at her mother, who seemed to be enjoying this. Suddenly, Virginia burst out laughing. She stood up and kissed her daughter on the head. As angry as Suzanna still was, her thighs stopped thumping against the table and she settled down.

"Oh, honey," Virginia said, dabbing at her eyes. "I know I should be insulted, but I am so flattered that you think Rio would try to seduce me . . . even if it were just for a place to live." Virginia had another fit of what Suzanna might kindly call "the giggles" but was so intense it was more like a "bout of braying." Her mother was practically honking with laughter. "That is so sweet of you to think that."

"OK," Suzanna said, when her mother had calmed down. "So . . . what's the deal, then?"

"Working with these kids, helping teach them something exciting, watching the wall come down one kid at a time has filled a void I didn't even know was there. Imagine what we could do if we actually start a real program for inner-city kids? Think of the difference it would make! I'm going to help set up the foundation or whatever it is and help teach. I have an extra bedroom and Rio is welcome to it."

"So that's the need?" Suzanna asked, relieved.

She felt like an idiot. A jealous idiot. She would have continued to berate herself, but she was so relieved that her mother hadn't stolen her fantasy man that all she could do was smile.

"But what about Rio's kids here?" Suzanna asked. "The last thing they need is to be dumped by the two of you."

"We've already worked that out." Suzanna noticed how comfortably her mother said "we." It sounded good.

"How?" Suzanna asked.

"These kids are all over eighteen. If they want to keep it going, they can. And those twins, Miles and Winnie? They are really motivated to make a success of it. Rio is helping them get set up at their high school."

"Eighteen is pretty young," Suzanna said.

"It is young. But a few months ago, these kids had no direction, nothing they cared about, and nothing to occupy their time. Don't you see? Rio started this impossible project with nobody interested and no money to see it through. Now he'll be reaching kids on two coasts. Just following his example will help these kids."

"That sounds like a gamble."

"Life's a gamble," said Virginia.

* * *

By the following morning, when Suzanna came into the kitchen to see her mother feeding Lizzy breakfast, she realized how much she wanted her mother to stay. But she knew it wasn't fair to place that burden on her, so she didn't say anything except, "I'll miss you, Mom."

Virginia looked up from the table, where she sat with Lizzy. She seemed to be reading Suzanna's mind.

"Don't tell your sister just yet," Virginia said.

"OK. But why?"

"Things are . . . more complicated with Erinn. I need to be the one to tell her. I'll figure it out."

Suzanna shared the news with her husband. To her surprise he seemed as deflated as she was to hear it.

"We have to let her go, Beet," Eric said. "In her time, she let Erinn go and then she let you go. It'll be practice for when it's Lizzy's turn."

Suzanna felt like crying every time she looked at her mother over the next couple of days. But Virginia seemed to be on top of the world. She was energized and full of purpose as more and more teenagers seemed to take part in dancing lessons. Suzanna watched from the front of the tea shop, but suddenly a crowd of kids closed around Rio and her mother. Suzanna moved closer. Was her mother safe in that crowd? When Suzanna got close enough to see what was going on she gasped. Not only Rio but her mother and several teenagers were doing the zombie choreography to Michael Jackson's *Thriller*! Even from a distance, she could see a boy with a tattoo sleeve, Miles, whom Virginia had mentioned. She thought she recognized the goth girl . . . what was her name? Suzanna couldn't remember, but she did know that she was Miles's sister . . . twin sister. She really needed to pay more attention to her mother's stories. The girl was transformed from a gloomy, stooped-shouldered teenager to a vibrant young woman, laughing along with the rest of the group. They looked almost professional! The entire group seemed to move from step to step with total ease. How long could they have been working on that? Was *Thriller* now in the country's collective DNA?

Suzanna jumped as a hand clasped on to her shoulder. She turned and saw Eric standing beside her.

"Oh! You scared me," Suzanna said. "I thought you were a zombie."

"Not yet," Eric said, smiling at the pack of crazy-quilt dancers hopping and lurching around the skateboard area.

"What?" Suzanna asked.

"These kids have given me a brilliant idea," Eric said.

"About being a zombie or a dancer?"

"You'll be the first to know, Beet."

* * *

The next few weeks flew by. Mr. Clancy's Courtyard gleamed in the Southern California sunshine. The walkway was smooth and even. The tree sculpture, to everyone's knowledge, was finished; it stood in the courtyard covered by a muslin drape. Eric had worked relentlessly on his brilliant idea and soon it would be time to unleash it on Venice Beach.

CHAPTER 25

VIRGINIA

Virginia realized with a jolt that she had run farther than she'd ever run before. Every morning she took Piquant and Lizzy out in the Baby Jogger and ran north toward Santa Monica. For the first few weeks she had clocked about a mile, which didn't even take her out of the Venice city limits. But now, she ran effortlessly past the Santa Monica Pier, past Perry's Pizza, where she needed to be on her guard as tourists took to the bike path on rental bikes and skates, on past the California Incline and the Annenberg Beach House.

She looked up at the cliff that towered over the Pacific Coast Highway. Erinn's house was just at the top of the cliff. She was literally minutes from her eldest daughter, but she hesitated. Should she call and let Erinn know she was in the neighborhood? Or would Erinn find that intrusive? Virginia loved her eldest daughter fiercely, but their relationship was never easy. Virginia had been putting off telling Erinn about the move east. She wasn't sure why. On the one hand, she knew Suzanna would be much more upset about her leaving and yet it had been simpler to tell her. Virginia and Suzanna had always had an easier relationship than she and Erinn.

She unbuckled Piquant and Lizzy from the Baby Jogger and the three of them spent a few minutes on the sand. Virginia felt emotions welling up inside her; when she went back to New York she would miss this precious child. As she watched Piquant and Lizzy playing, she knew her dog would miss Lizzy, too.

Virginia dug her phone out of her back pocket. She resolved to tell Erinn she was moving. She would do it, and she would do it now! Unless Erinn didn't answer the phone.

Erinn answered the phone before Virginia could change her mind.

"Hello, dear," Virginia said. "Lizzy and I are in your neck of the woods."

"Oh?" Erinn said, in a tone Virginia could not decipher.

"Yes, we're on the jogging path just below you. If you were in the park, you could look over and see us."

"But I'm not in the park." Virginia knew that Erinn was not being rude, just being . . . Erinn. When she was little, Martin used to call her Miss Spock. She was so serious, so literal minded, and actually had little pointed ears.

"I thought you might want to go out to breakfast," Virginia said.

There was a long pause at the other end of the line. Spontaneity was not one of Erinn's strong suits.

"All right. That would be nice. Shall I meet you at Back on the Beachwalk in ten minutes?"

Back on the Beachwalk had become one of Virginia's favorite restaurants since she'd come west. It was on the northern, more serene side of the bay area. She loved the hubbub of Venice, but when she wanted time to think, Back on the Beachwalk was the place she went to unwind. The restaurant had indoor and outdoor seating, the outdoor part being right on the sand. Virginia could also always bring Piquant, which was another plus.

She knew she'd mentioned the place to Erinn a few times and she was touched that her daughter remembered.

Once at the restaurant, Virginia settled Lizzy at the table and Piquant under it. She had just ordered coffee and two bagels when Erinn walked up to them. Lizzy clapped, and Erinn bent for a kiss. Virginia smiled. Erinn had never seemed particularly interested in children before, and Virginia was happy to see Erinn open herself up to Lizzy. Virginia knew better than to make this particular observation—Erinn could get prickly at the most innocent remark. Virginia passed Erinn a bagel.

"How is life at your place?" Virginia asked.

"It's a madhouse," Erinn said, sitting down and ordering coffee. "Dymphna and Blu, not to mention my cat, seem to have bonded over love of the rabbits."

Virginia laughed. "It could be worse," she said.

"I suppose. But I have to tell you, Mother, I just want my house back. Living in the guest room in my own house is driving me crazy."

" 'No one can drive us crazy unless we hand them the keys.' "

"Douglas Horton. You got that quote from me."

"No, dear. Actually, I got that quote from Douglas Horton."

Virginia took a deep breath and a sip of coffee.

Why was everything so hard with Erinn?

"I wanted to talk to you," Virginia said.

"I guess I'm not the only one being driven crazy by her living arrangements," Erinn said with a slight smile.

"What do you mean?" Virginia asked, breaking off a piece of bagel for Lizzy.

"It can't be easy living with Eric and Suzanna. I mean, it's pretty tight quarters over there."

"Actually," Virginia said, trying not to sound defensive, "we've done pretty well. I think Suzanna has been happy to have me there. Has she said anything to you to the contrary?"

"No, Mother, she hasn't. I just assumed you must be getting on each other's nerves by now."

"We're doing fine."

"Of course you are. What could I have been thinking?"

Virginia knew she was on dangerous ground. Erinn was very thin-skinned when it came to Virginia's effortless relationship with Suzanna.

"I'm sorry, Mother, I'm just in a bad mood."

"Is everything all right with Christopher?"

"Yes," Erinn said, sounding a little surprised. "Why would you think otherwise?"

"No reason, dear."

Maybe this was not the time to have a serious discussion.

"I just feel as if I'm out of step. Dymphna and Blu are getting along great—I mean, who could possibly get along with Blu?—and you and Suzanna apparently are sailing along without a ripple," Erinn said, looking like she had when she was ten years old and wondering why none of the other children liked her. "I just don't understand why I have so much trouble . . . *socializing*."

"Erinn, you say 'socializing' like it's a thing to wrestle to the ground. But it should come naturally. If you'd just relax a little. . . ."

"You've been saying that since I was five. I guess Suzanna got all the relaxing genes."

"Why are you so hard on your sister?"

"Probably because you always defend my sister."

"Are we really going to have this discussion *again?*"

"Oh, I'm sorry if I'm boring you."

Virginia could see Erinn was on the verge of tears. This was a very old wound. What could Virginia possibly say to comfort her eldest daughter? The truth of the matter was that life with Suzanna was easier than it was with Erinn. It always was and it always would be. It didn't mean that she loved one of her girls more than the other, but Erinn almost challenged you to love her.

"Dear," Virginia said carefully, "you and Suzanna are two very different people. You're like a glass of champagne and your sister is like a glass of warm milk. Both are fantastic, but you can't compare the two."

Virginia studied her daughter as Erinn looked out at the waves. Had this helped? Had she made things worse? Why wasn't there a road map for talking to your children—no matter what their age? Virginia put her hand on Erinn's arm and gave a small squeeze. She saw a tear glistening on her daughter's cheek. Every fiber in her body wanted to reach out and hug Erinn, but she knew that would make things worse.

If it had been Suzanna . . . Virginia thought, but put the brakes on that immediately. Erinn stood up.

"I just want to be a glass of warm milk sometimes, Mother," Erinn said. "And I don't know how."

Lizzy squealed as a seagull landed nearby. Virginia turned to coo at the toddler and when she looked back, Erinn was walking away.

She watched helplessly as Erinn's back got smaller and smaller. Her heart ached for her girl—and she still hadn't told her she was leaving.

CHAPTER 26

SUZANNA

The zombies were preparing their attack.

It was the first chance Suzanna had gotten to look at herself since she'd been turned into a zombie. The pale skin, the sunken eyes, the stringy and matted hair. Her clothes were torn and stained—disintegrated in the sun. She looked a mess, all right.

And somehow I still look fat.

Her sister, Erinn, came up behind her. Erinn looked equally undead and studied her own reflection alongside Suzanna's.

"I thought we weren't supposed to look in the mirror," Erinn said.

"That's vampires," Suzanna replied. "They have no reflection."

"I know that," Erinn said, in her tired "I know everything" voice. "I mean, I thought we weren't supposed to look at ourselves in case we hated the way we look."

"Dear God, how Hollywood is that? I don't think you're supposed to like the way you look once you're a zombie," Suzanna said.

A siren sounded and the sisters exchanged a glance. A male zombie in rags lurched past them, out the door of Suzanna's tea shop and onto the Venice Beach Walk, where he fell into lurch with a group of other zombies: men, women, and children. Suzanna and Erinn got in step behind him, trying not to bump into the door frame while attempting to match his pace, their arms outstretched, groaning in a low, feral tone. Suzanna felt clumsy as she tried to navigate her walkway. The zombie lurch was not as easy as it looked.

I'm the worst zombie ever.

Eric's brilliant idea was to have a Zombie 5K before the tree dedication. He thought it would be the perfect way to bring everyone, pro-tree, anti-tree, never gave a damn about the tree, together. Suzanna was surprised by Erinn's enthusiastic support until she realized that the 5K would take some of the spotlight off Alice. Suzanna was always surprised when her sister acted like any other insecure woman.

She had to hand it to her husband: The Zombie 5K was the perfect community activity. There were the runners, who would wear "tag football" streamers around their waists. As they neared the finish line, zombies would chase them and try to steal a streamer. This meant that anyone who wanted to participate but wasn't in good enough shape to run the 5K could participate as a zombie. In other parts of the country, there would be no shame in saying, "Hell, no, I'm not running 5K." But not in Southern California. This way you could pretend you just wanted to wear the crazy makeup and lurch around.

The zombies would hide until the runners had the finish line in sight and then they would attack. Eric thought that it would be better to have the zombies attack as the runners were starting to tire. It would give them an extra boost of adrenaline as they tried to escape and would give the zombies a fighting chance to catch the local athletes since they would be fresh out of the gate.

Rio, Eric, Christopher, Dymphna, and Bernard were the first to sign up as runners. Suzanna signed herself up as a zombie, not because she couldn't run a 5K (which she thought she could, given enough advance notice) but because she thought it might be a harmless, blameless way to chase after Rio. Mr. Clancy and Erinn were the next zombies to sign on. Erinn was perfectly happy to admit a 5K was not going to happen in her lifetime, plus she thought she could wear a GoPro camera on her head and get some great footage.

"You have no social shame, have you?" Suzanna asked Erinn when she explained why she had chosen to be a zombie.

"Since I don't even know what that means," Erinn said, "I guess not."

Everyone was surprised when Virginia signed up as a runner.

"I've been out with Lizzy and Piquant jogging every morning," Virginia said one morning after returning from a run. Lizzy and Virginia had become a real fixture on the Beach Walk. Ever since

Lizzy's Disneyland trip, the toddler had been sporting Minnie Mouse ears. Virginia had sewn a red polka-dotted ribbon to the hat, so it would stay on as Virginia ran through the neighborhood, pushing the Baby Jogger, which she also festooned with ribbons. Virginia had gotten so fast that losing the hat had become a real possibility! A local pet shop vendor had stopped her one day and handed her a tiny polka-dotted dog collar for Piquant. The three of them were a sight to see!

When Virginia and Suzanna had approached Donell with the sign-up sheet, Suzanna was aware that he seemed uncomfortable with her mother.

Oh, my God! Is this another man in love with her?

"Donell," Virginia had said to him. "You know we're having a dedication of the tree sculpture. We want everyone to put old prejudices aside and start over."

"Everyone?" Donell asked, sliding his sunglasses down his nose and looking Virginia in the eye.

"Everyone," she said, looking right back at him. "Clean slate."

Suzanna looked at the two of them, who seemed to be in some sort of standoff.

"All right, then," Donell said, beaming the first radiant smile Suzanna had seen in a while. He took the sign-in sheet and studied it, his smile fading. "A race? Are you kidding me? I'd be better off being an obstacle! How about I provide some sage for the winner?"

Virginia took the clipboard back with Donell's signature on it. Next to his name, Suzanna could see that he had written, *Will provide sage for life for the winner.*

Ah, the hyperbole of Angelenos—even when they were from Hawaii.

Alice refused to participate in the race.

"I need to look refreshed for the cameras," she had said to Suzanna when she was approached. "You know, for the dedication ceremony."

Most of the tea-shop ladies signed up as zombies since they weren't exactly race material, and Rio's teenagers signed up as zombies as well because it was way cooler than being runners. Suzanna worried that there would be more zombies than runners, but Eric had told her, "It'll all work out, Beet. This sort of thing . . . you have to rely on magic."

That was one of the things she loved about Eric. He had worked like crazy to get his MBA but here he was, believing in magic.

People started signing up one after another—like magic! Erinn put out the word on Facebook and it seemed that everyone she'd ever worked with over the years decided to come participate in the race. The macho competitiveness among them, including Cary, drove them all to be runners.

*   *   *

On the day of the race, Suzanna saw Erinn peeking out of the tea shop, where they had applied their zombie makeup.

"I know half of the people out there," Erinn said.

"I know," said Suzanna, surprised, as she scanned the crowd. She'd never thought of her sister as having a circle of friends, but there were all the guys Erinn had talked about over the last few years: Gilroi, Carlos, the young audio guy everyone now called Fetus.

"Is Jude here?" Suzanna asked.

"No, thank God," Erinn said, clearly agitated. "He's still out of town."

"I'm surprised you don't want to see him. You could lord your new age–appropriate boyfriend over him."

"No thanks. I don't want to see him or anyone else I know. I look like a damn fool," Erinn said, indicating her undead makeup. "Well, not a fool. Then I'd be wearing clown makeup. But these are my colleagues and I don't look *professional!*"

Suddenly, Suzanna grabbed a towel and started scrubbing at Erinn's face.

"What . . . ," Erinn said, but her voice was muffled in the terry cloth.

Suzanna held up a mirror. As Erinn looked, Suzanna scrubbed at her own face.

"I don't look like a zombie anymore," Erinn said, confused. "I just look like I'm wearing too much makeup!"

"Exactly," Suzanna said, taking the mirror and studying herself. "Nobody said we couldn't be *cute* zombies."

Erinn looked worried, but Suzanna knew her sister was relieved.

"Speaking of cute," Suzanna said, "where is Blu?"

"I have no idea. She said she'd be here, but she didn't sign up. Anyway," Erinn said as she put the GoPro camera on her head, "when she shows up, I'll get some footage of her. I'm sure she'll be turning a few heads, whatever she decides to do."

Suzanna studied her sister. There she stood, not wanting to face her colleagues in her excellent zombie makeup but perfectly happy to strap a thing that looked like a clunky coal miner's lantern onto her forehead.

Mavis, the local shopkeeper, had been elected as the zombie lookout. She wouldn't be involved in the chase, but she would let the zombies know when the runners were approaching. She'd given them a few false starts: "OK, Zombies, here they . . . ," she would begin and then stop. "Oh, no, that's just one runner. Hang on . . ."

But finally the runners were appearing in the distance.

"They're here," Mavis said. "For real this time!" She was scanning the horizon with binoculars. "Oh, Erinn and Suzanna, I can see your mom . . . she's got Lizzy *and* Piquant in the stroller!"

"I'm sure going to miss her," Suzanna said.

She turned to look at Erinn, who, even through her softened zombie makeup, looked stricken.

"What do you mean, miss her? You mean Mother? Is she ill?"

"No," Suzanna said, first wanting to kick herself, then her mother, for not telling Erinn. "She's going back to New York. It's complicated."

"Why didn't she tell me?"

Suzanna looked at her. "Because *you're* complicated."

The first runner—Suzanna thought it might be one of Erinn's ex-cameramen, Carlos—went by in a flash.

"Let's do this!" shouted a random zombie and then the lurch was on.

Suzanna caught Erinn's eye. Her sister looked irritated.

"What's wrong?" Suzanna hissed.

"We're never going to take down Mother at this pace."

"Who says we have to take down Mom?"

Their mother sprinted past them, polka-dot ribbons streaming behind her. Erinn dashed after her with surprising speed. Suzanna was about to give chase but then Rio was at her side. In a split second he was in front of her. She watched his tight ass flexing in his workout shorts. She noticed he still had both the ribbons tied to his waist. No zombie had gotten hold of him yet.

What could it hurt?

Suzanna put on a burst of speed. The flag on his right hip was inches from her. She reached out but it snapped itself away from her. She reached again. Rio, seemingly oblivious to her (what else was new?), dodged and weaved among the runners and the attacking hordes. Suzanna focused harder.

"Hi, Beet," Eric said as he loped past. He didn't even seem to be breaking a sweat. Suzanna was disconcerted for a moment. It was like a crazy romantic dream when suddenly something goes terribly wrong. What was her husband doing here, in the middle of an old-time fantasy? Suzanna stumbled and regained her footing. By the time she was balanced she could see Rio a few runners ahead, some of his students merrily chasing him. Suzanna almost ran into a zombie in front of her and jumped sideways. Something very shiny and blue caught her eye.

It was Blu, in her Superblu costume, running hellbent toward Eric.

Rio was forgotten in a flash. Suzanna couldn't believe Blu could run so fast in four-inch platforms. She didn't even want to imagine what other skills the girl might have.

Luckily, runners and zombies alike kept stopping to gape at Blu. From time to time that slowed her down and Suzanna was able to make up some distance. She could tell the instant Blu knew Eric's wife was in the picture—she probably had some practice—as the two women locked eyes.

Bring it, bitch.

CHAPTER 27

ERINN

Erinn ran as fast as she could. She raced past runners whose flags were in easy reach. She sped past without a glance. She could see her mother ahead of her and tried to catch her, but her GoPro camera kept falling down into her eyes. Erinn finally took it off and stuffed it in her pocket. As she watched her mother's back, still youthful and full of life, she knew that in a few years, that back would bend. Erinn felt she had wasted so much time just taking for granted that her mother would always be there. She watched as Virginia waved and shouted to people who a few short months ago were strangers and were now her friends. Didn't she still have a lot to learn from her mother, this woman who could still surprise both Erinn and Suzanna? This woman who could speak Spanish and knit and dance? What else didn't Erinn know about her?

Erinn saw Piquant look back at her from the Baby Jogger. She saw Lizzy's little baby hands reach out and pull him back.

This is my family.

Erinn sped up and overtook the carriage. Her mother was laughing as Erinn ran beside her.

"Mom," Erinn said, but she was winded.

"Mom?" Virginia said, smiling. "I thought I was Mother. You haven't called me Mom since you were ten."

"Mom," Erinn tried again.

"I'm not stopping, Erinn. You're a zombie and I'm not stopping until you grab one of my flags!"

With that, Virginia launched herself forward, away from Erinn. Erinn reached out again and grabbed hold of the flag. It came off in her hand. She looked at it as Virginia slowed. Virginia turned and looked at Erinn. Tears were running down Erinn's face, smearing the remains of her zombie makeup.

Virginia reached out.

"Baby! What is it?"

"Mom," Erinn choked. "Don't leave me."

CHAPTER 28

SUZANNA

It was as if all the other zombies and runners were gone. There was no sound. Suzanna even closed her mind to Blu in the electric-blue jumpsuit. She saw Eric ahead of her in his bright yellow T-shirt with both his zombie alert flags still intact. There were two of them after Eric. There were two flags. If they were children someone would say, "Suzanna, you need to share."

Like hell!

Suzanna felt herself starting to float. She willed herself to stay on the ground. She was not going to lose to Blu!

She reached out for a flag and Blu reached for the other. Suzanna suddenly launched herself at her husband's back, tackling him. Somehow he managed to spin around and catch her. They hit the ground with Eric on his back and Suzanna lying on top of him. Blu vaulted over them. Suzanna, atop a surprised Eric, looked up at Blu, who stared back at her, breathing hard. Blu give Suzanna a big grin, a thumbs-up, and ran off.

What did that mean?

Suzanna decided Eric was more important than Blu at the moment and she covered him with kisses. He was laughing.

"What are you doing, Beet?" he asked. "You made me lose the race."

"Don't leave me," Suzanna said between kisses. "I love you!"

They both sat up and looked at each other as runners and zombies leaped all around them. Suzanna rested her head on Eric's shoulder. She could feel his heart racing from the exertion of the run. Her heart was racing because she knew she'd been playing with fire—and so had Blu.

"Am I missing something?" Eric asked. "Why would I be leaving you?"

"For Blu!"

"Blu who?" Eric said, smoothing back her hair.

"Superblu!" Suzanna sniffled.

"So we could run off and be Superblu and O'Hara? I don't think I'm the rumpled detective type."

"This isn't funny."

"I wouldn't leave you for Superblu. Or any other Blu. Beet, listen, I love you. I know who you are, and I love you."

I know who you are, and I love you was the most remarkable statement Suzanna had ever heard. Because it was one thing for someone to love you when you were faking it. But Eric *did* know who she was and he did love her.

"I'm a jerk," Suzanna said, kissing him again.

"Well, yeah, sometimes," he said. He pulled her to her feet. By this time the zombies and runners were long gone and it was just the two of them. "And you have the most expressive eyes I've ever seen on a zombie."

"Don't make me cry," Suzanna said. "You'll ruin my makeup."

CHAPTER 29

ERINN

"Be careful with that," Erinn said.

She walked behind one of the movers as he hitched her Morris chair up the front stoop, through the hallway, and into the living room. Gone was the couch shaped like lips. Gone was the coffee table of the leering man. Each hideous piece, one by one, replaced with her own beloved furniture.

Of course, the paycheck was gone now, too. Video of Blu's lithe form streaking through the 5K in her trussed-up catsuit was all over the Internet by the time Alice unveiled her tree sculpture that same evening. A few days later, as Alice boarded a plane to Santa Fe, Blu had signed a movie deal. No small-time reality show would suffice for her now, and Alice was safely elsewhere, building metal sculptures made of pop-tops. Erinn wished Alice the greatest success. Just not in Los Angeles.

Erinn had to admit that there were times she missed Blu. But the removal of both women from her life returned things to normal. If you could call a backyard full of rabbits "normal." Dymphna was staying, which made Erinn happy. Maybe life shouldn't settle in too much, Erinn thought, and Dymphna would definitely see to that.

Suzanna had cautioned that watching movers manhandle your prized processions took a strong heart, and as her sofa appeared in the doorway, bumping against the door frame, Erinn gave up watching and went into the kitchen to feed Caro. She peeked into the backyard. It had become a habit, like checking a watch for the time. Just a quick glance to make sure all was well.

The backyard had been transformed. Christopher had surprised Erinn with a façade he'd built for the rabbit cages. Instead of ten stacked wire cages, the rabbits were now residing in individual units in what looked like a miniature Victorian house, the lines perfectly mimicking those of the guesthouse. Each habitat even had its own red door seamlessly set into the wire mesh. Christopher had also cleared out the side of the yard that Erinn only used for storage and enclosed it for the rabbits' play area. The backyard, once rampaged by rabbits, had sprung back to life, just as her living room was doing right now.

Erinn tapped softly at the back window over the sink. She didn't want to startle the rabbits. It was enough to get Caro's attention, though. He was lying on the top of the cages, in his favorite spot between two of the faux roof peaks, serving as guard cat for his friends. Caro jumped down and padded into the kitchen.

As the movers put the last lamp in place, Erinn saw them to the door.

Should she tip them? She pulled her cell phone out of her pocket. She'd call her mother and ask. But before she found her mother on speed dial she slipped the phone back into her jeans. Her mother would be leaving for the airport in an hour.

I'd better get down to the Bun.

Erinn checked her reflection before she left the house. She was pleased to see her mirrored antique hall tree back in its rightful place. Tucking a strand of hair (the part that constantly escaped her enameled clip) back in place, she decided she looked no worse for wear. Since Christopher had become part of her life, she did try to pay a little more attention to how she looked. Suzanna had suggested a new hairstyle, but Erinn had settled on an assortment of antique hairclips.

She stopped dead in her tracks at the front gate. Cary was leaning against Erinn's car, deeply engrossed in her iPad. Erinn headed over. Cary looked up at the approach of her footsteps.

"Settled back in to your own home?" Cary asked, as if having your boss remove your furniture and return it to you at her whim was business as usual. Which, Erinn guessed, for Cary it was.

"Yes," Erinn said, waiting for Cary to move. "It's lovely." Remembering her manners, she added, "Thank you."

"And Christopher?" Cary said, still languidly leaning. "He's good?"

"He's well," Erinn said, and again added, "Thank you."

"I suppose you're wondering why I'm here," Cary said, finally straightening up and slipping her iPad into her bag. "Shall we go for a walk?"

"I can't. I'm on my way to the Bun."

"Perfect. I could use some tea! I'll go with you."

Cary walked over to the passenger side of Erinn's car. Erinn unclicked the lock and they both got in. Erinn drove south, along Ocean Avenue. Summer was in full swing and so was the traffic. Cary made small talk as Erinn dodged and weaved around the tourists who invaded her town every year for four months.

"Well," Cary said. "I did it!"

"Pardon?" Erinn asked.

"I did it!" Cary said, turning in her seat to look at Erinn. "I sold *Budding Tastes* to the Fine Foods Network."

So much had transpired in Erinn's life in the last few months that it took her a moment to remember that *Budding Tastes* was the food-and-wine-pairing show that Erinn had wrestled into a junk-food-and-wine-pairing show.

"Why would the Fine Foods Network want to do a show about junk food?" Erinn asked. "That's an oxymoron."

"I think they must be trying to get the Honey Boo Boo and *Duck Dynasty* crowd." Cary shrugged. "You don't sound very excited."

"I am," Erinn said, although she wasn't. She had other things on her mind.

"I thought we were screwed when we lost *Red, White, and Blu,*" Cary said. "This could not have come at a better time. It's perfect."

"As Khalil Gibran said, 'To go forward is to move toward perfection,'" Erinn said absently.

"Uh, yes, I guess that's true," replied Cary.

Erinn was confused. Was Cary thanking her for coming up with the twist for the show? Offering her a job? Sharing the good news? Mercifully, they were within sight of the Bun. Once peak season arrived and parking became impossible, Suzanna always made sure there was a parking spot in the back alley for Erinn. Even so, summer traffic would keep her locked in the car with Cary for another several minutes.

"I'm sure it's going to be a terrific show," Erinn said.

"Well, I think that's true. That's what I wanted to talk to you about."

"I know I bring this up all the time, so forgive me for repeating myself. But aren't you supposed to be talking to my agent, not me?"

"Now that's just silly. We're friends!"

Erinn blinked. Was that right? Were they friends? She realized with a jolt that they were.

"Thank you, Cary. That's nice to hear."

"Good! I was thinking that you and I should be co-executive producers on this. I mean, I couldn't have done this without you."

"Very true." Two cars in front of Erinn finally moved forward and she was able to swing into the parking space behind the Bun. Virginia, with the eternally trembling Piquant in her arms, and Rio were standing by the SUV, suitcases beside them. Eric was bringing out the last bag as Erinn turned off the car. No one had noticed her car as she pulled in. She sat watching them, momentarily forgetting about Cary.

"So," Cary said, smiling. "What do you say?"

"I'm busy," Erinn said, absently, as they got out of the car.

"What?" Cary asked, stunned.

"I'm busy. I'm working on something of my own."

She looked at Cary's crestfallen face.

"I'm sorry," Erinn said. "But I had this idea for a Web series, and I'm . . . well, in the parlance of the day . . . I'm going to run with it. I hope it doesn't interfere with our . . . you know . . . our . . . ."

"Friendship? Of course not. Although I'm heartbroken, of course. So?"

"So?"

"So, what are you working on?"

"It's a Web series," Erinn said again, surprised that Cary was interested. "I got the idea right before that poor tree went up in flames. It seemed as if the entire neighborhood was coming together to learn how to spin yarn. It was really a beautiful sight."

"You're doing a show on community projects?" Cary asked.

"Of course not!" Erinn said, trying not to sound affronted. "No one would watch that! I'm doing a series on knitting. Start to finish. It will be like the whole food-to-table movement only it will be from the animal's back to yours."

"I'd work on that log line," Cary said, throwing out another industry term that Erinn finally understood.

"You're working with Dymphna, I presume?" Cary asked.

"Yes. Her name is Dymphna Pearl, you know."

"Brilliant." Cary beamed. *"Knit and Pearl!"*

Now it was Erinn's turn to beam.

Cary suddenly noticed the little group standing by the SUV.

"Ah!" she said. "Well, I'll go get some tea, then."

Cary gave Erinn a hug, which Erinn endured. She was not a big hugger but she guessed if her friend wanted to hug her, so be it.

Erinn walked toward the SUV, which was gleaming bright yellow in the sun. Erinn thought the car was perfect for Southern California. It looked as if it were always ready for an adventure.

"Are you sure you have everything?" Eric was asking Rio. Rio nodded. Eric turned to Virginia, handing her the car keys.

"Are you sure you want to drive? I can drive, if you want me to."

"Or I could drive," injected Erinn. "The airport is only twenty minutes away."

Shortly after the 5K, Erinn, Suzanna, and Eric had all been thrilled when Virginia announced that she had decided to stay in Los Angeles and continue Rio's efforts with the kids.

"I just think a seasoned hand might not be such a bad idea," Virginia had said. "I mean, the more I thought about it, if kids didn't need guidance, I wouldn't have had a job in the first place!"

"As a professor?" Eric had asked. "Or a mother?"

"Both," Virginia had said, looking at Erinn. "But being a mother was . . . is my top priority. These kids need a mother as much as they need a dance instructor—which is a good thing, since I mother better than I dance!"

Suzanna and Eric had laughed but Erinn stayed silent. She was still a little rattled by her declaration of dependence at the race, begging her mother not to leave.

"Besides," Virginia had said, patting Erinn's hand, "a really special kid asked me to stay. Who could say no to that?"

Erinn studied her mother now, as Eric and Rio loaded the back of the van with Rio's bags. A new relationship with a friend, a new relationship with her mother. This was proving to be quite a year.

"It's not a big deal," Virginia said. "If I'm staying in Los Angeles, I've got to drive!"

Erinn realized that Suzanna had come out the back door, Lizzy on her hip. They watched as Virginia got into the driver's seat. As Rio walked over to Suzanna, she hastily gave Lizzy to Erinn.

"I know you'll do great," Suzanna said.

Rio kissed her on the cheek.

"Suzanna . . . ," Rio said, but she stopped him.

"Everything is fine, Rio. If I ever become an alcoholic and need to do the twelve steps, I think you'll be on my list of amends, too."

Suzanna reached out and hugged him. Erinn studied their hug. It was effortless and heartfelt. Perhaps she should videotape Suzanna's hugging technique.

When Rio and Eric shook hands, Erinn heard Suzanna take a deep breath. Erinn looked at her sister.

"It's like *Casablanca*," Suzanna whispered. "When Ingrid Bergman decides to stay with the man who is best for her and not the loose cannon. Staying with Humphrey Bogart would have been a big mistake."

Erinn thought about saying it was the loose cannon who had made that decision, but she decided to let cinematic history rewrite itself.

Because this was the perfect ending.

EPILOGUE

SUZANNA

"Mother, you can't call a dance studio *Great Feets!*" Erinn objected over a family dinner in the Huge Apartment.

"Why not?" Virginia asked, serving chicken breasts stuffed with apples—another comfort food staple that Virginia made when trying to get her way.

"You know why," Erinn said, cutting into the chicken.

"It's fun," Virginia said. "The kids like it."

"I'm with Mom," said Suzanna. "Who cares if it's grammatically correct?"

"I do! Especially if my production studio is going to be in there," replied Erinn.

"Do you have a better idea?" Suzanna asked.

"I was thinking The Wolf and The Rabbit Productions."

"I forgot the peas," Virginia said, leaping up.

Erinn watched her mother head into the kitchen. She called after her, "I thought you'd like it!"

"Did I say I didn't like it?" Virginia asked, returning with a steaming bowl.

"Do you?" Erinn asked.

"You're talking about the Native American children's story, 'The Wolf and the Rabbit,' " Suzanna said. "The one Dad told us?"

"Of course," Erinn said. "I thought it was clever, since our last name is Wolf, Dymphna's knitting show features rabbits, and the story is about dance."

"Yes," Virginia said. "But it's a terrible story! Your father should never have told you kids about it—it's worse than Hansel and Gretel."

"All children's stories are terrible," Eric said. "I can't believe we're all not scarred."

"Who says we're not?" Erinn said. "Besides, you said it yourself, all children's stories are terrible, so why not?"

"I don't know if I remember that story," Eric said.

"Of course you do," Erinn said. "It's the one about the wolf who wants to cut off the ears of the rabbit, but the rabbit tricks the wolf into dancing until he's dizzy, and the rabbit gets away before the wolf can cut off his ears."

Lizzy suddenly let out a little whimper. All the adults turned to look at her. She was taking in a breath that promised to produce an ear-splitting bellow.

"Poor bunny," Lizzy wailed.

The sonic blast of her cry rocked the house.

Suzanna picked up Lizzy and rocked her, all the while glaring at her sister. Erinn reached out and patted Lizzy.

"Don't cry, Lizzy," Erinn said. "The rabbit still has his ears."

"Oh my God, Erinn!" Suzanna said, quieting Lizzy. "Face it, that name sucks."

"Not to mention, dear," added Virginia, "that the wolf sounds not only mean but stupid. It won't inspire confidence."

"Are you going to make sure there are no small children around every time you explain the name of your production company?" Suzanna asked. "And trust me, you'll have to explain it forever."

"At least it's better than Happy Feets."

"Great Feets," Virginia said.

"We need a name that reflects the fact that it's a TV studio. The name should reflect storytelling."

"Well, you shouldn't leave out the rabbits," Suzanna said.

"You can't leave out dance, either. It's half the equation," Virginia added.

"I think we should tie it to the Rollicking Bun," Suzanna said. "I mean, maybe we could sell the Angora yarn or knitted shawls at the Bun."

Suzanna was surprised that her mother and sister seemed to think this was a good idea. Of course it didn't solve the problem of the name. If anything, it added to the dilemma.

"When we were trying to think up a name for the Rollicking Bun, Fernando and I were at each other's throats," Suzanna continued. "Eric just said, 'Let me know what you decide and I'll order the sign.' "

Suzanna cut chicken, peas, and baby carrots into little pieces for Lizzy, who, if Suzanna had to be truthful, really liked them much better than kale. Suzanna thought about her old friend Fernando up on Vashon Island running his bed and breakfast. She missed him. She and Fernando had always fought passionately: about the name of the shop, about the menu, about the customers. They had fought for weeks over the name; Suzanna wanted to call the place the Rollicking Bun. Fernando was insistent that the name reflect his baking—the shop should be called the Epic Scone. Leave it to Eric to come up with the Rollicking Bun . . . Home of the Epic Scone. He solved problems even when he was staying above the fray.

"Eric." Suzanna turned toward her husband. "You always seem to come up with something that makes everyone happy. Don't you have any ideas?"

"I do have one suggestion," he said. "For what it's worth."

* * *

"Miles, Ray, be careful with that!" Virginia called from the unit in Mr. Clancy's Courtyard that used to be Rio's dance studio. The boys were carrying the new sign that was to hang over the door. Christopher had made it, and he had been very secretive about it. The sign looked like it was about the size of a surfboard but it was completely wrapped up in brown paper so no one could see it before the great unveiling.

Ray and Miles carefully guided the draped sign into the studio. The Wolf women, as well as Lizzy, Dymphna, Ray, Miles, Winnie, Mr. Clancy, Bernard, and several loyal tea-shop patrons were standing by to see the new studio's name. Ray and Miles held the sign while Donell did a sage blessing on the space. Then it was time for Christopher to rip off the paper for the reveal.

Carved into the sign were goofy-looking rabbits climbing up the lettering. Some of them, wearing ballet slippers, danced above the letters. To one side, a friendly wolf held a movie slate.

The sign read:

The Rollicking Annex...
Yarn and Yarns created here.
Please dance in.

Everyone cheered. Champagne was opened and everyone in Venice seemed to have a toast to offer.

"Thank God we got away from that awful Great Feets name," Erinn whispered to Suzanna. "I'm so happy Eric ran with my idea."

Moments later, Virginia refilled Suzanna's glass with champagne and said, "Eric really is a genius. I am so relieved he tossed that horrible Wolf and Rabbit story and saw things my way."

Suzanna looked over at her husband. He was in an animated conversation with the Grumpy Old Men. He seemed to sense her gaze and looked right back at her. There didn't seem to be anyone else in the room. At the moment, Suzanna couldn't imagine ever needing a Get Out of Jail Free card.

The studio suddenly filled with pulsing music. Miles and Winnie, those two sullen kids who were now glowing with purpose, dragged Virginia, Suzanna, and Erinn into the center of a circle of jubilant, spontaneous celebrants. The Wolf women reacted true to form: a hopeful Suzanna, a grateful Virginia, and an embarrassed Erinn. The three joined hands.

Everyone sang.

The music said it all.

We Are Family.

MOTHER'S CHICKEN AND APPLES

Serves 4

Ingredients

2 large skinless, boneless chicken breasts
1 cup chopped apple
1 tablespoon chopped walnuts
3 tablespoons shredded mozzarella cheese
1 ½ tablespoons Italian-style dried bread crumbs
1 tablespoon butter or margarine
½ cup dry white wine
¼ cup water
1 tablespoon water
1 ½ teaspoons cornstarch

Directions

Flatten chicken breasts.

Combine apple, walnuts, cheese, and bread crumbs.

Divide apple mixture between chicken breasts and spread evenly on each breast before rolling. Roll up each breast. Secure with cooking twine.

Melt butter or margarine in a skillet over medium heat. Brown stuffed chicken breasts. Add wine and ¼ cup water. Cover. Simmer until chicken is no longer pink, about 20 minutes.

Transfer chicken to warmed platter or plates.

Pour juices from pan into small saucepan. Combine 1 tablespoon water and cornstarch—add to juices. Cook and stir until thickened. Pour over chicken.

Serve.

MOTHER'S MACARONI AND CHEESE

Serves 8

Ingredients

1 pound of elbow macaroni
1 pound extra-sharp cheddar cheese cut into small pieces (Virginia
    sometimes switches off and uses Pepper Jack or Swiss. Pick your
    favorite cheese or mix them all together.)
$\frac{1}{4}$ pound butter
4 cups of milk
2 teaspoons salt
Fresh ground black pepper to taste
Potato chips

Directions

Preheat oven to 350 degrees F.
Cook pasta according to package directions until al dente.
While the pasta is cooking, heat the cheese and the butter in the
milk and stir fairly regularly until it blends. (This is not a necessary
step. You can just add the cheese pieces to the cooked pasta, but Virginia finds that the smooth sauce distributes more easily.)
Add salt and pepper and pour entire mixture into a large, buttered
casserole dish.
Sprinkle crushed potato chips across the top and bake for 30 minutes.

MOTHER'S CHOCOLATE MARSHMALLOW FUDGE

Serves 12

Ingredients

1 small can (5 ounces) evaporated milk
4 tablespoons butter (I use unsalted)
2 cups granulated white sugar
$\frac{1}{4}$ teaspoon salt (I leave this out if anyone has a health issue. But if they are eating fudge, how bad can things be?)
1 7.5-ounce jar Marshmallow Fluff
2 cups semisweet chocolate chips (make it butterscotch fudge by using butterscotch chips instead)
2 tablespoons pure vanilla extract (Don't give in to imitation vanilla—it will ruin everything.)

Directions

Line the bottom and sides of a 9 x 9 x 2-inch pan with aluminum foil.

Mix the milk, butter, sugar, salt, and marshmallow into a heavy-duty saucepan and place on stove over medium heat. Using a wooden spoon (preferably), stir constantly till the mixture boils. Lower the heat a bit and continue stirring for five more minutes. If you are working with a candy thermometer it should read between 230 and 234 degrees.

Now, take the saucepan off the heat and mix in chocolate bits and the vanilla. Pour immediately into the prepared pan. Let the fudge cool to room temperature before putting it in the fridge.

Acknowledgments

This book is about family.

To my brothers and your fabulous spouses: Thank you for being weird. The inspiration never ends.

Without my mother's guidance, nothing would get written—or at least edited. I love you, Mom. To my aunt, A. Jacqueline Steck: I miss you every day, but especially when I was writing this book. I will love you forever.

To my father, Joseph Bonaduce: You made writing look easy. I wish you were around so you could tell me how you did that. I am grateful for everything you taught me. I'm sure my editor appreciates the fact that you drilled "never miss a deadline" into me at a young age. I love you, I miss you—and thank you.

To my sprawling, supportive, fantastic family by marriage, what can I say except: There is never a dull moment.

To Patti, your generosity in accepting my family as your own makes me want to cry. To Liz, my partner in crime, thanks for always listening. To Anne, I'm constantly surprised you aren't my biological sister! To Clare, my kickstarter, where would this writing adventure be without you? And to Mary, thanks for introducing me to your brother.

To my husband's brothers: When I'm writing the good guys, if they are not my husband, they are one of you.

It's been said that you can't choose your family but you can choose your friends. I have made sterling choices. While I may have doubted myself on this road to authordom, my friends Nancy Barney, Melinda Wunsch-Dilger, Elle Fournier, Lisa Insana, Vivien Aladjem-Mudgett, and Patricia Rogerson never wavered in their faith. Thank you.

My friend and mentor Jodi Thomas says there are no stupid questions. There are. I asked them. Thank you, Jodi, for always answering with a straight face and for years of encouragement.

Many thanks to Charmaine Lorelli, for your time and kind words. To Jaidis Shaw, your thoughtful guidance has been invaluable. To Bruce Hsiao, thank you for sharing your amazing story.

To Amanda Spitzer, Beth Kinsolving, and Evelyn Dolphin, my proofreaders; Sharon Bowers, my agent at Miller Bowers Griffin Literary Management; and Martin Biro, my editor at Kensington Books; thank you for allowing me use of the possessive when speaking of you.

Finally and always: to the man who defines family for three generations, my husband, Billy—you raise me up.

If you enjoy the lives and loves of the Wolf sisters, be sure not to miss Celia Bonaduce's

A COMEDY OF ERINN

Erinn Wolf needs to reinvent herself. A once-celebrated playwright turned photographer, she's almost broke, a little lonely, and tired of her sister's constant worry. When a job on a reality TV show falls into her lap, she's thrilled to be making a paycheck—and when a hot Italian actor named Massimo rents her guesthouse, she's certain her life is getting a romantic subplot. But with the director—brash, gorgeous young Jude—dogging her every step, she can't help but look at herself through his lens—and wonder if she's been reading the wrong script all along. . . .

An eKensington e-book on sale now!

CHAPTER 1

Erinn Elizabeth Wolf leaned on the fence that kept visitors from sliding down the bluff into the ocean. She glowered at the young couple snuggling on *her* bench—in *her* park. The young man and woman occasionally looked at the water, but spent most of their time sinking into each other's eyes.

The sun was just dipping into the water. The world was suddenly filled with coral, russet, violet, periwinkle, and cornflower. Erinn was getting impatient, very impatient. She decided to take matters into her own hands.

She joined the couple on the bench. Nudging the young woman aside with her hip, she heaved her oversized bag onto the bench and hunkered down.

"Look at that sunset," Erinn heard the young woman sigh softly. "God's masterpiece."

Erinn snorted.

"God wouldn't have a prayer creating a sunset like that," she said. "This is a masterpiece only city smog could produce."

The couple ignored her. It was obvious Erinn was going to have to crank up the annoyance factor. She studied the couple. Gauging that they were liberal arts students from one of the local universities, Erinn formulated a plan. With a quick prayer, asking forgiveness from her beloved Democratic Party, Erinn said, "Since he's now out of office, I think Dick Cheney is really coming into his own, don't you?"

The couple left their spot on the bench—he frowning, she beaming with politically correct good will.

That's one way to get your bench back.

Erinn glanced at the rapidly advancing sunset and realized she had not a moment to spare. She reached into her bag and pulled out a battered, hand-held video camera. She quickly and expertly adjusted her settings and started panning steadily over the horizon. She was getting pretty good at her camera work—if she did say so herself.

The view at Palisades Park in Santa Monica, California, was the billion-dollar vista featured in movies since cinema's golden era. Although Erinn had lived in Santa Monica for nine years, she never got used to the incredible beauty the park offered.

Whenever Erinn was shooting, she was nimble—and confident in her movements. But as soon as she shut the camera off, a transformation took place. She suddenly appeared heavier and slower, as if gravity had taken hold of her—as if she were rooted to the earth. When the sun had gone, Erinn stowed her camera and made her way home. She didn't walk far, as she was the owner of another masterpiece—one of the few remaining Victorian houses on Santa Monica's main drag.

While Erinn would never be mistaken for the stuff of fairy tales, the courtyard of her house looked like something out of *Beauty and the Beast*. The old climbing roses that crawled up the lacy wooden pillars also disguised layers of peeling paint on the porch. An uneven walkway curled quaintly toward the side yard.

She retrieved a large silver key from a keychain that looked like a medieval jailer's and fitted it into the front door lock. The door squeaked open, and Erinn was home.

She shrugged off her coat, hung it on an old-fashioned hall tree, and carefully put her camera aside. She caught a glimpse of herself in the mirror and rearranged a few bobby pins, hoping to control her wild, coarse hair. Even with her hair pulled back in a severe ponytail, corkscrew tendrils tended to escape. Her hair was still mostly pepper, but now with a sprinkling of salt. Erinn had made no attempt to halt the aging process, which she knew was practically a sacrilege in Southern California—but she stood firm against useless vanity. Even so, without the weight of the camera bag on her shoulders, hints of the graceful young woman she used to be were still evident in her posture and the way she moved. Almost miraculously she had remained an extremely attractive woman.

Not that she cared.

Not that anybody cared.

The doorbell rang. She peered out. A man in ripped jeans, a tight T-shirt, and carrying a skateboard was trying to open the gate. Erinn instinctively stepped out of sight, but kept her eye on the man. He managed to get the latch open and headed up Erinn's path. He marched up to the porch and knocked.

It suddenly occurred to Erinn that this must be someone who wanted to rent the guesthouse.

"Damn it, Suzanna," she cursed under her breath.

Her younger sister, Suzanna, was worried that Erinn would lose the house if she didn't generate some income. She had placed a rental ad on craigslist without Erinn's knowledge or consent. Erinn balked when she heard about it, but promised her sister she'd keep an open mind and at least meet with a few people.

The man, in wraparound sunglasses, knocked on the door again.

She yanked open the heavy wood-beamed door.

"Hey there, how you doing?" asked the young man, as he removed his glasses. He put out his hand by way of introduction. "Craigslist."

He had the casual gait of a man—Erinn would put him at about twenty-eight—at ease with himself. He was also extremely well built, with biceps peeking out from under the sleeves of his snug T-shirt.

"That's an interesting mode of transportation," Erinn said, indicating the skateboard.

"Yeah," he said. "It's a pain in the ass sometimes, but it's a real chick magnet."

"Pardon?"

"The babes really go for a guy on a skateboard."

"*I* don't."

"Well, you're not a . . ."

He propped his skateboard against the house and stepped inside, without invitation. Erinn followed him. He walked around, whistling appreciatively.

"Wow, this place is awesome," he said.

He walked into the living room and started to pull open the curtains.

"Dude! You have an ocean view . . . why do you have the curtains shut?"

"If you must know, I like to keep to myself. I like the privacy," Erinn said. "Besides, I find Southern Californians vastly overestimate sunshine."

"Well, it's a cool place anyway," he said as Erinn closed the curtains. He squinted in the darkness. "You could do a spread in *Better Caves and Gardens*."

The cat rubbed against the young man's legs.

"Sweet! I love animals," he said, scooping up the cat. "Whoa! This is one fat cat!"

Erinn reached out and patted the cat, a large, flat-faced, silver point Himalayan.

"His name is Caro," she said.

"Hello, Car-ro," he said, pronouncing two *r*'s.

"It's pronounced with one *r*," Erinn said. "Car-o. It's Italian for 'dear one.' "

"Isn't that what I said?"

"No . . . you said '*Car*-ro' . . . that's Spanish for 'truck.' "

"Well, no offense, dude, but Truck's a much better name for this guy," said the young man as he put the cat down and headed toward the kitchen.

Erinn kept her face impassive. This boy was not winning her over. "And my name, in case you're interested, is Erinn."

"Wow, nice kitchen, Er . . . Do you mind if I call you 'Er'?"

"Massively," said Erinn.

"What about Rinn? Or Rin Tin Tin?"

Does he want the guesthouse or did he just come here to insult me?

"Why would you call me Rin Tin Tin?"

"Just shortening the process, dude. That's how nicknames are made. You start out with something that makes sense, like Rinn, and pretty soon you're Rin Tin Tin. It's totally random."

"I didn't catch *your* name," Erinn said.

"Jude . . . Raphael."

Common ground at last.

"Ah!" she said. "As in the artist!"

"As in the turtle," Jude said. "Hey, let's go check out my guest-house!"

He stood and followed a stormy Erinn into the backyard.

If love could have kept the place up, Erinn would have had no worries. But like everything else about the Wolf residence, the yard was looking a little down-at-the-heels. The one-room guesthouse was nestled in a patch of large fig trees. It was a miniature Victorian, complete with a tiny porch and hanging swing. Its bright red door stood out from the greenish tone of the rest of the exterior, and its window boxes overflowed with geraniums.

"This is it," she said, trying to hide the pride she felt in the place.

Jude stood back and looked the building over.

"Huh."

Erinn turned on him.

"Is there a problem?" she asked.

"Nah," he said. "I'm just not really big on these gingerbready kind of places, ya know? They're kinda gay."

"Gay?"

"I mean . . . not in a bad way. Like . . . not even in a gay way, you know?"

"Shall we go inside?" asked Erinn, since she hadn't the faintest idea.

She clicked on the light but didn't step inside. Her eyes scanned the room lovingly. Jude stood on the porch, looking in over Erinn's head. The room had an open floor plan, and every inch of space counted. A small kitchen was fitted into one corner and a bathroom was tucked discreetly into another. There was a wrought-iron daybed that functioned as a seating area as well as a bed and a tiny, mosaic-tiled café table and chair set. Even in this small space, there was an entire wall of bookcases. Erinn turned to Jude.

"Is this gay as well?" she asked as she walked into the room, Jude at her heels.

"Hey! If you're gay, I don't care. Really," Jude said. "I'm, personally, not gay. I'm, you know, metro/hetero. But whatever floats your boat, I say."

"Thank you. I was so worried it might be offensive to you somehow, if I were gay."

"Whatever, Erinn. I mean . . . gay is as gay does, right?"

"Well, obviously, that's true," Erinn said. "But I don't do as gay does, because I'm not gay."

"Whoa . . . you know that old saying . . . something about . . . you're protesting a shitload."

"Are you perhaps thinking of 'The lady doth protest too much' from *Hamlet*?"

"Moving on, Erinn," Jude said. "Your sexuality isn't the only thing in the world, right? There's food, the beach, the theater . . ."

Erinn winced and walked around the room, trying to ignore the cretin who was taking up much too much space—and oxygen—in her little sanctuary. She started opening blinds to make the room seem somehow bigger.

"I don't go to the theater," Erinn said.

"What do you mean?" asked Jude, trying out the daybed. "Erinn Elizabeth Wolf, the famous New York playwright, doesn't go to the theater? That's crazy!"

Erinn almost choked, she was so surprised by this comment. Any use of her full name by someone other than her mother usually meant she was being recognized. Jude had his back to her and was studying a line of books in the bookcase. He turned to look at her.

"Did you realize your initials are E.E.W.? EEEEEEwwwwwwww."

Erinn tried to ignore Jude's inept attempt at winning her over with a nickname. But she definitely wasn't finished with the conversation.

"You . . . you've heard of me?" she asked.

"Sure. I was a theater major. You're in the history books."

Erinn tried—and failed—to hide her dismay. She was surprised to hear that, at forty-three, she was already considered a relic and consigned to history. She tried not to let on that Jude had delivered a verbal slap.

"Not the *history* books, exactly . . . but . . ." he said.

"But . . . like . . . you know," offered Erinn, who could see he did not mean to hurt her feelings.

"Well, yeah."

Erinn sat down at the mosaic table. Jude continued to look around the room and stopped to admire a photograph. It was a close-up of a wrinkled old man playing checkers.

"This is cool," Jude said.

Erinn studied the picture, lost in thought, remembering the first time she saw Oscar sitting in the little park across from her loft in

Manhattan. He was always so focused on his game. That was nearly twenty years ago . . . by now, he was probably dead, or just another lost New York memory.

"I took that years ago," she said.

"You took that? Awesome."

Erinn warmed to the praise.

"Well, I've always been interested in the visual arts. I'm actually learning how to shoot an HD camera and I'm thinking of trying my hand at editing, too. I like to keep up on those sort of things."

"Hmmm," Jude said. "That's pretty cool for somebody . . . uh . . . not totally young . . . to be into that stuff."

"Let's talk about you, shall we?" Erinn asked as her good will ebbed away.

"Sure," said Jude, grabbing the chair opposite her. "Well, let's see . . . I'm in the business . . . television mostly. I mean, in this town, isn't everybody?"

Erinn looked at Jude thoughtfully. What could Suzanna have possibly been thinking? She'd been hoping to rent to a fellow artist, but everyone who applied seemed to be from *television*. Erinn realized that her mind had wandered, and she tried to tune back in to whatever it was Jude might be saying.

". . . but, you know, until I can produce my own work, I pick up assignments wherever I can."

Erinn watched Jude as he picked up the rental agreement on the table.

"Well, I don't think you really need to read that just yet. . . ." she said, trying to grab the document that would have damned her to her own personal hell should he sign it.

Jude picked up a pen from the table. Erinn watched in silence as he lost interest in the document and started doing curls with the pen, watching his bicep rise and fall with the motion. He was mesmerized. Erinn coughed, hoping to get his attention. Jude looked up and smiled sheepishly.

"I read that you should work out whenever—and wherever—you can," he said.

"Oh? You read that?"

Jude laughed. "Well, I downloaded a workout video to my iPod so I could listen to it while I was skateboarding. Same thing."

Erinn arched an eyebrow. Jude suddenly looked up at her.

"What about Tin Lizzy? That would be an awesome nickname for you!"

"You know, Jude, I'm not sure this is going to work out."

He looked up. "Oh? Why not?"

"Well," Erinn faltered. "I just think that, if two people live in such close proximity to each other, there should be some symbiosis . . . if you get my drift."

Jude looked at Erinn for a minute, then smiled.

"Oh, you mean 'cause I'm in such good shape," he said. "Don't worry about that. I can help you get rid of that spare tire in no time."

"No, no, no," Erinn said. "I appreciate your offer. Although I wasn't aware I *had* a spare tire."

"Oh, big-time."

"It was more along the lines of, well, I don't feel we're . . . intellectually compatible."

Jude frowned.

"I'm not smart enough to rent your *guesthouse*?"

He held up the rental agreement and waved it in her face.

"Is there an I.Q. test attached to this?" he asked.

Erinn stood up so fast she knocked the chair over, and stormed out of the guesthouse. Jude sprinted after her, and Erinn wheeled on him.

"I'm sorry, Jude, but clearly this isn't going to work."

"Tell me about it. You think you're some sort of god because you wrote one important play a hundred years ago? Nobody can even make a joke around you? I'm out of here."

"I assume you can see yourself out?"

"If I can find my way around your huge ego, yeah," Jude replied, as he walked toward the main house. He stepped over the cat, which was sunbathing on the walkway.

"See ya around, Truck."

Apparently, Jude had not succeeded in giving *her* a nickname, but poor Caro did not escape unscathed.

Erinn went back into the kitchen, stung by Jude's comments. To distract herself, she decided to make a pot of soup. She pulled out her large stockpot, added some homemade chicken stock, and started scrubbing tubers in a fury. *Who does he think he is, talking to me that way?* she thought. *I dodged a bullet with that one.*

The phone rang. Erinn wiped off her hands and reached for the cordless, hesitating just long enough to grab her half-moon glasses, and checked the caller I.D.

It was Suzanna.

Erinn put the phone down without answering it. She took off her glasses and returned to her soup.

© William Christoff Photography

Celia Bonaduce is a producer on HGTV's *House Hunters*. She is the author of the Venice Beach Romances and lives in Santa Monica, California, with her husband in a beautiful "no-pets" building. She wishes she could say she has a dog. You can contact Celia at www.celiabonaduce.com.

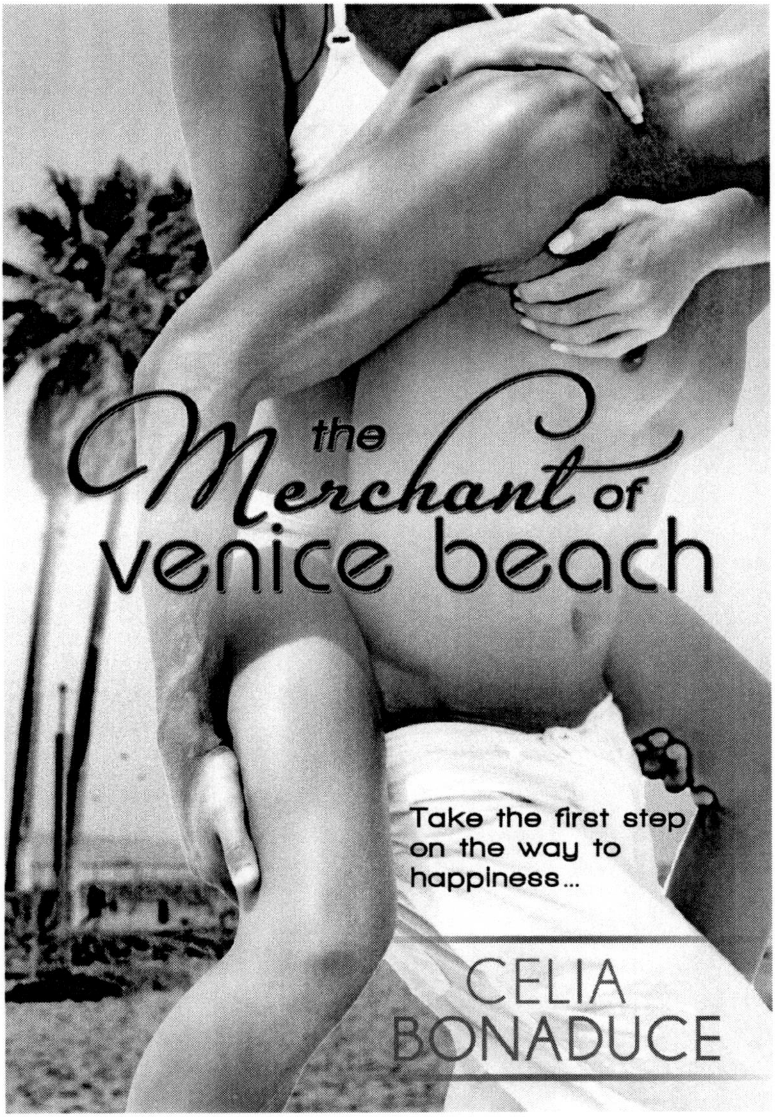
the Merchant of
venice beach
Take the first step on the way to happiness...
CELIA BONADUCE

The Merchant of Venice Beach

The Rollicking Bun—Home of the Epic Scone—is the center of Suzanna Wolf's life. Part tea shop, part bookstore, part home, it's everything she's ever wanted right on the Venice Beach boardwalk, including partnership with her two best friends from high school, Eric and Fernando. But with thirty-three just around the corner, suddenly Suzanna wants something more—something strictly her own. Salsa lessons, especially with a gorgeous instructor, seem like a good start, a harmless secret, and just maybe the start of a fling. But before she knows it, Suzanna is learning steps she never imagined—and dancing her way into confusion.

"*The Merchant of Venice Beach* has a fresh, heartwarming voice that will keep readers smiling as they dance through this charming story by Celia Bonaduce."
—Jodi Thomas, *New York Times* bestselling author

CPSIA information can be obtained at www.ICGtesting.com
Printed in the USA
BVOW01s0836230414

351365BV00001B/1/P